Einze

The Urge

Fall of a Stoic

Cover art by Cherie Fox

Copy-edited by Victor Serrano

Copyright © 2024 by Einzelgänger

All rights reserved. This book or any portion thereof may not be reproduced or used in any manner whatsoever without the express written permission of the publisher except for the use of brief quotations in a book review.

ISBN: 9798326983893

Independently published

Second print, November 2024

www.einzelganger.co

Thank you supporters and subscribers.

— Einzelgänger

The Urge: Fall of a Stoic

1. Titus 6
2. Ariadne 15
3. Seer 26
4. Shed 36
5. Alcander 46
6. Hephaestus 53
7. Custody 59
8. Hunt 66
9. Epictetus 72
10. Handbook 81
11. View 86
12. Tiberius 91
13. Furtum 97
14. Gold 103
15. Helvidius 118
16. Party 126
17. Cave 134
18. Dionysus 139
19. Woman 149
20. Urge 158
21. Chaos 170
22. Thalassa 181
23. Ritual 195
24. Brundisium 204
25. Neptune 212
26. Elysium 220
27. Nysa 231
28. Helios 244
29. Gladius 253
30. Scorpius 264

31. Noctua 274
32. Magnus 282
33. Aelianii 289
34. Athens 300

1. Titus

The day Titus Laelius Faber set the district on fire remained vivid in the memories of many Romans. His failed attempt to distill ammonium from horse urine caused papyrus scrolls in his study to ignite. Only when flames seized the bookshelf and raced through the room via scattered togas did Titus realize the unfolding disaster.

His house by the Tiber became the epicenter of a fierce inferno. About thirty slaves scrambled with buckets of water to douse the flames. Residents fled screaming through the streets, a mother whisked her children to safety a block away, and some jumped into the river to swim to the opposite bank.

Wandering like a lost stray dog past the burning buildings, Titus overheard snippets of conversations among bystanders—two slaves had suffocated in the smoke, and one was crushed to death attempting to carry the gravely ill Lucius Septimus out of his house. The aged ex-senator did not survive the blaze, inciting the wrath of his family toward Titus.

With a shake of his head, Attius Laelius Crassus slumped onto the living room couch. Titus roamed aimlessly back and forth.

"His days were numbered anyway," he said. "Let's be honest, father. The man was old, blind, and sick. He couldn't even remember his own name!"

"Who are you to speak of the dead in such a manner? Your words are as reckless as your actions!"

Titus gazed at the flickering candle on the table. His mother's sobs echoed from the kitchen. Attius slammed his fist on the table.

"You should count yourself lucky to be walking free! The Septimii would love nothing more than to see you crucified. And I might agree with them! But you're still my son. Do you realize the effort and bribes it took to convince the court to give you another chance?"

Titus nodded, head bowed.

"Nicopolis is your last chance. Promise me you'll abandon your bizarre experiments there."

"But father, I can make reparations. I'm on the verge of a breakthrough. I'll more than compensate the Septimii."

"Just promise me! Or the whole deal is off! And then you can figure out where to go on your own. Do you understand what's at stake? Be wise for once. Think of your family, your mother."

Titus sighed. His mother's incessant weeping continued.

"I promise."

The Septimius family was outraged when Attius Laelius Crassus sent his son to Nicopolis, entrusting him with fourteen properties and a handful of lands to manage and assigning him a charming little house at the forum. The Laelii were drowning in real estate in southern Epirus.

Though he bore the significant responsibility of property management, Titus hardly lifted a finger. A handful of well-trained slaves maintained the properties, and the fate of the lands was in the hands of the farmers, who used the soil as they pleased without interference. Titus delegated rent collection to his loyal servant Remus, who had traveled with him from Rome to Nicopolis.

No sooner had his father's words left his ear than Titus scoured the marketplace. Returning home with a crate full of firewood, glassware, precious metals, and various tools, he managed to obtain a jug of pig urine from a local farmer through Remus, though Titus refused to disclose its purpose.

"Any news from your sister?" asked Remus, placing the jug of urine on Titus' workshop table. Titus lifted the lid, releasing a warm vapor that made Remus gag, though he managed to keep his stomach down.

"Nothing."

Titus poured the pig urine into a kettle simmering with a brown concoction.

"No news is good news, I guess," said Remus, fanning away the vapor.

The clinking of glass echoed through the backyards as a kaleidoscope of smoke rose from the kettle through a hole in the ceiling. Titus, dancing like a chef in his kitchen, added various herbs and powders to the boiling mixture. Remus paced the workshop.

"You promised your old man."

"Oh, please don't bring this up again."

"If he finds out, there'll be hell to pay. And I imagine the neighbors aren't too thrilled about your activities either. People talk. Rumors reach Rome faster than carrier pigeons."

"Come on, it won't come to that. I'm extra cautious this time. What could possibly go wrong? Besides, I've taken some precautions." Titus pointed to a bucket of water in the workshop corner.

"That won't help much if your house catches fire again."

"Weren't you supposed to collect rent today?"

Remus tossed a bag of coins on the table.

"Done."

"If I didn't have you…"

"Wouldn't it be better if you went yourself for once? Then you could meet the tenants too. They're curious about you."

"Curious? About me? How is that even possible?" said Titus, shaking his head. "I prefer you do it. You're more suited for it than I am."

Titus glanced once more at Remus' well-defined muscles. And then there was his piercing gaze that seemed to peer right into your thoughts. The tenants thought twice before refusing to pay, such was the servant's intimidating presence, unlike with Titus himself, whose scrawny frame couldn't even make a street cat flinch.

"Some rumors are already circulating," Remus mentioned. "They say you're turning flowers into diamonds and crafting bronze coins from cow manure."

"Bronze coins from cow manure? How do they come up with these things? Let them talk."

"I'm not comfortable with this, to be honest. You never know what kind of people you might attract. Even in Nicopolis, there's no shortage of thieves. Your father warned you. Be careful."

"Don't worry about it," said Titus, turning away from Remus' penetrating gaze. "My father can say what he wants, but I'm an adult with my own will. I know what I'm doing. And as I said, I'm on the verge of a breakthrough. I'm certain it will be done before the end of the month."

"You've been saying that for two years now. Do you really think it's even possible? No one in the history of mankind has ever turned stone into gold, as far as I know."

"History doesn't predict the future. Humanity makes progress all the time. And I'm on the verge of pushing our species into a new era—an age of abundance where there's enough wealth for everybody!"

***

Despite his solitary life, Titus soon made a friend in Nicopolis. He met Arrian of Nicomedia at the market, and they struck up a conversation about Titus' passion—metallurgy—as well as other topics such as the city of Rome and the corrupt politicians manipulating the system. Arrian, who harbored ambitions to hold a governmental position in Rome, invited him to a political gathering he was organizing.

Out of a sense of duty to Arrian, the Roman tinkerer mingled among the crowd. In the Odeon, a massive building at the forum, a crowd gathered, primarily prominent Greeks and a few Roman dignitaries. "A special guest from Rome traveled to Epirus on behalf of the Emperor," Arrian informed him, while leading him through the tribune. "Gaius Julius Maximus." Yes, Titus knew him. In Rome, they called him Gaius Maximus Mentum because of his enormous chin.

After securing a spot for Titus in the Odeon, Arrian disappeared, likely overwhelmed with responsibilities. Titus observed the crowd in the round amphitheater. And then he appeared. A massive chin poked through the entrance, followed by a stocky little man who strutted as if he had just conquered all of India. The gigantic chin shone in the bright sun, as if someone had rubbed it with olive oil. Laughter emanated from the audience. "Mentum," someone called out. Titus chuckled.

From the very first word out of Gaius Maximus' mouth, Titus felt bored, wishing he was back in his study.

Arrian briefly appeared from behind the scenes and then disappeared again—who knows where. Titus observed the folk on the grandstand. Two city guards kept a watchful eye on the feasting, drinking, noisy crowd, composed mainly of men, though some were accompanied by their wives and children.

On the third row, to the left of the entrance, he saw her. She had long, straight, reddish hair flowing past her shoulders and wore a stola. Their gazes met. She smiled. Next to her was an older couple. The man of the couple had a notably broad, protruding jaw. The woman was petite and slim, and her similarly reddish hair led Titus to suspect she was her mother.

By the time the event concluded, Titus remained seated, casting discreet looks at her. A group of musicians played to mark the end, and some attendees began to leave. The unknown girl's eyes frequently glanced in Titus' direction. He stood up, squeezed past people on the benches, down the steps, past the front row. His heart raced. The closer he moved toward the woman, the more his body shrank, like a snail's feeler retracting upon touch.

The man with the broad jaw whispered something to his wife. Grinning, they watched Titus approach. The girl continued to smile at him.

A loud male voice rang out from the front row.

"Look, there's that crazy Laelius."

A group of merchants laughed and drank wine.

"Yeah, that's him. Laelius! Laelius!"

"What's he doing here? He never goes out."

Titus felt as if all eyes in the Odeon were on him. He grew dizzy. Hunched over, he waved his hand and quickly walked to the corridor leading outside, leaving the mocking laughter of the crowd behind.

A week later, Titus attended a poetry performance in the Odeon. Once again, he met surprised faces, but the astonishment at his presence seemed lessened. From the stands, he saw her again. A group of young men surrounded her like hungry wolves waiting for an opportunity to catch her attention. However, their advances, murmurs, and laughter swiftly ended as the broad-jawed man chased the youths away.

Titus' body trembled at the thought of speaking to her. Despite her finding him in the audience and smiling at him, he convinced himself that the gods deemed it too soon for such an encounter. Thus, after the performance, he withdrew in silence.

It wasn't until two visits later, during a concert by a group from Thessaloniki, that he finally made his move. That morning, Titus hadn't managed to eat a bite. Pale as a ghost and shaking as if standing naked in the Alps during winter, he approached his target, bypassing the curious young men who kept their distance. The broad-jawed man looked puzzled as the mysterious Roman bowed.

"Laelius?"

On that day, the broad-jawed man, named Ptolemaios, and his wife Galyna introduced their daughter, Ariadne. She blushed when Titus, with shaking hands, mixed up the sequence of his names.

A week later, spurred by her daughter's encouragement, Galyna convinced her reluctant husband to let Ariadne spend time with the Roman. "He's an odd fellow, but he's wealthy and comes from a respectable Roman family," he supposedly told his wife, thus granting Ariadne permission to meet Titus in Nicopolis' public spaces.

2. Ariadne

One summer morning, Ariadne slipped unseen into Titus' house through the backyard. She had brought pastries from the market. She wore an off-white stola, revealing one shoulder. Her auburn hair clung to her forehead.

"Are you alone?" Ariadne asked.

"Remus is fishing. At the lagoon."

She dropped the bag of pastries on the ground, seized Titus by the collar of his chiton, and pinned him against the kitchen wall. Titus' heart raced. He gasped like a hound on a summer day. Ariadne kissed him. Her body odor overwhelmed the scent of rose perfume.

"What did you tell your father?"

"He thinks…" Ariadne paused between kisses, "… I'm at Eirene's."

"Eirene," Titus echoed between smooches, "… isn't she the one with the big…"

Ariadne pressed him even harder against the wall. She leaned her forehead against his. The pupils in her green irises pierced his soul.

"What are you saying? Do you find her attractive?"

Titus laughed.

"I… was just… joking."

"Say I'm the only one for you."

"You are the only one."

"Liar." Ariadne's lips met Titus' again. She sucked on his tongue so hard he feared it might tear from his mouth. Titus grabbed her, carried her to the living room, and threw her on the couch. He wanted to devour her like a wolf eyeing fresh meat, driven by an urge he couldn't explain, as if his body acted on its own.

After the deed was done, Titus gazed into Ariadne's eyes. Her gaze was as fierce as a Scythian on the battlefield. She laughed and kissed him. Titus caressed her thighs. They were the most beautiful thighs he had ever touched, even more so than those of all the prostitutes in Rome combined. He just couldn't get his hands off them.

"I have to go," Ariadne said.

"Why so soon? Remus will be away for a while longer."

A wave of sadness swept over her face. Titus lifted himself up.

"My parents are expecting me…"

"Stay a bit longer."

Titus kissed her neck, her cheek. He clasped her waist. Ariadne pushed him away.

"Stop, I really have to go."

Ariadne stood up, dressed herself, and left the house.

Dusk was falling. Titus leaned contentedly against the fence in his backyard. "What a day." He took a sip from the wine jug. He heard the front door open and close. Remus appeared in the backyard with a fishing rod and a bag full of fish.

"It smells like roses inside," said the servant, his voice carrying a mix of disapproval and amusement.

"That sounds about right," Titus said, grinning. Like a Spartan who had just crushed an army of Persians, he took a gulp from the jug.

"Messing around before marriage is frowned upon here. You're playing with fire."

"Playing with fire is my specialty."

"You have an agreement with Ptolemaios. What will that family think if you betray their trust now?"

"She's the one taking the initiative, not me."

"That says something."

"What do you mean by that?"

"If she can't even be faithful to her own flesh and blood, why would she be faithful to you?"

"It'll be fine. Remus, believe me, she's completely smitten with me. You should have seen how she tore the toga off my body. Besides, since when do slaves understand love?"

Remus sighed, shrugged his shoulders, placed the bag

of fish on the ground.

"Maybe I don't. But I do understand loyalty. Be careful what you wish for."

Remus went inside.

Clouds drifted across the moon. Titus took a big swig from the jug. Remus' words still echoed in his head. But he knew this was more than a mere game, more than desire.

This was special.

Titus hadn't spent much time in his study lately, which didn't bother him too much. Ariadne was not exactly a homebody. She also loved drinking wine. She took Titus to theater performances, art exhibitions, and music events. Nicopolis was no Athens or Rome; there was still a great deal to do.

That afternoon, they lay in the shady backyard of the Odeon.

"Remus is on the Apollo Hill. Let's go to my place," Titus said.

"Don't you like it here?"

"Yes, but I long for you."

"I long for you too, but…"

"But what?"

"Do you want just my body, or…?"

"I want all of you, in every way."

"Why?"

"Why what?"

"Why do you want me?" She looked as if she genuinely meant the question.

Titus tried to verbalize the reasons he fell for her. But he found it difficult to pinpoint what exactly he loved about her, aside from her beauty. Could it be her character? The way she spoke? How she looked into his eyes? His father taught him what to look for in a woman. Things like modesty, honesty, obedience, virtue. "Find yourself a good Roman wife and you'll be a happy man," he often said. Maybe that's why Titus had looked for a woman resembling his mother; someone trustworthy and stable, someone humble and predictable, someone he could rely on, embodying certainty in an uncertain world. Ariadne seemed more like the opposite of that. And she wasn't even Roman.

A group of dressed women in fashionable dresses passed through the garden, leaving a trail of perfume in their wake. Titus' gaze briefly followed the women as they passed. "Ow!" The slap echoed through the garden, startling a group of ducks bathing nearby into flight toward a pond. Titus clutched his leg.

"I saw you gazing at them!"

"I didn't do it on purpose! It just happened. I didn't think about it."

"Don't do that. Not as long as you're with me. Promise?"

"I can't promise that."

Ariadne smacked his thigh again. She grabbed his collar and kissed him. Titus pulled back his head.

"Not here," he whispered. "Have you lost your mind?"

"Come on, let's go to your place. I'll teach you to make promises to me."

By the time Remus returned from Apollo Hill, Ariadne had already left Titus' house. Remus didn't even seem to bother commenting on the smell of roses; a subtle headshake was enough to communicate his disapproval.

Since her visit, Titus hadn't heard from Ariadne for a while. Normally, she would pop in daily, even if just to vent about her day. Because Titus hadn't seen her for a week, he decided to visit her at home.

Galyna let him in and took him to Ariadne's bedroom. They stood in the doorway. Ariadne was in bed, in broad daylight.

"Is she sick?" Titus whispered.

"No," Galyna said.

"What's the matter, then?"

"She has this from time to time. It'll pass on its own."

"I told her she should go to the temple!" a voice came

from the hallway.

"Yes, yes!" Galyna responded. She looked at Titus and whispered, "My husband is convinced the gods can help her. But we can't get her into the temple no matter what."

Titus entered the room and crouched by the bed.

"Hey... what's wrong?"

Ariadne was curled up under a blanket, staring at the wall in a deadened manner, clutching a doll made of cloth, wood, and ceramic. She didn't respond. A tear rolled down her cheek. Titus touched her shoulder.

"What's the matter?"

Galyna sat beside him.

"You better leave her alone for now. It really does pass on its own. Don't worry."

Titus went back home.

On a cool afternoon in September, Ariadne excitedly talked about a traveling group from Britannia that would perform in the theater in two market weeks. But when Titus informed her that he would be in Athens visiting his sister on that day, her excitement vanished like snow in the sun.

From the steps of the Odeon, she stared ahead. A gentle breeze swept across the market square. Most merchants had already started packing up their goods. Cats prowled around the fish stalls, begging. A dog devoured a pig's stomach he had stolen unseen from the butcher. Titus stood up and pointed to the market.

"If you want to hunt for bargains, now's your chance."

"So, you're leaving?" Ariadne's eyes narrowed. Her breathing quickened. She tried to hide her trembling hands by clasping them tightly together. "And you're telling me this now?"

Startled, Titus tried to assure her he would return. He sat close to her and firmly grasped Ariadne's hand.

"Believe me, just three weeks. My sister really needs me. Her husband is…"

"And don't I need you?"

Titus fell silent.

"Why are you leaving me behind… I don't want to lose you like…" The young Greek slapped her leg. She shook her head. "I don't want you to go."

"Lose me like who? What are you talking about?"

"Nobody."

"Come on, tell me."

Titus' concerned eyes scanned her face as if trying to read her thoughts. With trembling hands, Ariadne blew her nose into her handkerchief. She stared at two cats fighting over a fish head on the ground.

"A long time ago, my father went to Egypt on a

business trip. I was seven. He was a merchant and often away. He promised to bring back a souvenir. I wanted a doll. A doll from Egypt."

"And... did you get your doll?"

"No. He never came back."

Titus looked at her, puzzled. A brief smile crossed Ariadne's face, like the sun peeking through during a cloudy, rainy afternoon.

"Ptolemaios is my stepfather. My real father... my mother lost hope that he would ever return. Shortly after, she met Ptolemaios. They got married. No one ever heard from my father again."

Titus was silent for a moment. He stroked her chiton.

"Did you ever look for him?"

Ariadne made a face of disgust.

"Who says he wants to be found? Maybe he started a new life in Egypt. He probably has a wife and a few children there. He must be happy without me. I don't want to interfere."

"I'm not buying that! Why would he just leave you like that?"

Ariadne rested her head on Titus' lap. She smiled. Her pupils were dilated enough to swallow the whole city. She squeezed his hand as if she never intended to let go.

"I've never felt this way about anyone before," she

said.

Titus wrapped his arm around her and kissed her forehead. It felt as though his heart was pumping a starry night sky through his veins, tingling every capillary and organ. Thoughts of marrying her and starting a family danced in his mind. And once he finally succeeded in turning stone to gold, the world would be theirs. Nothing could come in between them. They would travel to Marseille, visit the new amphitheater in Carthage, drink wine in Athens. He would take her to Alexandria and reunite her with her father or, at least, find out what happened to him.

On the journey to see his sister, Titus couldn't eat. He asked the charioteer to stop several times due to an upset stomach, arriving a day later than expected. From Athens, he sent her no less than twelve letters in three weeks. When he got back, the exiled Roman proposed to the Greek Ariadne, who said a resounding "yes." Titus celebrated the engagement with Remus and a jug of Falernian wine.

On the seventh day before the kalends[1] of December, 866 years since the founding of Rome (112 AD), Titus Laelius Faber married Ariadne, daughter of Echemus and Galyna, stepdaughter of Ptolemaios. They moved into a charming house in the heart of Nicopolis. Ariadne's family provided this house, located three streets from the forum, as her dowry. From the cozy veranda, one could step into a

---

[1] The kalends is the first day of the month in the Roman calendar. In this case it's the 1st of August.

spacious living room connected to an open kitchen, while the back housed three snug rooms and a garden. Titus claimed the largest of these rooms as his new study.

Two years after the wedding, their son Ares was born, and a year and a half later, their second son Faustinus. Happiness seemed boundless until Titus received sad news from Rome shortly after Faustinus' birth. Titus' father and family patriarch, Attius Laelius Crassus, had died of a stroke.

3. Seer

Shortly after the death of Attius Laelius Crassus, a power struggle within the family led to the squandering of their capital, allowing their wealth to vanish into unknown pockets. After two years of mismanagement, the once wealthy Laelius house faced significant debts, forcing Titus to sell twelve out of fourteen villas and nearly all land around Nicopolis. Only two villas and a modest piece of land with a shed remained, along with Remus, as he sold all his other slaves. Ariadne spent days crying on the couch.

"Can't you think of something? What will happen to us? Do we have to sell the house too?"

"How am I supposed to know that? As if I've ever been in this situation before! I'll come up with something. I still have my two hands. I can probably find some work."

He envisioned a future of hauling heavy rocks or teaching a bunch of whiny kids on the street for a meager wage. Or perhaps he would end up begging in the forum. Surely, it wouldn't come to that. He still managed two villas and a piece of land. To his relief, the family could just get by with the rent and lease income.

"But what about our plans? We were going to Marseille, Salona, and Malaga. What about drinking wine in Athens?" Ariadne asked.

"We can't afford that right now. That's why my

experiments are a priority. I'm on the verge of a breakthrough and..."

"When you met me, you were also on the verge of a breakthrough! When is this breakthrough coming?"

"Believe me, dear, it won't be long. Once I succeed, I'll take you wherever you want. Malaga, Carthage, Gaul, Britannia. In fact, if it really turns out as I imagine, we could build holiday homes in any city you desire! We could even start our own empire. Imagine, dear, our own little empire by the Iberian Sea, or somewhere between Syria and Judea. We will be gods among men. No one could harm us. Wouldn't that be wonderful?"

More determined than ever to turn stone into gold, Titus hardly left his study. He sent Remus out daily to buy old metal, used glassware, and pottery at a low price. Occasionally, he scoured the market himself for second-hand glass bottles and tools, bringing home large quantities, to Ariadne's annoyance. Smoke and fumes from his study filled the neighborhood with a variety of scents, from melting bronze or silver to a pungent mix resembling dog vomit, elderly feces, and drunkard's urine.

Plautia, the neighbor, came to complain. She was an elderly, distinguished lady living with her husband, Sejanus, and spent most of her time on the balcony and veranda. She was always up-to-date with neighborhood and citywide news.

Not too long ago, she mentioned that Alcander Cassius, a young Greek with Roman roots, had returned to

Nicopolis after studying literature and rhetoric in Athens. He came back to manage the local family business, including numerous plots of land and properties, some of which had belonged to the Laelii until the Aelianii family bought them. Alcander Cassius was infamous for his lavish parties and numerous concubines. Rumors suggested he was now seeking a marriage partner.

Months passed since the Laelii family's downfall. Titus spent his days in his study, and Ariadne was rarely home, unusual for a Greek married mother. One evening, Ariadne left abruptly, stayed out all night, and hadn't returned by the next morning.

With Faustinus in his arms, a nervous Titus paced the house. Ares played on the floor, trying to kick his father's calves as he passed. The neighborhood cat, a black and white tomcat, walked meowing through the living room. The animal had no permanent owner and had been taking advantage of the generosity of the people in the neighborhood for years. He had no competition. With his imposing presence, he had driven all the other cats away. Ares liked to pull his tail, upon which the cat would hiss and dash off through the backyard.

Footsteps sounded on the terrace. The front door opened.

"Where have you been?" Titus asked.

"At my parents' house, like I told you," Ariadne replied.

"Again with your parents? You visit them quite often,

don't you? Have you forgotten you have a husband and two children?"

"Why are you so possessive? You sound like my stepfather. Let me be free! I feel suffocated!"

"Possessive? Suffocated?" Titus placed Faustinus on the couch. He grabbed Ariadne's shoulders. "I just want to know where my wife is. Is that too much to ask? Is there someone else?"

"How dare you?" Ariadne pushed Titus away and slapped him. "How could you even think that? What kind of person are you?"

"Why are you acting like this? What have I done to you?"

Ariadne stumbled into the kitchen, tripping over the threshold. After Titus helped her up, she frantically searched the cabinets while leaning on his arm.

"Wine. Where's the wine?"

She released Titus' arm and collapsed. The pile of dirty kitchen linen on the floor cushioned her fall. Titus sighed. Ares ran to his mother and jumped on her back. Faustinus cried.

"We opened the last jug yesterday, with dinner, remember? Just before you left?"

"Why hasn't Remus fetched more? What good is that slave for? You should have sold him, too."

"Don't talk about him like that!"

Ariadne's eyes filled with tears. She pushed Ares away and rolled across the greasy kitchen floor. Like an upturned beetle, she flailed her limbs, smearing her tunic with floor grease. Ares laughed out loud, while Faustinus' shrill cries filled the room.

Titus placed Faustinus in his crib in the bedroom. In the kitchen, he poured an orange brew into a cup and handed it to his wife.

"I hate that sour stuff!" The neighbors likely heard the ceramic shatter. "Wine! Give me wine!"

Ariadne grabbed a decorative bowl from the counter and smashed it to the ground. *Does she have any idea how much that bowl cost?* Titus wondered. Then she pulled cups and bowls from the cabinets. Among the shards, lying on the greasy kitchen floor, she fell asleep crying. Titus laid her in bed. He watched her breathe unevenly through her mouth. He turned her onto her side, filled a bucket with well water, and placed it by the bed.

Ares played in the backyard, terrorizing a group of ants with a stick as they tried to escape through the young grass. When his father emptied a bucket by the cypress tree, he curiously approached his mother's vomit and poked it with the stick. Titus noticed Plautia and Sejanus watching them from their balcony. They probably heard every detail of the argument. *Oh well, what does it matter?* Such outbursts were more routine than exceptional nowadays.

In his desperation, Titus visited the temples at the forum, offering sacrifices to Juno and Venus, the protectress of marriage and the goddess of love. When these offerings seemed to have little effect, he decided to see a seer who lived just outside the city. This seer, named Timotheos, was renowned for his ability to read the gods' will through animal behavior. Even the Praetor visited him from time to time, as Titus had heard from Plautia, who spoke highly of the man.

Timotheos lived in a modest villa surrounded by a tall, white wall. Titus marveled at the large number of animals around the villa. Countless rabbits hopped through the backyard, cats lounged in every corner, and the villa's roof was teeming with birds. A cheerful shepherd dog greeted Titus on the property by jumping up against him.

As if expecting Titus, Timotheos opened the gate to the backyard. The seer sported a long white beard and his Eastern-looking robe revealed skinny, white-haired wrists. Without uttering a word, the seer led his guest to a windowless, dark room at the back of the villa, where the scent of incense greeted them. Five small oil lamps warmed the space.

"This is the room," Timotheos said. "Here, they tell us about what is to come, and what they plan to do."

"Who?"

"The gods, of course. They usually don't speak directly to us. They talk to the animals. The animals then speak to us. That's what those temple priests don't understand. They build temples for Apollo and worship him in stone. But Apollo doesn't speak to them in those temples. They don't listen to their complaints and pleas either. The gods only speak to us through nature."

On an altar lay flowers, mountain crystals, and other items that all radiated something sacred, as if they emitted a glow without being light sources. A Persian carpet lay on the floor, featuring an apple tree with long, twisting branches. Various birds perched in this apple tree, and at its base was a pond with fish and ducks, with various animals populating the landscape with mountains in the back.

Timotheos invited Titus to sit on the carpet. The seer took an oil lamp from the altar and placed it between them. He poured a dark brown brew into a cup and handed it to his guest. "Drink up." The drink was odorless but tasted bitter. Reluctantly, Titus finished the last sip. The seer then asked him the reason for his visit.

"I want to know how to save my marriage."

The seer nodded in agreement and made elegant gestures around the small flame of the lamp, which flared up and started moving like a Greek temple dancer.

"Gods weave the future; your path is your own choice. I can ask a favor of the gods for you, a glimpse into what is to come."

From a basket in the corner of the room, Timotheos took some white flowers and dipped them in a bowl of red wine. He placed the bowl next to a statuette of Zeus on the altar, knelt, and motioned for Titus to follow.

The seer raised his hands and turned his palms outward. With his eyes closed, he mumbled in a language unknown to Titus. The oil lamps in the room began to burn brighter, and the flames danced up and down. Chickadees chirped, pigeons cooed, blackbirds sang, chickens clucked. Titus looked around with wide eyes. *Is this some clever trick? Or am I hallucinating from the bitter drink?* He decided not to think too much about it and surrender to the experience. His marriage was at stake, after all.

Soon, the bird sounds faded but lingered in the background. The Persian carpet felt warm, the tree's branches twisted, and the animals came to life. A rooster searched for food in the grass; a snake slithered along the tree stump.

"Roosters crow in the morning; hens lay eggs in silence. Shadows brew, whispers of hidden truths, lovers lost in distance, revelation inevitable," said Timotheos.

Titus could make little sense of it. He looked back at the carpet. He saw rain clouds gathering over the landscape. The animals fled to bushes and plants. From the cloud cover, a lightning bolt appeared. The seer shook his head and mumbled again in the strange language. The sky turned red, and volcanoes spewed lava in the distance. From cracks in the ground, scorpions crawled over the landscape and then into the tree.

The seer turned pale. His old limbs trembled. It seemed as if Titus and the seer had become part of the carpet, now nestled in the landscape under the tree.

"Zeus whispers trials. Great changes. Passions unbridled."

An owl hooted from the top of the tree. The scorpions halted their movement. In the sky, a flock of seagulls appeared, so numerous they shaded the tree. The seagulls took turns diving, snatching the scorpions in their beaks and devouring them alive. The black creatures fled back into the crevices.

With closed eyes, the seer took a deep breath. "Many voices, paths given by the Gods. Revenge, love, wisdom. We cannot prevent our desires. Following them is our choice."

The clouds cleared, and the sky turned blue. Chickadees, blackbirds, and other birds returned. Rabbits hopped by the tree trunk. Ants crawled out of holes, along branches, over leaves. The Persian carpet lay as it had been before.

As Titus left the house of Timotheos behind, he glanced back. The seer was watching him. Titus could read the concern on his face from a distance. *What is so terrible that it even shakes a seer?* Titus couldn't make much sense of his words or the appearance of scorpions, seagulls, and the owl. Facing challenges and uncovering secrets sounded unsettling. *But isn't this just what seers do? Make people scared and confused so they keep coming back for more?* He found it amusing that even the Praetor fell for this charlatan's arts.

The northern gate of Nicopolis was near. Titus was startled when a black scorpion, as large as his palm, approached him. And to his amazement, an owl hooted from a tree along the path. Out of the corner of his eye, a seagull took a dive, grabbed the scorpion in its beak, and flew away. When loud thunder sounded in the sky, Titus, shaking his head, quickened his pace, longing for his study.

4. Shed

Shortly after her husband, Dimitrios, died from a mysterious illness that slowly rotted away his tongue and intestines, Flavia moved from Athens to Nicopolis. Flavia was five years older than Titus, but her many wrinkles made her appear fifteen years older. Ares and Faustinus enjoyed visiting their aunt, who lived just two streets away in a small house with a large front garden full of plants and flowers. She had turned her backyard into a vegetable garden, where she also built a small pond to keep carp. Flavia herself had no children, at least not anymore. She had given birth to five children, four of whom died from infectious diseases, and one from food poisoning.

Ares and Faustinus spent the night at Flavia's, who had offered to have them over. She spoiled her nephews with freshly baked bread and blueberries from her garden, entertained Ares with exciting stories about the barbarians from the north, and rocked Faustinus to sleep with tender love. Flavia was alarmed to learn that Ares showed a particular interest in the bloody scenes that unfold on the battlefield. She was "truly startled" when Ares asked her to explain how prisoners of war are tortured and what torture methods are specifically used. "But how long does it take for a person to die if all their bones are broken?"

Recently, Ares had been waking up in the middle of the night, crying due to a recurring nightmare. Flavia witnessed this for the first time.

"Scary men are coming to get me."

"What kind of scary men? What did they look like?"

Flavia's wide eyes looked at the toddler. He didn't answer, so his aunt picked him up, rocked him back and forth, and soothed him with her angelic voice, singing him a song. Flavia had previously mentioned to Ariadne that dreams have a deeper meaning, but her sister-in-law immediately dismissed the idea as superstitious nonsense. According to Ariadne, the dream was simply Ares' way of dealing with the sudden poverty the family was facing, emphasizing that Titus was to blame.

Out of concern, but also due to a strong interest in dream interpretation, Flavia took her nephews to a local healing place to seek explanations and possibly a solution. However, the healers couldn't provide much useful information, except that the scary men symbolized "fear" that could have arisen from an unstable living environment. To avoid an argument with her sister-in-law, she asked Titus not to tell Ariadne about her trip.

In the morning, a bang started the neighborhood, followed by a loud crash as if an entire market stall full of glassware had been toppled from three stories high onto a stone floor. Various neighbors from the adjacent houses came outside. The dog of their elderly, stone-deaf neighbor Mr. Evagrius, barked as if he was about to be clubbed to death. The neighborhood cat, who was sleeping in the doorway just before the bang, jumped a meter into the air out of fear.

After chasing the neighborhood cat off the porch, Titus slammed the front door shut. Sweat ran down his upper body, and his eyes were red. Shards littered the kitchen floor. A strong scent of wine, vinegar, burnt wood, and molten copper tingled in his nose.

"I've been clear about this from the beginning. Why is it suddenly a problem?"

"It always was for me! But you're just too blind to see that."

"I can't read minds, can I?"

"If only you could. Because apparently, you have no clue about what I've been trying to make clear for *four years* now."

"Ariadne, by Jupiter, what are you talking about?"

Ariadne sighed. She collapsed onto the couch in the living room. An empty wine jug stood on a side table, next to an iron cup from which she took a sip.

"This is exactly the problem. I'm not even going to bother anymore. Go back to playing in your little room."

Titus grabbed the empty wine jug and threw it against the wall.

"You know how important this is for us. It's my only hope to get out of this mess. I'm on the verge of a breakthrough, believe me!"

"Why don't I believe a word of this? Do you have any

idea why? Go find a job!"

Ariadne marched to the bedroom with firm steps. She returned shortly after in a dark red chiton, holding a drawstring bag in her hand. The sweet scent of roses and lavender overpowered the smell of wine, vinegar, burnt wood, and molten copper. The dark red eyeshadow made her gaze even more intense than it already was.

"I'm going to my parents."

"Sure, go back to your parents again."

Without casting a glance at Titus, she walked out and slammed the door shut. Illuminated by an oil lamp, Titus saw the dark circles under his eyes in the hand mirror. A full moon had already risen above the fence in the backyard, shining as if it urgently wanted to tell Titus something.

That evening, there was a grand symposium at the Odeon, entirely dedicated to a new commemorative statue of Emperor Augustus unveiled at the entrance. The affluent society found any excuse for a celebration, with slaves scurrying about with wine jugs. Nonetheless, Augustus would likely have been delighted by all the hustle and bustle in the city he had founded.

The silence in the house remained uncomfortable for Titus. The absence of his wife and children's voices was somewhat like a marketplace without street musicians. Background noises seemed to come to the forefront, such as the voices of Plautia and Sejanus, the wheezing and coughing of Mr. Evagrius, and the meowing of the neighborhood cat sitting on the porch.

From his couch, Titus heard the rattling of a wagon pulled by horses approaching and then slowly fading into the distance. Boisterous youths paused briefly at the garden gate at the front of the house but soon headed toward the forum. Titus let his thoughts drift with the crickets' singing until a deep voice interrupted the harmonious chorus, which slightly irritated him.

"Hello? Titus? Titus!" The visitor pounded on the gate. Titus recognized the voice. He picked up the oil lamp from the side table and opened the door. The figure in the blue chiton pulled back his hood, revealing a pale face. It was Arrian, standing slightly bent in the doorway to avoid hitting his head.

"What's wrong?" Titus asked.

Arrian's eyes bulged. He huffed and puffed as if he had run from Marathon to Nicopolis.

"Your wife," he said.

Arrian poured two iron cups with fruit juice made from the apricots and berries he had hastily bought from the evening market. He stared at the bowl of olives and the now stale bread on the table that Remus had picked up from the baker that morning. Shaking his head, Titus walked to the kitchen, grabbed a jug from the countertop, sat opposite his guest, and took three big gulps. His eyes were red, as if he had been standing in smoke.

"At the Odeon? A black wig? Alcander Cassius, you

say? Isn't he that wealthy snob?"

"I've had my suspicions for some time…"

"Why didn't you say anything?"

Arrian's shoulders slumped. A long, audible sigh escaped his lips.

"Wasn't it obvious? I mean, she comes home late at night, or even early in the morning. Isn't that unacceptable for a housewife with two children? I don't understand how you tolerate this, Titus. I would never have let it go this far."

"We talked about it. She kept saying she was going to her parents. She said I didn't trust her. That I suffocated her. I tried to trust her, to give her space…"

Sighing, Arrian stood up.

"Come with me. I'll show you something."

Titus and Arrian rode through the northern gate of Nicopolis on horseback, racing through the countryside. A disgustingly large villa loomed closer in the distance. Apparently, the building, surrounded by fields and plantations, boasted more than twenty rooms, three bathrooms, a bathhouse, a bakery, and an inner garden that made any city garden in Nicopolis look bleak.

Titus stopped his horse at a small shed, dwarfed by the villa that lay about a hundred passus behind it.

"This is one of the few properties I have left," said

Titus. "The land around I leased to a farmer. Grumpy guy. Not around much."

"Olive trees," said Arrian, inspecting the surroundings, glaring over a flock of sheep and a few goats grazing in the dark. "Your little shack grants us front-row seats for what's to come. A scary coincidence, isn't it? The gods must have meant it this way."

Arrian bumped his head against the doorpost as they entered the shed. It smelled musty inside. There was a bed, a simple wooden table with two stools, several full and empty wine jugs, a storage cabinet, and a wooden chest. A hatch in the floor led to a crawl space.

They stuck their heads through a small window overlooking the terrace of the ridiculously large villa that belonged to none other than Alcander Cassius. Titus had heard about the young man's extravagant morning rituals, like daily bathing in a warm bath filled with rose petals, having his hair carefully styled, and sometimes spending entire afternoons in front of the mirror, but knew little else about him.

A few oil lamps illuminated the terrace of Alcander's villa. At the entrance, a chubby little man sat on a stool, wearing a notably shiny bronze helmet. Two guards with dogs and torches patrolled the outer wall to the left of the terrace. Though they spoke loudly, Arrian and Titus couldn't understand what they said. The light from the full moon shone through the window, illuminating the table where Titus placed two mugs of diluted wine.

"Are you sure they will come?"

"Patience."

In the meantime, they saw the guards with their dogs walking past the outer wall three times. The chubby doorman had fallen asleep. Titus rubbed his eyes. Shortly after, the sound of wheels on gravel and the dull thud of hoofbeats grew louder in the distance.

"I hear something."

"Here they come."

Pulled by no less than four horses and accompanied by an old, experienced rider, a luxurious carriage stopped right in front of the terrace. The vehicle looked too grand even for a Roman emperor. The doorman woke up with a start, ran to the carriage, and helped Alcander step out.

Titus' heartbeat quickened when he saw Ariadne emerge from the carriage, wearing a jet-black wig. Hand in hand, she and Alcander walked across the terrace and into the villa. Titus' hands trembled. His pounding heart began to hurt as if the pulsing muscle wanted to burst out of his throat. Arrian looked at him.

"Didn't I tell you?"

Titus took a big gulp of wine, squeezed through the window, and crossed the field toward the villa.

"Wait, what are you doing? Titus!"

Titus took another large gulp, threw the jug ahead of

him where it landed with a thud on the soft, tall weeds. He marched through the fallow ground. The guards had just walked to the back. The drowsy doorman on the terrace had fallen asleep again. Emerging from the darkness, Titus charged onto the terrace and kicked in the door before the sleepyhead could notice.

"Wait! What are you doing?" The drowsy doorman, startled by the noise, leaped up and ran after Titus but tripped over his own feet and fell flat on the ground, while Titus ran unhesitatingly on.

Like a rampaging wild boar, the Roman stormed through the villa, from room to room, making his way to a space fit only for an imperial residence. In this room, he found Ariadne naked on a couch studded with gems. Alcander tensed his right bicep in the mirror. The drowsy doorman, now with a bloody nose, had meanwhile alerted his colleagues. Three men and two dogs strong, they ran through the villa's corridors.

Ariadne screamed.

"Seize him!" Alcander gestured with his arms toward the guards.

Titus looked at his wife.

"What have I done to you? Can't you show me a shred of respect?"

"Nothing happened between us!" Ariadne burst into tears. Titus puffed up like a pufferfish.

"Nothing happened? *Nothing*? Then why are you

here?" he snapped. "Why are you naked?"

"Don't yell at me! I hate it when people yell at me!"

"I'm not yelling! I'm calm!"

Alcander sighed and shook his head. The barking of the dogs grew louder. With a lot of noise, the guards stormed into the room.

Titus got away with just a few scrapes. Over his shoulder, he saw the guards and dogs returning to the villa. Though the soft, damp ground had cushioned his fall, he grabbed at his lower back. Mud covered his clothes. He wept. A shadow approached him. He felt an arm around him.

"It's going to be okay. Everything will be okay," said Arrian.

5. Alcander

Startled by the loud thunder, the neighborhood cat had hidden in a crevice between Titus and Mr. Evagrius' houses. The old neighbor's dog lay trembling under a table on the veranda a few meters away, posing little threat to any intruder. Titus sprawled out on the couch, finding solace in the patter of the rain as if it quenched the heat of his turbulent thoughts after days of inner inferno.

Since the revelation, his emotions swung wildly, though he tried to shield his sons from his turmoil by maintaining a calm and happy façade. Once they were asleep, he alternated between tears and rage, occasionally pounding the walls with his fists. In his sorrow, he reminisced about the early blissful moments of their relationship, realizing those moments had become increasingly rare post-marriage. Perhaps this decline was due to his frequent retreats to his study, or maybe he retreated to avoid confronting the painful reality that their marriage was but a shadow of its former fiery romance.

Titus leaped up as his eldest son, Ares, walked into the living room, sobbing.

"Did you have that dream again?" Titus lifted Ares and soothed him. "Come on, no one's going to take you away. It's just a dream. Dreams aren't real, remember what I told you? And if they do come, they'll have to get past me first."

Titus assumed a fighting stance, playfully jabbing the

air with his fists, eliciting giggles from Ares.

"When will Mom come back?"

"Daddy doesn't know."

"Why don't you know?"

"Because I don't."

"Why not?"

"Just because, Ares, just because!"

Titus had informed Ariadne through a letter of his intent to divorce her on the grounds of adultery. As the head of the family, he had a strong legal standing, and an adulterous woman had few rights in the Roman Empire. "That wretch can forget about custody," Titus had told Remus. He also expected to retain the house, originally received as a dowry from her family.

When putting Ares to bed, Titus shared fairy tales his mother used to tell him, about forest nymphs who protect the trees, plants, and animals, and who dance and sing their way through the woods. His mother claimed that these mythical beings truly existed and, indeed, that she herself had once seen one. Although Titus believed his mother wholeheartedly in his younger years, he later viewed her stories as mere flights of fancy.

The storm had passed. Mr. Evagrius' dog crawled back to its master, who dozed off in a chair next door. The neighborhood cat emerged from its hiding spot. As the crickets resumed their chorus and people began to roam the streets again, a knock sounded at the door. Titus opened it to find an unexpected visitor.

"What are you doing here?" Titus trembled, unsure whether to erupt in anger or maintain a calm composure.

Alcander, assuming the role of a monarch, settled on the couch in the living room, directing one of his bodyguards to pour him a drink. Titus turned pale but remained silent. Through the doorway, he noticed Plautia, while swiping the street, trying to sneak a peek into his home, before one of Alcander's men shut the door.

"It's a charming little house indeed. I'm wondering if we should sell it or rent it out," Alcander said, gazing around.

"What are you talking about?" Titus asked.

"Didn't you hear me? I'm deciding what to do with this house after you pack your things and leave."

"What? Leaving my house?" Titus clenched his fists. "She cheated on me! I'm entitled to part of the dowry! That's the law!"

"Cheated? What are you talking about?" Alcander replied. "Ariadne told me you forced her to frolic with other men. What was she doing in the Odeon then? Earning a few denarii, perhaps? While you sat at home doing nothing? You had to after the Laelii fortune dwindled and you sold off your lands and properties, right? Poor woman, sent out by her husband to solicit."

"This is absolute nonsense!"

"Calm down, Titus. And let's not forget the fire you started that claimed four lives, getting you banished from Rome for life. I'm well aware of your antics in the city. One Great Fire[2] wasn't enough for you? Yet you continue your dangerous activities here on my native soil. You're a murderer, a threat to Nicopolis, and a pimp."

Woken by the shouting, Faustinus cried from his crib, and Ares wandered into the living room, hiding behind his father's legs.

"Who are you guys?" Ares asked.

"Ares, go to your brother," Titus said. "Dad will be right back. I just need to sort some things out with these gentlemen."

"Oh, Titus, are you afraid I'll harm your son?" Alcander sneered. "Believe me, I care about these children. In fact, I'll do everything in my power to ensure they grow up safe and prosperous."

"Stay away from them, you and that harlot!"

Ares froze, and Titus hugged him tightly, trying to shield him from the unfolding drama. Faustinus' cries filled the room.

"I'll give you until the kalends. And that's generous of me," Alcander said with a smirk before leaving the house with his bodyguards following him, as faithful as dogs.

---

[2] Alcander refers to the Great Fire of Rome that in the year 64 AD destroyed more than half of the city.

Titus kicked the half-filled wine cup off the table.

The next day, the rainy weather had given way to a clear blue sky. Titus stood in the backyard, surveying his surroundings. Remus sat on the grass, stretching his legs out, while the neighborhood cat perched on the fence, closely watching Ares and Faustinus as they ran around the garden, laughing. Ares threw a stone at the cat, hitting it squarely on the flank.

"Ares! You shouldn't do that!" Flavia scolded as she stormed out from the kitchen into the garden. Startled, the cat jumped off the fence into Mr. Evagrius' yard, inadvertently plunging into the pond. Mr. Evagrius' dog started barking, causing Ares and Faustinus to burst into laughter. Titus glanced over at Plautia and Sejanus' balcony, where Plautia, with a goblet in hand, peeked into the garden with a sidelong glance. Titus scratched his head and sighed.

"Let's go inside," he whispered to his sister.

Flavia slumped on the couch, her shoulders hunched forward, and her large eyes staring blankly ahead. The laughter of Ares and Faustinus echoed from the garden. Titus poured two mugs of diluted wine and sat down on a stool at an angle to his sister.

"I understand why you're asking this... but do you realize how risky it is? A woman with two young children? All the way to Iconium? I wouldn't even know the way," Flavia said.

"You won't be traveling alone. I'll send Remus with

you."

"And once we get there, then what?"

"Our cousin, Lucius Junius Silvanus, has recently become a magistrate in Iconium. He can help us."

Flavia scoffed and laughed. "That country bumpkin? You two can't stand each other, remember?"

"If not there, then Rome," Titus said with a deep sigh. "As long as you're far from here."

Flavia paced the living room toward the kitchen, while Remus' cheerful voice, calling out indistinct things to the children, drifted in from the garden.

"Rome? If Alcander and Ariadne get custody, they'll come looking for us. Then we'll have to flee from place to place. Even if we stay out of the authorities' grasp, you'll be charged with kidnapping. And how do you think that'll be for your children?"

"Then so be it."

"Titus, my health isn't good. It hasn't been for a long time, and you know it. I understand what you want, but this is madness. As your elder sister, I refuse to cooperate."

Titus stood up and walked to the back door. Staring into the garden, he saw Faustinus perched on Remus' shoulders while Ares tried to hit him with a stick, and the wiry servant darted across the grass like a prancing horse. Titus pondered the things that could go wrong if Flavia and Remus traveled east with his children. They could fall prey to bandits, get stranded without money, or worse, be killed in a political conflict. The thought of losing his loved ones filled him with sorrow. He stared ahead, nodding in agreement.

6. Hephaestus

Arrian revealed that Ariadne's family had taken the rumor of Titus prostituting their daughter for months as the truth. The evidence? Eyewitnesses claimed to have seen her in the city's most upscale brothel, wearing a pitch-black wig. One of these witnesses, an elderly Greek widower named Theophanes, even claimed to have slept with her, although he admitted to being nearly blind. However, his friend Eustathius, who was old but still had good eyesight despite slight dementia, supported the story, adding that she accepted two bronze coins and a glass of wine as payment.

The rumor spread quickly through the neighborhood. Some residents glared at Titus during his strolls. Yet Titus' close neighbors—Mr. Evagrius, Plautia, and Sejanus—didn't seem to take the rumors too seriously. Plautia even brought him homemade bread with olives multiple times and shared the latest neighborhood gossip to the point of annoyance.

Since the glares started, Titus had barely shown himself in public. Distraught, he asked Flavia to take the children for a while, claiming he needed time to reflect. Nevertheless, he quickly immersed himself in his experiments, with Remus providing all the necessary supplies. Every day, the servant scoured the market for stones, metals, and rather dubious ingredients like worn-out ladies' slippers and ram testicles. Everything went into a large iron pot simmering over a gentle fire in the study.

Day and night, smoke in all the colors of the rainbow escaped through the hole in the ceiling. The city guard asked Titus three times to cease his activities. The fourth time, he bribed them with a few coins to stop bothering him.

After three days of continuous simmering, Titus entered the living room, his face covered in soot. He walked into the garden with a charred stone in his hand and threw it at the fence with force. Remus, lounging in the garden reading, jumped up and watched as tiny black grains scattered across the grass.

"Doesn't look like gold, does it?"

"Know when to shut up, Remus."

Titus lit an oil lamp and grabbed a wine jug from the kitchen. He instructed Remus to fetch the latrunculi pieces and the board, then filled two cups with wine. "Cheers," said Titus, raising his cup and emptying it in one gulp. He arranged the game pieces. "What do you think of all this? Do you believe I did it?" asked Titus.

"I don't even think you're capable of it."

"Why not?"

"You're a good person. And... I don't think pimping is in your nature."

"It's all absurd, isn't it?" Titus made his opening move on the board. "Your turn."

Remus moved his piece and looked back at Titus, who

was staring at the board.

"Do you think she'll come back?" Titus asked.

"If she does, would you take her back?"

Titus shook his head. Images of his wife flashed before his eyes—her laugh, her auburn hair sticking to her forehead, her white thighs. He remembered their first meeting, the sunny afternoons in the Odeon's backyard, lying together under the large oak.

"I'm just wondering." After a pause, he continued, "I'd never take her back. Not after what she's done."

As usual, Remus easily defeated his master. And again. And yet again. More wine. Another try. Even more wine. With a grin unbecoming of a man who had just lost yet another game, Titus grabbed a full jug and stepped onto the porch, barely avoiding the neighborhood cat, and wandered into the night. Remus wanted to follow, but Titus ordered him to watch the house.

Titus staggered past the forum like a drunken sailor, encountering giggling couples and shouting vendors. Past the forum, he found himself in a street lined with pubs and brothels on either side. It was bustling. Shouts and murmurs formed the backdrop to loud music and songs by street performers. Titus looked around. The thought of Ariadne hanging out here and prostituting herself sent a pang through him. Was he starting to believe those ridiculous rumors? He could hardly imagine it.

A group of men playing a dice game at a table looked

up as Titus approached the terrace. "Look, it's that crazy Laelius. What's he doing here?" said a muscular man with droopy eyes.

A man with a weathered face and only four teeth stood up. "His wife left him for that rich snob."

A third man, skinny as a shrimp, flailed his arms. "He had his wife turning tricks because he's broke. And now that he's got no wife, he's turning tricks himself!" The skinny shrimp turned to Titus. "Hey, Laelius! How much for a suck?" jeered the skinny man, flailing his arms wildly. The group erupted into laughter.

"Ah, Zeno, yours is so tiny, you'll probably get it for free!" The muscular man toppled off his stool, roaring with laughter.

Titus ignored the group, taking a seat at a table and ordering a mug of wine. He watched the passing crowd, ordering another mug, and then another, and yet another. Suddenly, like a blow to the face, Titus spotted two familiar figures in the crowd—Ptolemaios and Galyna. He took a big gulp. His heartbeat thudded in his throat, his hands clenched into fists. He stood up abruptly, his chair clattering onto the cobblestones.

"Ptolemaios!" he shouted.

The crowd fell silent, and the street musicians ceased their playing. Ptolemaios turned around, his expression shifting from surprise to hostility. Galyna grabbed her husband's hand.

"What are you doing here?" Ptolemaios said.

"They've betrayed me! It's all lies!"

"Lies? Are you still in denial after everything you've done to my daughter? I had higher expectations for you, Roman. I thought you came from a good family. How wrong I was."

"You know damn well I would never hurt her! Let alone make her prostitute herself! What disgusting lies spread by that daughter of yours and her new... whatever he is! That's your daughter for you! Not a shred of integrity! Well done! Great upbringing!"

"You shut your mouth about my daughter! You've disgraced our family!"

The crowd gathered around the quarreling pair. Galyna wept. Just as Titus was about to land a punch on his former father-in-law, the city guards appeared.

Angry shouts echoed across the forum as the city guards dragged the struggling Roman along. A curious crowd followed Titus right up to his front door, three streets away. Ironically, the city guards imposed house arrest on Titus in a house that was no longer his.

"You'll regret this!" Titus yelled as the city guards slammed the front door shut. Amidst all the murmuring and groaning, a loud, raw voice boomed, "This isn't over yet! And your daughter, the whore, will regret it!"

From the living room, Titus peered out the window and saw Plautia, Sejanus, and other neighbors mingling with the crowd. He stuck his head out the window.

"Nicopolis will feel the power of Laelius!" he roared. "I will transform myself into a god! Do you hear me? I will burn like Hephaestus and set this disgusting city ablaze!"

Remus lifted Titus and laid him on the couch. Mr. Evagrius' dog barked incessantly.

"Go home, everyone, leave Mr. Laelius be," yelled one of the city guards, who remained on the porch like a statue for the rest of the night. After some murmuring, the crowd began to disperse, and soon the street was empty. Titus looked around. The living room spun. He closed his eyes and fell asleep.

7. Custody

Titus was sprawled on the floor when he opened his eyes, vomit clinging to his cheek. The walls around him seemed to dance. The birds sounded off-key, the neighborhood cat's meow felt like stabs in his ears, and the barking of Mr. Evagrius' dog felt like punches to his stomach. The thought of fresh rye bread made him nauseous. As water was the only thing his stomach could handle, Remus went to the aqueduct that afternoon, returning with four full jugs.

When Flavia learned of Titus' house arrest, she immediately visited him with Ares and Faustinus. "I don't know what came over me," Titus told his sister. "I wasn't myself, as if possessed by an evil spirit." At Titus' insistence, Flavia agreed to look after the children a bit longer. She reported that the news of his week-long confinement spread like wildfire through the city.

Days flew by. The house, which once started as a safe haven of love and happiness, had slowly decayed, and now felt more like a dungeon. The walls closed in, suffocating Titus. Or was it his head that had swelled? Breathing also became heavier, as if the air had thickened. Plautia brought him figs from North Africa, but she couldn't get much out of the Roman and returned home disappointed. Mr. Evagrius brought over a jar of top-grade garum, which his dog had apparently been drooling over all morning. Even the neighborhood cat made a brief appearance, rubbing its body against the garum jar before the elderly neighbor chased him away. Arrian was in Patrae for a project involving Emperor Hadrian's aqueduct construction, otherwise, he would have surely visited.

One rainy afternoon, Flavia stormed into Titus' study, in tears. Her thin limbs were shaking, and her large eyes bulged. Through grand gestures, she conveyed that Alcander and Ariadne, accompanied by a legion of heavily armed personal security, had barged into Flavia's house and demanded the children. "What could I have done against that?" Flavia said, wiping away her tears. In anger, Titus threw a pan containing a yellowish liquid that had been simmering on a low flame against the wall.

That same week, Titus was visited by Gaius Lucullus Flavus, a local praetor dealing with civil matters in and around Nicopolis. Known for his exceptionally tall, thin frame, Gaius wobbled as he walked. The city was well aware that this man could eat like a lion without gaining an ounce.

"I understand this is a tough time for you. It's all quite sad," Gaius said, sipping wine Remus had poured for him.

"Thank you for your sympathy," Titus replied, shaking his head. "What does this mean for me?"

"After careful consideration and lengthy discussions, the decision was made that it's in the children's best interest to be placed temporarily under the guardianship of Alcander Cassius Aelianus. This meant they would receive their daily care and upbringing under his supervision."

"Consulted with whom? The jackass who stole my

family? How much did he pay you to bring me this news? This whole thing stinks. They are my children! I am their father!"

As Gaius reached for his wine cup, Titus stood up and kicked it off the table, the contents splashing against the wall. Gaius flinched, squeezed his eyes shut, and let out a frightened yelp but quickly straightened up.

"I won't be intimidated by you. This is the decision, and I—"

"Intimidated? What are you talking about, you weakling? I am just angry! Wouldn't you be angry if *your* children were unjustly taken from you?"

Gaius sighed, dropped his head, and looked down at the table.

"I have no children."

"How fortunate for the children you don't have." Remus chuckled as he cleaned the wall with a damp cloth. Titus shook his head. "Listen, Gaius, I demand this decision be reconsidered. I am the pater familias. I have rights too!"

The Praetor stood up, his tall frame towering over Titus and Remus. "I'm afraid this decision cannot be changed. If you wish to see your children, you must ask the guardian's permission."

Gaius staggered to the front door.

"I don't need permission! I will come and get them

personally! They are my children!"

Gaius turned in the doorway, his finger trembling as he pointed it in the air. "You'd better not, or you'll be committing a serious offense."

"So what if I do?"

"Then you'll have to deal with the city guard. They've been ordered to enforce this arrangement. And yes, they will use force! So be wise, Laelius, or you risk more than you're willing to lose."

The rest of the day, Titus didn't speak a word. Plautia told him the next day that Alcander invited Ariadne and her family to a dinner party that same week. Apparently, the entire twenty-three-member family had shown up, laughing, feasting, and drinking merrily. The lovebirds were also preparing for a trip to Olympia—yes, with the children. Eyewitnesses had rarely seen Ptolemaios in such a good mood, reportedly eating and drinking for ten. Galyna even shed a tear of joy after Alcander gave her a personal tour of his ridiculously large villa.

Titus' house arrest was over by then, but it seemed as though he voluntarily continued his punishment. Almost daily, he sent Remus out to gather everything from rocks from the Pindos mountains to silphium from Cyrene, which was sold in small quantities at the market, and was not exactly cheap. Plautia had come to the door a few times to complain about the hammering at night. Later, when the city guards also paid a visit, Titus reluctantly agreed to work only during the day.

"The breakthrough will not take more than a few days," Titus had told Remus, who then relayed the "good news" to Flavia, asking her to look after Ares and Faustinus for a bit longer.

A shimmering green-blue smoke attracted a group of magpies, which perched on the edge of the hole in the ceiling. Titus searched through a stack of papyrus sheets for a description of how silphium combined with certain specific ingredients could invoke the wrath of Jupiter. The neighborhood cat was sleeping in a corner of his study until a sudden crackle and flash scared it, causing it to scream and jump out the window into the garden. Mr. Evagrius' dog started barking hysterically.

Not long after the spectacle, four city guards, Plautia, Sejanus, and a group of anxious neighbors came to inquire. After Titus apologized multiple times and promised that his experiments were absolutely harmless, the people dispersed with reluctance on their faces. For the next few days, the city guards patrolled the street often, but everything seemed quiet except for some smoke coming from behind the house.

Nights became warmer, and warm summer rains alternated with brief periods of sunshine. Remus reminded Titus that he had only ten days left until the kalends, urging him to hurry with the move. But the Roman seemed unconcerned by this warning, spending all day carefree in his study.

At Remus' insistence, Titus invited a legal advisor named Decimus Aemilius Maximus for a house visit early one morning. The advisor's bald head shone as if he rubbed olive oil on it several times a day. With his chest puffed out, he entered the living room.

"Divorce and infidelity are my specialties. Look, a divorce is like being fired from a job you hated anyway. The only downside is you no longer get paid." He chuckled, making a circle with his right thumb and forefinger, inserting his left index finger into the circle and moving it up and down. "Get it?"

Titus gave an uncomfortable laugh and glanced at Remus, who was quietly chuckling and shaking his head in a corner of the living room after serving wine to Titus and the guest.

"Come on, man, get over it. You're about to enter great times! You have the absolute best lawyer sitting on your couch. If you go with me, your kids will be running around here again soon, and your wife—or rather, ex-wife—will foot the bill. This wine is delicious, by the way. Truly exquisite! Athenian?"

Titus took a sip from his cup.

"I hope you know what we're up against."

"Oh, don't worry about it. There's no opponent I can't take on. I'd even sue Zeus and win if I had to! Just tell me who it is, and consider it done."

"Alcander Cassius Aelianus."

Decimus' smug smile vanished faster than light. He pulled a cloth from his toga.

"Ah, you mean *the* Alcander Cassius Aelianus?"

Titus nodded. The advisor paled, his hefty torso shrinking like a tormented ant. He wiped his forehead with the cloth as if his pores had suddenly started secreting olive oil. He struggled to form words but only managed a few syllables. Remus frowned and looked at Titus, who awkwardly scratched the back of his head. The advisor sighed and groaned, slowly regaining some color in his face.

"I... I... remember now that I'm completely booked for the foreseeable future."

He got up, thanked Titus for the wine, and exited the door. Remus stared out in disbelief, shaking his head. Titus, defeated, sat in his chair, staring at the half-full cup of wine on the table.

In the afternoon, Arrian arrived at the doorstep, having been informed by his servant Leonidas about Titus' drunken escapade and house arrest. When Arrian entered his study, Titus dropped a copper rod from his hands and burst into tears.

"They took my children."

8. Hunt

Titus dragged himself across the square, down the street, and eyed the bars on either side. It was still dark outside. Unlike that evening when he had clashed with Ptolemaios, it was deserted. Here and there, a drunk stumbled into an alleyway. A group of musicians was about to leave. Titus nearly stepped in a puddle of vomit with his boots. Remus had set out these high, dark brown boots for him the previous night. The boots were as good as new, given that Titus never ventured outside the city. The water bag, which Remus had filled the previous evening, was almost unused as well. At the end of the street, he turned the corner and saw Arrian already waiting by the gate in the distance, accompanied by his two Celtic greyhounds—both leashed—and Leonidas.

"We're heading a little northward, then toward the coast," he said.

Arrian proudly led his dogs through the immense city gate. At the gate, a group of students, led by an old literatus who gave a naughty boy a whack with his stick. The children reminded Titus of his sons. Plautia had told him the previous night that they had left with Ariadne and Alcander for Olympia that afternoon. If Titus hadn't promised to join Arrian early in the morning, he might have drowned his sorrows in again.

Although the area around Nicopolis consisted mainly of farmland, there were still patches of forest. Just before the west coast was a broad strip where many city dwellers regularly escaped the hustle and bustle. Some walked, others played latrunculi in the shade, others trained their bodies sheltered by the trees, and a few practiced discus throwing. And of course, one couldn't forget the lovebirds and families who enjoyed simple foods. Arrian, on the other hand, visited the forests for another reason.

Leonidas unleashed the dogs. They ran through the maze of trees and bushes like freed slaves encountering freedom for the first time. With Leonidas' extensive expertise in dogs, Arrian had trained his Celtic greyhounds to be obedient yet effective hunting dogs. As much as they loved dashing through the woods, often far from their master's sight, they always returned immediately when Arrian blew on an acorn cap.

"Did you know Xenophon of Athens was a great hunter? He was a master at setting traps. He knew all about using nets. He even used caltrops to catch bears. But I keep it simple."

Titus nodded. Arrian's whistle hurt his ears. The Celtic greyhounds, barking and frenzied, raced back to their master. Leonidas rewarded them with pieces of bread. According to the slave, the rabbit population had grown significantly over the past few years. But due to the noisy presence of city dwellers, the creatures had hidden in bushes and burrows. After Leonidas had sent the dogs ahead, Arrianus elaborated extensively on why he had once come to Nicopolis.

"I wanted to be a student of Epictetus," the

Nicomedian said.

Arrian enthusiastically recounted how he had been interested in Stoic philosophy since he was a young boy and that his parents had even managed to obtain an original letter from Seneca the Younger to Lucilius during their vacation in Rome, which they brought to him in Nicomedia, his birthplace.

"Epictetus teaches us not to be influenced by things that are not within our power."

Titus gazed at the sun rays that had found their way through the canopy to the forest floor.

"And what things are within our power?"

"Only our opinions, goals, desires, attitudes—in other words, our own choices."

"So this Epictetus believes that nothing else in life is within our power besides our own choices?"

"Can you prove him wrong?"

The Celtic greyhounds had vanished from sight, although there was some rustling from the bushes in the distance. Arrian blew on the acorn cap, and a few moments later, the beasts hurried back to their master like the wind.

"Adultery, the loss of wealth or a loved one, or even your children, people lying and cheating... All these things we consider so terrible are not within our power. Epictetus teaches us to become aware of this and to focus on things that are within our control. He teaches the power of reason: the unique human ability to think clearly and make conscious choices by distinguishing good from evil."

As they walked along the path, the dogs eagerly sniffed the edges, until one of them disappeared between the bushes and hurried toward the coast. Leonidas' eyes followed the beast closely. With a gentle smile, Arrian caught a glimpse of a creature darting from bush to bush.

"Do not wish for things to happen as you want, but wish for them to happen as they do. Then you will live happily. That is rationality. That is a choice only humans can make because they can oversee the workings of nature."

"How can I wish for all this injustice? It's wrong. It shouldn't happen. I can't imagine wishing for it!"

"But it is the will of the gods. It's about accepting what happens, even if it's unjust. But by acceptance, I don't mean that we justify or condone immoral actions. You can disapprove of injustice and still accept it. Acceptance acknowledges that, however unpleasant the situation may be, it is reality. You can never win a fight against reality. But if you desire whatever comes your way, then you can never lose."

Leonidas laughed as he saw the dog emerge from the bushes with prey in its mouth. The rabbit was still alive because Arrian had trained his dogs to catch but not kill the prey. He took the rabbit and showed it to Titus. The dogs circled the group, tails wagging, and Leonidas rewarded them with bread. When Arrian released the rabbit, the four-legged animals remained seated obediently.

"The past cannot be undone," Arrian continued, "and we usually have no control over the present, because most of it is not up to us. Let go of these things and you will experience inner peace. Come with me to Epictetus. He can help you with this."

Titus laughed, knelt down by one of the dogs, and stroked its fur.

"You know what would give me inner peace? Justice. That's what needs to happen. Thank you for wanting to help, but I don't believe your philosopher can solve my problems."

Arrian took a deep breath and blew on the acorn cap. The dogs jumped up and sprinted through the bushes.

"I understand you want justice, a virtue esteemed highly by the Stoics. Begin by embodying justice, for this is within your realm of control. You may then try to persuade others of your innocence and advocate for just actions. That's the Stoic way. But whether your fellow man does what you wish is another question. Justice, or fair treatment by others, is not up to you."

"But why do people fight for justice if it's not up to them? What's the point?"

"This is exactly what Epictetus tries to make clear. You only have control over your actions. What you want is in the hands of judges—their disposition, whether they can be bribed—in other words, factors beyond your control. The justice you desire is ultimately not up to you, no matter how hard you fight for it. That doesn't mean you shouldn't fight for what's right! However, you need to be realistic, and the outcome might be quite disappointing; that's what happens when you desire something beyond your control."

"I appreciate your wisdom, but I believe the justice I seek is indeed within my power. With the right means and contacts, I can ensure this justice."

"I'm sorry if I sound harsh, but what means? What contacts?"

"I'll find a way."

"Then I hope the gods grant you that justice soon. If you change your mind, friend, you're always welcome." In the distance, Leonidas was making wild gestures. The greyhounds sprinted through the bushes, barking loudly. "I think they've found a fox den."

Arrian hurried through the bushes, past the trees, toward his servant. Staring at the dry branches and tree stumps on the path, Titus trudged forward. A large, black scorpion crossed the path. Titus stopped, waited for the creature to disappear into the bushes, and continued walking. The voices of Leonidas and Arrian and the barking of the dogs slowly faded into the distance. A man in a dark red toga and a hood approached him and greeted him with a friendly nod. The man seemed familiar to Titus, although he couldn't recall where he had seen him before.

9. Epictetus

Things weren't going well for him. Remus had visited every legal advisor in Nicopolis by now, but the response was always the same: suing Alcander Cassius was doomed to fail unless one had enough money to bribe almost the entire judiciary of Nicopolis and its surroundings. And since Alcander had made himself virtually untouchable through bribery, Titus could do little against that rich snob through legal means. Once that realization sank in, he decided to give that philosopher Arrian was so enthusiastic about a chance.

Arrian welcomed Titus with joy. Epictetus didn't have a fixed place where he held his lectures. Often, he and his students gathered in the city park, sometimes even by the large oak just outside the city. But, as Arrian explained, in recent months the wealthy patron Caius Aelius Octavianus had opened one of his properties for Epictetus' lectures. The property, near the forum, was regularly used for meetings and educational purposes. And since the patron himself was a Stoic student, he hosted the philosopher and his students for free, as long as he could have a front-row seat. Arrian admitted it wasn't very Stoic, but it provided Epictetus and his students with a temporary location.

The lecture hall on the ground floor was huge, fitting a hundred people. The ceilings were high, and the walls decorated with paintings, with columns on either side separating the main hall from the corridors. The hall had four doors, two leading to the hallway and the other two to a large patio. Well before the lecture began, people eagerly filled the wooden benches, which even had backrests. The hall was packed. The audience included craftsmen, intellectuals, aristocrats, and politicians. Even slaves were welcome, if their masters permitted them. Caius Aelius Octavianus sat in the front with a proud smile in his finest toga, accompanied by his two teenage daughters whom he intentionally exposed to Stoic philosophy from a young age. Then there was the noisy quaestor Tiberius Sellus who had come all the way from Rome and had previously interrupted Epictetus during lectures. Arrian and Titus managed to get a second-row seat.

Then he finally entered through the door, as if a demigod was entering, but one on crutches. Nobody knew exactly why Epictetus limped, and nobody dared to ask him. The majority claimed his former master had broken his leg in anger, others believed he suffered from rheumatism. Epictetus slowly hobbled to the lectern. He carefully surveyed the audience.

"A large gathering. Is that a good sign? It depends. Are you here because you want to become rich or famous? Or maybe to vent about your neighbor or your master or slave, or perhaps even about Zeus himself? Or are you here to learn how to be free? And no, by being free, I don't mean that you can do whatever you want. By being free, I mean that you're not dependent on things that are beyond your control. If you want to be free, you're welcome. If not, you're better off staying away."

Titus stood up. His heart pounded in his throat. His

hands trembled. He swallowed several times before he spoke.

"I... am new here. I come to seek your advice." From inside his chiton, he pulled out a piece of papyrus with notes that fluttered between his fingers and landed on the floor. He left the notes on the ground. "I've been through a lot lately. I don't know how to move forward. I... I don't come to complain, but I want to share my story so you can help me."

With a lump in his throat, he recounted how he lost his wealth, his wife left him, took his children and went on vacation to Olympia with Alcander Cassius, and also how his reputation was ruined by false rumors. The philosopher interrupted him.

"Why do you complain about things that are unimportant? You're upset over the loss of what was not yours in the first place. What did you expect? That you would be inseparable into the underworld? Do you really think, like the fools among us, that everything you cherish will never disappear?[3] Don't be so silly. If your former wife was to be with you for eternity, she would still be by your side. Your wife, your children, your house, your reputation, your precious metals, and even, yes, even your

---

[3] Several footnotes reference Arrian's notes of Epictetus' lectures, either as literal quotes or paraphrases. I have incorporated these references in the novel to lend credibility to Epictetus' statements in these fictional dialogues. I have used Elizabeth Carter's English translation of *Enchiridion* and W.A. Oldfather's English translation of *Discourses* as sources. This part is based on *Discourses*, 3.24

body are not your possessions.[4] Zeus has lent them to you. He takes them back whenever he wants.[5] This is the feast of the gods.[6] They lead the universe well and justly.[7] So don't call it a tragedy or a catastrophe, but accept it with contentment.[8]"

"But what do I have left if all these things are taken from me?" Titus wiped his tears on his chiton.

"The gods have made us humans to be happy and balanced.[9] Zeus has given us the means to do so. He has given us things that are ours, and things that are not ours.[10] That your wife leaves you is not up to you. But how you deal with this event is indeed up to you. That you feel miserable about this situation is not someone else's fault; it's due to your own deficiency."

"Wait, this is not right!" Titus said with a trembling voice. "Now you're blaming the victim! Isn't my wife to blame at all? And what about that scoundrel? They caused all this, didn't they? It certainly wasn't me who committed adultery. It wasn't me who spread all sorts of lies. Come on, philosopher. This makes no sense. I miss any form of justice!"

Titus felt his heart raging like a group of Spartan

---

[4] Epictetus, *Enchiridion*, 1
[5] Epictetus, *Enchiridion*, 11
[6] Epictetus, *Enchiridion*, 15
[7] Epictetus, *Enchiridion*, 31
[8] Epictetus, *Discourses*, 1.12
[9] Epictetus, *Discourses*, 3.24
[10] Epictetus, *Discourses*, 3.24

soldiers on the battlefield outnumbered by the enemy.

"Why do you call yourself a victim? You are suffering for your unreasonableness. Why should Ariadne suffer because you consider what belongs to another as your own?[11] Things like wealth, fame, power, relationships, and even fair treatment are ultimately up to the gods; they are beyond your control. The only thing within your control is how you deal with these circumstances.[12] If you remain undisturbed by these things, then you will also experience no sorrow. But if you keep lamenting about things that don't concern you, then you are nothing more than a slave."

Cheers came from the back of the hall, followed by the rest of the attendees. Titus sat down and stared blankly ahead. Epictetus turned to his audience and explained that if you let your happiness depend on things that are not yours, you're in an unreliable position. Arrian added, unasked, that Lady Fortuna just needs to take these things away from you, and she's gotten a rise out of you.

"Or she brings you joy by giving you what you desire. And so, you are dependent on her whims, and she plays you like a puppet. If you focus on what's not within your control, suffering is inevitable sooner or later," said Arrian.

Although the lecture was over, aspiring philosophers filled the hall to the brim. Tiberius Sellus, who, to

---

[11] Epictetus, *Discourses*, 3.24
[12] Epictetus, *Enchiridion*, 1

everyone's surprise, had remained silent during the entire lecture, finally contributed his aphorisms and fallacies. Caius Aelius Octavianus proudly walked through the crowd with Epictetus by his side, trying to quickly resolve some personal issues. Soon, Arrian joined in the conversation, to the irritation of the host.

Titus walked into the patio. Not a cloud in the sky. The sound of an owl echoed through the courtyard, sending shivers down his spine. A scorpion hurried across the courtyard. Titus took a few steps back and waited until the creature disappeared under a crack in the old stone wall. Among the conifers, he saw a man standing with his back to him, by the fountain in the middle of the patio, surrounded by a sea of withered plants. Just like the man he had encountered the previous day in the woods, he wore a dark red toga and hood, shielding him from the fierce sun. The man turned around. Titus' heart skipped a beat.

"That Epictetus is quite a phenomenal speaker, isn't he?"

Titus examined the man from head to toe. Now he was sure. It was the same guy as in the woods. He still seemed familiar, but he couldn't remember where he knew him from, or who he was, for that matter. His face was too smooth for a gladiator, but too rough for a politician. His skin seemed to see little sunlight. His eyes had the depth of a well, but also the sparkle of the lagoon on a sunny afternoon.

Titus made brief eye contact and glanced at the tops of the conifers towering over the walls surrounding the patio.

"Arrian was right," said Titus. "Epictetus' words are useful. I feel better now."

"Fantastic. I think I heard him say that a true philosopher does not wish for life to go as he wants, but as it goes. Did I hear that correctly?"

Titus stared at the fountain. A brief burning sensation appeared in his stomach. He thought about how deeply he wished life had turned out differently, that he had never lost his fortune, that his father was still alive, that his wife had never deceived him, that he had finally discovered the secret to turning stone into gold and thus being carried on the hands of the Roman people along the Tiber. He felt small, insignificant, powerless. *How could I wish for all this?* Sighing deeply, he shook his head.

"Yes, that's correct."

"Ah." The man frowned, dipped his hands into the fountain, and took a sip of water. "So, you should accept in contentment that your wife commits adultery and falsely accuses you of being a pimp, right? Zeus has taken back your wife and children and assigned them to another."

"That seems to be the gist of it, yes."

As if struck by a stray arrow, Titus cast a blank stare ahead. The tops of the conifers danced like courtesans in the brothels near the forum. The sound of crickets drowned out the nonsensical background chatter. Titus imagined himself watching impassively as his former wife strolled hand in hand with Alcander Cassius through the sacred precincts of the gods in Olympia, or as he himself walked undisturbed through the marketplace in Nicopolis while the people laughed and scorned him. Again, a burning sensation filled his stomach, spreading to his chest and throat. His legs felt heavy, as if Sisyphus had placed his boulder on his shoulders.

"Are you suggesting Epictetus is wrong?"

"Oh, not at all. I wouldn't dare. Perhaps I'm completely mistaken. But I do wonder if we truly must accept everything that Epictetus claims is 'not up to us' with contentment, especially those things that deeply revolt us inside."

Titus sighed deeply, his fingers and toes curling as the burning sensation seemed to climb into his hands and feet. Hoping for relief from these unpleasant sensations, he pushed his body up and down with his calves.

"But what else can we do? Whether the gods are good or bad, or not gods at all, many things are not within our control. Epictetus is entirely right about this. My wealth, my wife, even my children are not mine. The gods can apparently take them away from me. As long as I'm attached to these things, I'm vulnerable. So, what I really need to do is let go of all this."

"Is that so? Look, according to the Stoics, we should focus on things within our control and not desire things beyond our control, like fame, wealth, or even our loved ones. If we do, Lady Fortuna plays us like puppets—I get that. But aren't the many things beyond our control precisely the fine things in life? What would life be worth without walks with your loved ones through the olive groves, the sight of the temple of Zeus, the enjoyment of a Falernian wine? Following the Stoics might create inner peace, but it also stops you from truly living."

Titus remained silent. After a glance at the dancing conifers, the man walked back inside, looked around, and left the building. Titus stayed in the patio for a while longer, staring at the fountain, until Arrian called him back inside.

10. Handbook

Arrian arranged a spacious wagon to transport Titus' belongings to the countryside. In haste, Titus had gathered his clothing, some mugs, jugs of wine, and materials from his workroom, including a glass bottle shaped like an oil lamp, stones of every color of the rainbow, and a lump of copper as big as a fist. Carefully, Remus kept the fragile items together while the cart trundled over the bumpy road northwards. A few men helped unload in the burning sun. They didn't seem to have their hearts in it.

"Can we go now?"

"Just a moment." Arrian inspected the cart. "Take it back to Claudius. Let the horses drink on the way."

Titus sought shelter in the shed. It was surprisingly cool inside. There wasn't much furniture. He had placed that ugly old chair he got from his father in the corner. There were no separate rooms. Titus had to sleep, entertain guests, and work all in the same space, which he also shared with Remus. Outside, at the front of the shed, was an open kitchen, almost unused and perfect for his experiments. "At least we have no neighbors who'll come to complain," said Titus to Remus, although the possibility of that scoundrel Alcander interfering with his activities crossed his mind.

Titus lay on the floor, repeatedly tossing a bronze coin into the air that just missed the ceiling.

"It smells a bit musty. I wonder what Epictetus would say about a musty-smelling shed," said Titus.

"He wouldn't worry about it. Just like he wouldn't worry about those accusations."

Arrian poured two cups of wine. He peered through the back window overlooking Alcander's enormous villa. Titus flung the coin against the wall. He pointed toward the front door, toward Nicopolis.

"I have a right to that house."

Arrian sighed. "You know, as much as you dislike it, your wife acted according to her nature, like everything in this world. We are all the result of previous events that shape who we are."

"That doesn't make her lies and deceit right."

"It's in human nature to do the right thing, but also to do evil. That applies to Ariadne too. I knew her father, Echemus. He was a good friend of my old man, as he visited my hometown a lot. He was a trader. He often sailed across the Mediterranean. When Ariadne was seven years old, he traveled to Egypt…"

"… and never returned. I know the story."

"But did you also know that Ariadne, for many years after her father left, slipped out of the house daily and waited for him at the west gate? She became a local attraction, I've been told. They called her 'the gatekeeper.' She waited and waited, sometimes from early morning until dusk."

Titus shook his head with a sigh. He pictured young Ariadne at the west gate, hoping with every figure that appeared in the distance that it would be him, and how she returned home disappointed every nightfall. He felt a lump in his throat.

"The most important man in her life disappeared," said Arrian. "No one here knows what happened to him or whether he's still alive. Such events mark a person. Not to justify it, of course, but…"

"I would never have left her like her father did. I've been faithful to her, not sleeping around like other men. I loved her and still do. I would have done anything for her."

"Yet it happened. Her nature enabled her to do so. Lady Fortuna determined it that way. Some people are so scared of being abandoned that they forget how to love. No matter how hard you try, they never truly commit. They always have one foot out of the door. Some leave because they cannot bear closeness. It's not nice, but it's understandable. Whatever her precise reasons are for her infidelity, take Epictetus' advice. Accept. Do not despair about what the gods have determined."

From his travel bag, Arrian took out a bundle of papyrus sheets.

"I'm working on something. Think of it as a summary of Epictetus' most important lessons. Like a handbook, small enough to take with you. It's not finished yet, and I'd like it back. But for now, you can borrow it. Let me know what you think when I see you again."

After Arrian left the shed, Titus did nothing but gaze through the window. He monitored every ant entering Alcander's villa, every movement of the drowsy doorman at the gate, every sigh of the overheated watchdog lying in the shade of the terrace roof. He ignored Arrian's papyrus bundle for the rest of the day.

The most exciting event that day around Alcander's villa was the black cat that sat on the drowsy doorman's face, precisely with its butthole on his nose, right after it had pooped in the bushes. The cat was surprised that the man wasn't amused. With threatening gestures, the guard chased the cat onto the roof, where it remained huddled for the rest of the day. Oh, and the egg seller came by, managing to sell his entire stock of quail eggs and a full crate of grapes to Alcander's personal chef.

Bored, Titus eventually picked up the papyrus rolls and sat down on a stone stool by the window.

"Some things are within our control and others not. We can control our attitudes, opinions, purposes, and desires—our own choices. We have no control over health, wealth, fame, or power—things that do not concern us."[13]

The death of his father Attius, his once wealthy family falling into poverty, losing his house, selling the lands around Nicopolis: were these things truly beyond his control? Titus examined his hands, the hair on his arms.

---

[13] Epictetus, *Enchiridion*, 1

He felt the air flowing through his lungs, the muscle pain in his thighs, his dry throat. A pang of panic shot through his chest.

Is my body also not my own?

The burning sensation in his stomach returned. The thought that Ariadne had fallen for another, and that this was entirely beyond his control, left him feeling powerless. His wandering eyes refocused on the notes.

"But if you regard only that as your own which is truly yours, and what is not in your control precisely as such, then you will have achieved it: no one will ever force you to do what you do not want, no one will ever hinder you, you will blame no one, you will have no enemies, and you will never suffer any harm."[14]

Titus stared through the window at Alcander's villa, imagining Ariadne and his children living their affluent, abundant lives there, laughing and dancing, and being happy. And then he saw himself sitting in his shed, impoverished but serene and fully accepting of the world around him. He placed the papyrus rolls on the side table next to the chair.

Am I indeed supposed to let go of everything that is not within my control?

---

[14] Epictetus, *Enchiridion*, 1

11. View

The day after moving, Titus sat fresh and bright in class. Arrian, with a grin as wide as if his hounds had caught a whole nest of hares, joined him. Rumor had it that Tiberius Sellus had an important meeting with some magistrates that morning, attending a ceremony to honor the gods in the temple square. This allowed Epictetus to lecture with notably fewer interruptions.

After class, Arrian dropped Titus off at the shed with horse and cart. Usually, he'd stay and chat, but that morning he left quickly due to expected visitors from Patrae. Opening the shed door, Titus found Remus sitting on the ground, looking distressed, flanked by two sweaty men glaring as if they wanted to nail him to a cross. Something moved in his peripheral vision. Titus froze and slowly turned his head. His hands trembled.

"I see you're continuing your dangerous activities here. How many stones have you turned to gold so far?" Alcander tossed a round glass bottle with a long, thin neck to one of the sweaty men, who barely caught it.

"Get out of my house."

"Well, I expected that renowned Roman hospitality my family always talk about. This is quite disappointing."

Alcander closely examined the small bottles and jars on a wooden table in the corner. Titus tried to recall Epictetus' words that had echoed in the lecture hall that morning, along with Arrian' notes. A deep sigh followed, his voice trembling.

"Be welcome. How can I help you?"

Surprised, Alcander looked at his sweaty bodyguards, who nodded and laughed.

"That's better. I like it in this shed. From here, I can enjoy a beautiful view." Alcander stood and walked to the center of the room. He smiled and took a big step toward the window. "I bet you enjoy it too."

"Why are you here?" asked Titus.

Alcander laughed. "Slave," he barked. "Pour us some wine. Can't you see we're thirsty?"

Remus gave Alcander a deadly look, then glanced at his master. Titus nodded. Remus stood and walked outside. Alcander sat in the ugly old chair in the corner, next to the window. The two sweaty men sat on the ground, backs against the wall, facing each other.

"Isn't it beautiful around the lagoon? Even though I thoroughly enjoyed our vacation in Olympia, I must admit that nothing compares to these meadows, the forests and mountains in the background, and, in the distance, the shimmering inland water on a sunny summer day. Epirus is my home; here lies my heart."

Remus entered the room with a jug and four mugs on a tray. Reluctantly, he poured the wine, handed the mugs to the group, and sat by the door. Alcander took a mug, toasted, and looked at Titus.

"Go ahead."

"Do you really think I'm trying to poison you?" Titus took a big gulp, inhaled deeply, and exhaled slowly, trying to relax his body.

"You never know." Alcander laughed and emptied his mug in one gulp. "Look, what I want to say is… I love the people of Epirus, and they love me. Ask around here, the farmers, the workers in Nicopolis, the fishermen. Everyone is enthusiastic about me."

As the two sweaty men took modest sips of their wine, they glanced at each other cautiously. Remus rolled his eyes. Titus chuckled, trying to keep his lips sealed, but couldn't contain himself.

"If everyone is so happy with you, why do you always walk around with two bodyguards?"

One of the sweaty men spat out the wine as if he'd choked on it and ran out, coughing loudly while his helmet fell off. Remus burst into laughter. The other sweaty man maintained a serious but tense expression. Alcander stood and approached Titus, who had meanwhile taken a seat on the stone stool.

"This morning, a farmer brought me a box of apples. They're the most beautiful apples you can find in Epirus. Bright red, flawless, shiny as gold, and they taste deliciously sweet. But occasionally, there's an apple with rotten, brown spots among them. This apple is dull and nasty. And if you leave that apple in the box, it will spoil the other apples too. So, what do you do with such an apple?"

Titus shrugged. "You sit on it?"

Alcander smashed the empty mug against the wall behind Titus.

"You throw it away! You are that apple! And I don't want rotten apples in my backyard. You're a danger to the surroundings, a plague that must be eradicated."

"Give me back my house, and you'll be rid of me."

Alcander laughed heartily and shook his head.

"Then you'd be out of my sight, but your stench would still linger in the streets of Nicopolis. The stench of a pimp, a worthless father."

Titus rose to his feet, his breathing quickened, his jaw clenched, his hands balled into fists.

"Then it seems you're stuck with me here."

"I'll offer you a thousand denarii."

Remus choked. The sweaty guard, recovering from his coughing fit, quietly re-entered the shed and sat back against the wall after hastily adjusting his helmet. Through hand gestures, the other guard futilely tried to indicate his helmet was askew. Titus stared in disbelief, shaking his head.

"A thousand denarii? For this shed and the parched patch of land around it?"

"For the shed, the land, and for you to leave Epirus and never show your face here again."

Titus chuckled softly, his eyes scanning Alcander from head to toe. Remus frowned at Alcander, then at the guard with the tilted helmet who was nervously fidgeting with his tunic.

"I wouldn't dream of it."

Alcander moved so close to Titus that their noses would have touched if the wealthy Greek wasn't almost a head taller. Smirking, he patted Titus on the head. Titus, hands trembling, met the uninvited guest's gaze. The guards readied their swords. Like a wolf stalking a rival, Remus eyed Alcander's bulky form, anticipating his next move.

"Or you come live with me, little dainty boy. I'll make you one of my concubines. I'm sure your former wife would love to watch how I tear you apart."

Titus almost vomited by the thought of it. Alcander stepped back. With a gesture, the guards stood and followed their leader out. Titus collapsed onto the stone stool. Remus leaned his head back against the wall and closed his eyes.

12. Tiberius

The lecture hall in Caius Aelius Octavianus' building was packed. The host himself took his place in the front row, beaming like a child. His daughters sat next to him, the youngest having already dozed off before the lecture began. Her elder sister quietly enjoyed the attention from the boys in the hall, whose parents had also mandated their attendance.

Arrian, also in the front row, brought along a bundle of papyrus sheets on which he furiously took notes. Titus sat beside him, looking pale. Alcander's visit the previous day had left a deep impression on him. That night, he had vainly tried numerous sleeping positions until the songbirds and blackbirds announced the dawn with their singing.

Tiberius Sellus attended again, this time bringing his son along—who, Titus noticed, fixated on the shiny hair of Caius' elder daughter. The Roman quaestor, as usual, managed to draw all the attention to himself. His deep, authoritative voice immediately put many into a submissive stance. However, he made little impression on Epictetus. That morning, the philosopher discussed harming and being harmed. When he asserted that one should not harm someone who has harmed them, Tiberius Sellus objected.

"People who treat me well, I treat well; those who treat me poorly, I treat poorly. I've lived by this all my life. I firmly believe in 'do good and receive good, do evil and deserve punishment.' I recall when my business partner deceived me and stole money. I personally ensured he paid for it because he deserved it. And recently, I caught a thief trying to break my front door lock. I grabbed him by the scruff and gave him a beating he'll never forget. It felt like justice, and moreover, the thief will think twice before robbing me again. Now, what's wrong with that?"

Epictetus nodded and limped a few steps toward the Quaestor.

"Imagine someone steals money from you. Consider it from the perspective of the thief and his moral choice, rather than the perspective of possession.[15] The thief might have snagged some denarii, but the price he paid is invaluable.[16] He'll realize he's not a good person, suffer a loss of self-esteem, perhaps feel shame. He'll sleep restlessly, always looking over his shoulder outdoors, as the city guards are after him. Nobody will trust him, everyone will avoid him. In other words, he has harmed himself through his actions."

Titus listened intently. The thought that his former love Ariadne had hurt herself through her actions brought a reluctant smile to his face, though he couldn't fully grasp how exactly. So far, it seemed he was the one paying a heavy price for the lies she and her lover had spread. It appeared they had emerged unscathed from the situation. He felt a burning sensation in his stomach again.

---

[15] Epictetus, *Discourses*, 2.10
[16] Epictetus, *Discourses*, 2.10

Tiberius Sellus wasn't easily discouraged. "Your argument overlooks the victim's position," he said. "What do I care if the thief can't sleep at night because of his actions? My concern is that he's making others' lives miserable and must be punished. So, he may have harmed himself through his action, but he has also harmed me! And I've repaid that harm!"

Titus crossed his arms and nodded. It was like the loud Roman could read his thoughts. *How could Ariadne and Alcander ever atone for their deeds if the gods let them go unpunished?* After all, they lived in wealth and abundance, unaffected by any adverse consequences of their actions. This contrasted starkly with the turn Titus' life had taken: poverty, social exclusion, sorrow, separated from his children.

Epictetus responded without hesitation. "First, realize what harm means. What have philosophers said?[17] Didn't Seneca write that it's much better to heal a wound than to avenge it?[18] What have you really lost if your money is stolen? Nothing that was truly yours. You've just made your own life miserable by clinging to what doesn't belong to you," he said.

As Tiberius Sellus vehemently protested this argument, Epictetus turned to Titus and limped toward him while speaking.

---

[17] Epictetus, *Discourses*, 2.10
[18] Lucius Annaeus Seneca, *Of Anger*, 3.27. I have used Aubrey Stewart's English translation of *Of Anger* as a source.

"The same applies to adultery. What do you lose if someone cheats on you? Also, nothing that was truly yours. But what does someone who commits adultery lose? Their status as a self-respecting person, someone who is in control of themselves, someone decent, with quality as a citizen and neighbor.[19] Who can trust her now? These are the truly important matters, not measurable by what has happened to you. So why would you seek revenge against someone who has so tarnished themselves, thereby harming yourself?[20]"

Waving his arms, Tiberius Sellus stood up and wondered aloud how he would harm himself by beating a thief. Epictetus invited his students to answer this question. Arrian stood up.

"It might be tempting to seek revenge on the thief, but this only brings negative consequences. Giving in to your desires only breeds more desires, following your fears leads to more fear, and thus, the path of anger and revenge leads to more anger and revenge. What really matters is that you act virtuously and prioritize your peace of mind."

"That's complete nonsense!" Tiberius Sellus said. "I don't see how my beating would lead to more beatings. That's what you're implying, right, Arrian? I believe the opposite is true. My beating ensures that the thief will behave better in the future. He won't make more victims and therefore won't receive more beatings from angry victims. In this case, anger leads to less anger!"

---

[19] Epictetus, *Discourses*, 2.10
[20] Epictetus, *Discourses*, 2.10

"How do you know your violence won't lead the thief to make more victims? That's quite presumptuous. Maybe he won't try to rob you again, but he's likely to try it on others. This means you've disturbed your peace of mind for nothing," Arrian said.

"For nothing, you say? If the thief leaves me alone, then my violence wasn't in vain!"

"That may be," Arrian said, "but who says another thief won't try to rob you? Will you lose your temper again? Will you let your fists fly? Will you let every thief unsettle you? If so, you're giving these rogues the power to disturb your peace of mind!"

"Then so be it! I won't let these street rats rob me without retaliation! You better believe it! They need to feel the consequences of their actions, or they'll never learn!"

The debate between the Quaestor, Arrian, and Epictetus was getting out of hand, leading Tiberius Sellus to grab his son's hand and storm out of the lecture hall, cursing. The young man managed one last glance at Caius' smiling elder daughter before his father pulled him outside.

Although Titus tried his best to internalize Epictetus' words, he couldn't stomach the idea that Ariadne and Alcander got away with their deeds so easily. He attempted to accept that the matters he worried about simply weren't his to control. He understood the logic, but the burning sensation in his stomach seemed to protest against the Stoics' claims. His wife's betrayal felt like something inside him had died, and the loss of his children felt like losing a part of himself.

After Tiberius Sellus' performance, the rest of the discussions barely registered with Titus. He vaguely remembered statements about the importance of conforming to the role nature has given you and how Socrates successfully resolved all sorts of conflicts without ever losing his peace of mind.

After the lecture, Titus walked out to the patio. Arrian kept him company for a while but was soon called inside by Caius Aelius Octavianus to participate in a debate about the flaws of the Epicureans. Titus wandered around, frequently glancing toward the lecture hall's door. He hadn't seen him yet, the man in the dark red toga.

Will he still show up?

After the last guests had left, Titus left the building, disappointed.

13. Furtum

By now it was midday in Nicopolis. Titus faced a long walk home, as his shed lay on the outskirts of the city, nearly level with the stadium. However, his legs had grown accustomed to the trek. To stay out of the public eye, Titus, clad in a gray hood, navigated through alleys and side streets as inconspicuously as possible, avoiding plazas and markets like the plague.

He couldn't resist passing by his old house one more time and found a familiar scene. The neighborhood cat napped on the terrace, there was an occasional bark from Mr. Evagrius' dog, and his old neighbor Plautia threw bread scraps out the window for the birds that had been waiting all morning on the rooftops. He paused briefly, trying to catch a glimpse inside his house, but it appeared dark and deserted. Hearing Plautia and Sejanus stepping onto the porch behind him, he continued on, turning right into the first alley.

The alley, narrow and long, flanked by high walls hiding gardens, bore signs of vigilant residents who had fortified the tops with nails and glass to deter burglars. A surprisingly large rat, overtaking Titus from behind, quickly disappeared through a crack in the wall, startling him. He also noticed cockroaches, as large as baby feet, patrolling the wall edges like city guards. Halfway down, a figure emerged at the exit. Unable to make out who it was, Titus slowed his pace.

A lanky young man with stick-thin legs and arms stared pointedly at Titus. Laughter echoed behind him. Turning, Titus saw two more youths approaching. One had a neck like a frog, the other sported a canary-yellow chiton. The figure at the alley's end now advanced, brandishing a knife. Titus raised his hands in surrender. The one in the canary-yellow chiton yanked Titus' hood off. The frog-necked youth stepped closer.

"Isn't that Laelius?" asked frog-neck.

"The pimp?" added canary-yellow.

"Then he must have money," said stick-legs.

Titus turned pale, his hands trembling slightly. Drawing a deep breath, he recalled Epictetus' words and a passage from Arrian's notes, albeit with difficulty.

"Spilled a bit of oil? A bit of wine stolen? Tell yourself: This is the price for serenity. Nothing comes for free."[21]

Without any resistance or retort, Titus handed over his purse to stick-legs. The youths laughed and ran off. Titus, maintaining his composure, informed the first city guard he encountered about the incident and continued home.

Back in his shed, Titus flipped through Arrian's notes, sighing. The bandits had stolen his entire rent, likely necessitating a loan from Arrian or Flavia to get through the month. Epictetus' teachings reminded him that it's not

---

[21] Epictetus, *Enchiridion*, 12

circumstances but the opinions formed about them that disturb peace of mind. However, he wondered what was so wrong with a disturbed peace of mind.

In malevolent circumstances, isn't it appropriate for peace of mind to be disturbed? Aren't emotions like fear and anger useful indicators that something is not right?

From afar, Titus heard familiar sounds—a piercing shriek, a hearty laugh. He leaped up and peered out the back window. Alcander's gold-trimmed carriage parked outside his villa. Ariadne, laughing, held Faustinus in her arms, while Alcander lifted Ares from the carriage. The drowsy doorman rushed down the porch, hauling various items inside: a side table, a decorated vase, a carpet, all undoubtedly expensive.

Ariadne hugged Alcander, sharing a tender kiss, after which the wealthy Greek smirked toward the shed. Like a snail, Titus withdrew into his abode. From the shadows, he watched as Alcander took his eldest by the hand, Ariadne carried the youngest inside, and the drowsy doorman tripped over the black cat that had darted onto the porch. A voice from outside interrupted his watch.

"Don't look at that."

A figure blocked the view. From his purse, Remus pulled out a small knife and began scraping moss growing in the crevices around the window.

"Move aside."

"I have work to do."

"Remus, I'm warning you…"

Glancing over his shoulder while clinging to the wall, the slave said, "They've gone inside already."

Titus pounded the wall in frustration, grabbed a jug from the pantry, filled a cup to the brim, and downed it in one gulp. Remus, catching the familiar scent, peered through the window. Seeing Titus gulp down another cup, he shook his head and resumed his moss clearing with a sigh.

By dusk, Remus had cleared the entire outer wall of moss. Titus, busy in the outdoor kitchen on the other side of the house, furiously worked with iron pots, glass bottles, and a variety of colored stones arranged on a table. As he poured a yellow liquid from a small stone bowl into the large metal pot over the fire, he took a hefty swig from a jug. Three empty jugs rested by the front door.

"Ah, glad you could join! You know what the Stoics say? They say not to worry about things beyond your control. What's beyond your control, you ask? Almost everything! Can you believe that?"

Remus sat beside the wine jugs, staring at the fire. Titus, examining the stones closely not just with his eyes but also with his fingertips and nose, picked up a purple, crystal-shaped mineral, held it to his ear for a few moments, licked it, and tossed it into the large pot.

"I've lost my wife and children. I'm broke. Everyone in Nicopolis thinks I'm a pimp who prostituted his wife. And according to Epictetus, none of this is within my control. Ah, what is within my control, you ask, my dear friend? I'll tell you. What's within my control... is this."

He scooped a boiling mixture from the iron pot with a large metal spoon and poured it into a clay mold.

"Oh, it looks fantastic! Just needs to cool down a bit, and I think my fortune has finally turned. The name Laelius will echo throughout the empire for centuries, not as a pimp or a menace to society or whatever that Greek scoundrel makes of it, but as a revolutionary!"

Titus hurried to the front door, stumbled over the step but remained upright, rushed to the pantry, and grabbed a full wine jug. Back outside, he poured two cups of wine.

Remus watched intently as the now gold-colored substance solidified. "It can't be..." he murmured.

"Come on. I can't wait to buy that bastard's villa. Then I'll invite the whole town and turn it into a huge bonfire."

The gold-colored substance solidified further, and by sunset, it seemed Titus had forged a genuine gold bar. Remus lit a torch. With special tongs, Titus carefully lifted the bar from the mold and submerged it in a bucket of water. Remus cleared the table of stones and covered it with a cotton cloth. Titus removed the bar from the water and placed it on the table. Remus and Titus exchanged glances, cheered, and hugged each other tightly. But Remus' joy turned to shock.

"Wait."

"What is it?"

The bar developed dark cracks and speckles. In seconds, Titus' creation crumbled into grayish dust, leaving a wisp of smoke. Titus stepped back, knocked over the table, and stormed inside, stomping and cursing.

14. Gold

It was foggy on the meadows that morning, cool and serene. Remus had left for Nicopolis without money, hoping to at least scrounge up some bread and olives from the market with a promise that Titus would pay once the rent came in. Titus too was up early. He had lit the fire in the outdoor kitchen and once again laid out various stones and tools on the table. On the counter, next to the large pot, stood bottles of the most diverse sizes filled with liquids in every color of the rainbow.

Searching for his last supply of silphium, Titus searched through the shed's cupboards.

"Why don't you look in there?" a voice said.

Titus nearly jumped to the ceiling. He turned to see a figure in his shed. It was the same man he had seen in the woods after hunting with Arrian and whom he had spoken with on the patio; the man who still seemed familiar, wrapped in a dark red toga. Frowning, the man pointed to the pouch hanging on the wall next to the front door. Titus' hands trembled slightly.

"What are you doing here?"

"Did you miss me?"

The Roman tilted his head, looking as if he saw mountain goats speaking fluent Persian.

"I saw you were waiting for me. On the patio. After

the lecture?"

"That's ridiculous. I hardly know who you are. I don't even know your name. Are you spying on me? Why do you just barge into my house?"

"You can hardly call this a house."

"Who are you?"

"My name is Magnus."

"Magnus, huh? Unfortunately, I don't have time to philosophize, as I'm in the middle of something very important."

Titus emptied the wooden chest at the back of the shed against the wall. The floor became littered with stones, minerals, papyrus scrolls, wooden pots, and iron tools that wouldn't be out of place in a torture chamber. Squatting, he threw the contents of the wooden pots onto the ground.

"Just look in the pouch."

Sighing, Titus stood up, walked to the front door, and pulled the pouch off the wall. His mouth dropped open in astonishment.

"How did you know that?"

Magnus laughed and walked to the window.

"Just a feeling. What a lovely view."

"I don't want to talk about it."

Titus glanced through the window. He saw Faustinus

sitting on the porch with a ball. Ares snatched the ball away. Faustinus began to scream. Ariadne ran out of the front door, shouting.

"Are those your children?"

Titus shrugged. With rapid, forced movements, he crushed some of the silphium in a mortar and mixed it with a sparkling sandy substance. He rushed outside and threw the contents of the mortar into the large pot where a yellowish substance simmered. With a long, iron spatula, he stirred the pot. Amidst the stones and minerals stood the clay mold. Using the iron spoon, he poured some of the substance into the mold. Excitedly, Titus and Magnus watched as the substance began to solidify and form into a bar.

"Oh no, I forgot something. Hey, since you're here, can you keep an eye on things? I'll be right back."

Titus turned the corner, grabbed the bucket next to the house, ran to the well, and filled the bucket to the brim. With the full bucket, he ran back around the corner. The bucket slipped from Titus' hand when he saw Magnus holding a gold-colored bar overhead with a large, iron tong.

"What are you doing?" Titus exclaimed.

He ran to Magnus and snatched the tong from his hands. He inspected the bar from all sides, sniffed and licked it, and tapped it a few times with the nail of his index finger.

"I've done it! I've turned stone into gold! I can't believe it!"

Tears streamed down his cheeks. He ran around the shed cheering, but suddenly stopped and walked to the pot where the yellowish substance still simmered.

"Wait, let me try again."

Using the large iron spoon, he scooped some of the substance into the mold again. Soon, the stuff showed dark speckles and the smell of burnt cat feces was barely tolerable. Titus gnawed on his index finger and groaned, pacing back and forth along the table. The brew was still soft but solidified quickly.

"Maybe some water to cool it down?" Magnus suggested.

"You're right."

Titus grabbed the bucket and ran as fast as Arrian's greyhounds around the corner. Frantically, Titus rushed to the well, filled the bucket, and stormed back to the shed without spilling a single drop. He poured the water over the mold. After the yellowish brew around the gold bar further cooled, it turned gray and disintegrated into dust. Titus slammed his fist on the table and fell to his knees.

Magnus examined the mold closely. He dipped his index finger into the dust.

"I think…"

Magnus gently blew the dust off the gold bar.

"I think it worked."

Titus leaped up. He saw a shimmering precious metal hidden beneath the dust. He shouted out loud. His thoughts scattered in all directions, like fruit flies in a pear orchard that, in their madness, no longer knew which fruits to feast on. Rome would welcome him as a hero, and he would present his discovery to the emperor. The world would be at his feet. King Osroes of the Parthians would beg for the secret recipe, and wars would even be fought over it.

He would buy back all his properties and lands. Then he would finally settle scores with that filthy rich Greek in that large, stinking villa by bribing the entire judicial system. But first, he would restore his name in Nicopolis. He would show that insufferable folk what he's made of, what his genius has led him to.

Remus appeared in the distance as a tiny dot amidst countless fields with the city of Nicopolis in the background. Titus waved to him with the gold bar in his hand and made jumps of joy. He ran a lap around the shed, pausing near the window to make mocking arm gestures toward Alcander's villa. However, it seemed no one noticed him: the drowsy doorman was sleeping on a stool. The black cat strolled along the wall at a snail's pace, and the villa's owner was nowhere to be seen.

With a bag of bread, olives, and a pound of goat cheese he had managed to wheedle from the market, Remus hurried onto the property. When Titus shared the news, Remus cheered loudly for his master. He examined the two gold bars lying on the table closely. They shone in the sun, flawless without any cracks or speckles. Titus jumped up, looked around, and then into the distance.

"Where's Magnus?"

"Who's Magnus?"

"Oh, an old friend from Nicopolis. He just appeared—he was just here visiting."

Remus examined Titus from head to toe.

"An old friend?"

"Yes."

Titus wrapped the two gold bars in a cloth and hid them in the crawl space under the shed. Then he gathered all the ingredients he had carefully noted on a piece of parchment and placed them in a wooden crate. The next morning, Remus had left early for Nicopolis to rent a horse and cart, so they could transport all the supplies to the market. Titus immediately dismissed Remus' suggestion to test the recipe a few more times. "There's no time to waste."

At the edge of the forum, right in front of the temple of Tyche, a crowd gathered. A large, white cloth supported by four wooden poles formed the roof of Titus' stall. Underneath, a table displayed jars, bottles, and stones. Remus had lit a fire and stirred the large, iron pot in which a yellowish substance bubbled.

Like a mad wizard, Titus dropped the necessary ingredients into the pot with graceful, dancing movements.

The crowd watched as he added a few drops from a glass bottle with a long neck, a pinch of pink powder from a decorated old box, three stinking leaves from an unnamed plant, dried droppings with a strong smell that made some gag, a fish head, a bull's testicle, and, of course, a dose of dried silphium from the pouch that Remus carried.

"That crazy Laelius has really gone mad," an old woman yelled, exciting laughter from the crowd. Titus pretended not to hear her. Plautia and Sejanus pushed their way through the crowd. The burly city guard who had watched over Titus' old house weeks before also attended. From the front row, he watched intently as Remus stirred the pot.

After Titus added the last ingredient, he turned to the crowd. Realizing all eyes were on him, his hands shook. His heart raced as if he had just sprinted from Marathon.

"De-dear citizens... of... Nicopolis! As I have already announced... you are about to w-witness... something... that has never happened before... in the history of mankind!"

Arrian, too, had come to watch the spectacle and waved and whistled from the crowd to his friend. To Titus' surprise, even Ptolemaios and Galyna were present, causing his eyes to quickly scan all the faces.

Had she come, now that the climax of my life is finally here?

How she would regret having traded him in and having ever doubted his potential. She would beg him tearfully to take her back. Then he would reject her, and she would be sad for the rest of her life. Perhaps she would wait for him every day at the gate while he traveled far and wide.

"Is something going to happen?" someone from the crowd called out.

Titus was startled, pushed his chest forward, and took a deep breath.

"Today... is a historic event. Because today, I, Titus Laelius Faber, will turn stone into gold!"

Exclamations of wonder erupted from the crowd. The city guards looked at each other in expectation. A group of children jumped up and down.

"First see, then believe!"

"It's coming right up! Remus, scoop it!"

With his sinewy hands, Remus grabbed the large, iron ladle, scooped some of the yellowish brew from the pot, and carefully poured it into the mold that Titus had meanwhile set on a second table, fully visible to the crowd. At that moment, a group of musicians, hired by Titus to make this unforgettable, historic event even more special, began to play.

All eyes were on the yellowish substance in the mold. The cooling process was rapid, but time seemed to stand still for Titus. When the solidifying substance already looked quite like a gold bar, exclamations of amazement came from the crowd. Titus imagined how Nicopolis would honor him, how a statue of him would rise next to that of Augustus, and how he would even get his own temple. And once he had won over the people (including the authorities), and they no longer saw him as "that crazy Laelius," he would stand strong against Alcander Cassius. In fact, he would have the scoundrel arrested for pimping, infidelity, and slander.

Arrian held his breath. With a serious look, he watched the solidifying, now shimmering substance. From the crowd came cheers. The thickening bar began to tremble, and black smoke rose from the edges of the mold. Dark brown cracks and fissures appeared. A pungent smell of cat feces and burnt wood spread over the forum.

Soon, the crowd scattered, with some gagging into alleys and others coughing across the square. Ptolemaios and Galyna had fled into the temple of Tyche, and Plautia and Sejanus had hidden behind a market stall. The city guards, who had rushed to the square because of the smell, tried to calm the suffering crowd.

"That crazy Laelius," the old woman shouted. "He tried to make gold from stone but produced cat feces!" Titus stared at the mold, which had turned the substance into black ash. The yelling around him sounded as if it happened in the far distance. He saw people moving along, but their faces had become vague and unrecognizable, as if he was drunk but without the euphoric feeling. Suddenly, he felt a hand on his shoulder. He turned around. It was Arrian.

"Come on, let's get out of here."

Remus and Arrian loaded the gear into the cart, lifted Titus onto a horse, and the three of them rode through the jeering crowd out of the square, through the northern gate, back to the old shed. The rest of the day—and evening—Titus sat staring under an olive tree in the fields with a jug of wine.

The next morning, Remus pulled weeds from the front garden as if he had done it before. With a worried look, he watched as Titus recklessly threw various ingredients into the large pot on the fire. Since the incident in the market square, Titus had not spoken a word. Remus' announcement that he was going to get bread and olives in the city was met with an affirmative grunt from Titus.

Titus crushed the very last bit of silphium in the mortar and threw it into the brew. Titus stirred and stirred until the substance began to sparkle and took on a golden glow. With a desperate sigh, he scooped some of the concoction into the mold. The concoction hardened.

Titus paced nervously back and forth while his gaze fixated on the mold. Raindrops fell over Epirus, soon followed by drizzle. Black cracks appeared in the solidifying mass. Smoke rose from the edges. The smell of cat feces spread through the front garden. Cursing, Titus stormed into the shed, grabbed a jug of wine, returned to the open air, and put the jug to his lips.

"It's not working, is it?"

Startled, Titus' eyes searched the weeds in the front garden. By the mold stood Magnus. Titus straightened his back and took a deep breath.

"It worked once before, so it should work now!"

Magnus laughed, watching as the raindrops mingled with the concoction in the mold.

"I don't think so."

"What do you mean? You were there!"

Magnus shook his head.

"I really only saw you produce cat feces."

"What are you talking about? You held those gold bars in your own hands! They were real gold bars, beautiful, shiny, and splendid, just as they should be, made by me and me alone!"

Magnus slipped his hand into his toga, under which he had a small bag strapped to his body.

"Do you mean one like this?"

"Yes, exactly like that one!"

Titus snatched the gold bar from Magnus' hands, examined it closely from all sides, and noticed three names stamped on the bottom: Lucianus, Scipio, Claudius.

"But wait a minute. Where did you get this from?"

"I took this from the temple of Tyche, just like the other two."

"But that can't be…!"

Like a mad dog, Titus ran inside, flung open the floor hatch, jumped into the cellar, grabbed a bundle wrapped in cotton, and dashed back outside. He shook the gold bars out of the bundle onto the table. The same names—Lucianus, Scipio, and Claudius—were stamped on the bottom of the bars.

"How can this be...?"

"Those also come from the temple of Tyche. You're quite easy to fool, you know. Perhaps your desire blinded you?"

"You sly, filthy, vile, twisted... Why did you do this?"

"Just for a laugh."

"A laugh? What's funny about this?"

"Well, I found it quite amusing."

"Amusing? Do you realize what you've caused? The whole city is laughing at me! My reputation is ruined! My dream is shattered!"

"Good!"

"What do you mean, good?"

Magnus grabbed Titus by the shoulders and shook him.

"Listen to me. You're wasting your energy on a goal that is physically impossible to achieve. Don't you see what you're doing? Turning stone into gold cannot and will never happen!"

Titus fell silent as the rain blurred the view of Nicopolis.

"You know it. But you refuse to accept it. Your desire is too strong, your imagination too vivid. But take it from me. It's impossible. Accept it. Don't live in a lie."

Titus felt dizzy. The surroundings began to spin. He saw stars. His stomach cramped. A dream he had pursued for so long seemed to have crumbled. He had believed in it so fervently.

Have I been unwilling to see the truth all this time?

Maybe Magnus was right. Maybe he had been pursuing an impossible goal and knew this deep inside.

"Impossible or not, this is my life's purpose. What am I without my life's purpose? I really wouldn't know. It's all I have left."

"Maybe it's time for a new purpose. Perhaps this is the moment to find out what you truly want."

"But this is what I truly want."

"Is it? And why is that? Have you ever thought about it?"

"I want to leave something valuable for humanity."

"Ah. And the power and influence that come with it don't interest you at all, do they? Imagine being able to turn stone into gold. Imagine being the only person in the world who knows how. What power and influence you

115

would have! Everyone would be at your feet. The Emperor, kings of distant lands. Rome would welcome you back with open arms. You would be a god on Earth."

"It's more complicated than that."

"Try me."

Titus stood there for a while, with a confused look on his face.

"I guess... I wanted people to accept me, especially those who never believed in me. Those people wouldn't be able to ignore me anymore."

"Your family, your acquaintances in Rome, those bullies on the forum... Ariadne?"

Titus nodded. "I would finally be somebody. Not a burden to his family, not a banished pyromaniac, not a husband whose tinkering never amounted to anything," he said.

"Or... a poor wretch who's lost almost everything, lives in this old shed, sharing the room with his servant. Someone who's powerless against those who continue to wrong him to this day. Imagine how he could make them all pay. He could have the entire Aelianus family banished to the desert by imperial decree! And Ariadne would finally be punished for her adultery!"

"Yes. That would indeed be wonderful. And I'd be lying if I said these fantasies never crossed my mind. But if I'm supposed to believe you, they will never become reality and my efforts have been in vain, my ambitions mere illusions."

"So what do you really want? To contribute to humanity? Fame? Wealth? Influence? Or... maybe just revenge?"

"I don't know."

"Then it's high time you found out."

15. Helvidius

Relentless thunderstorms turned the fields around the shed into a veritable mud pit. In the front yard, around the outdoor kitchen, stood numerous glass bottles and jars, partially filled with rainwater from the persistent storms. The mold on the table was always full. Some days, Alcander's villa became invisible, hidden by the wrath that Zeus had unleashed on Epirus, according to the temple priests. The rain cursed market traders and coach drivers, but blessed the farmers. Zeus' actions were never purely good or bad; they depended on the perspective of the person who experienced them.

Titus hadn't shown his face in Nicopolis for a week. He had sent Remus to fetch not just the usual groceries but also an extra-large supply of wine. However, the rain that had fallen on the roof for days relaxed him so much that he left the wine untouched. After heaps of scorching sun, it felt as though his body had been removed from a hot oven, given the chance to cool down—a sensation that applied to his overheated mind as well. The rain extinguished the fireplace of his thoughts, though it rekindled from time to time.

Titus lay in bed with the sound of rain pounding in the background, closing his eyes. He found himself on an expansive plain with erupting volcanoes in the distance. The sky was red. Smoke rose from cracks and holes in the ground. Thunder rumbled in the sky. It rained sulfur. The air was suffocating. Barefoot, he walked through a soft but slimy bed of worms and maggots. Cockroaches and spiders attempted to climb up his legs.

A figure descended onto the plain with its back to Titus. He wore a dark red toga. *Could it be Magnus?* The figure turned slightly, peeking over its shoulder. *Yes, it was Magnus.* His face was as pale as death. His irises glowed. He laughed, turned away again, and vanished into the distance as quickly as lightning.

In a nearby chasm, two large claws clung to the edge. A sinewy body covered with black scales pulled itself up from the depths. To Titus' horror, he saw the gigantic scorpion with teeth as sharp as the mountains of Cappadocia. The creature charged at him. He began to run.

"Help, help!"

Around him, more giant scorpions emerged to the surface. He felt a hard shove, followed by several blows to his shoulders and head. Crouching in pain, he begged the creatures to stop, but the shoves and blows continued. The gigantic beings surrounded him. Their enormous stingers moved aggressively up and down. Lying on his back on the soft bed of worms and maggots, one of the creatures delivered the first sting. Titus screamed. He had never felt such intense pain before. The scorpions, now in great numbers, took turns stinging him, quickly and mercilessly, like a swarm of bees punishing an intruder.

Amidst the pain, Titus felt two hands on his shoulders gently shaking him.

"Titus! I'm here. Titus," said a voice, familiar and

hopeful in his precarious position. Overwhelmed by pain, he tried to respond.

"Re... mus... help... me... Re... mus."

As if Moses had extended his hand, the red sky split in two, and a bright light poured out onto the barren plains. Some scorpions turned to dust, while others quickly crawled back into the crevices. The opening swallowed the entire sky, spreading until the light blinded Titus.

An owl's coo sounded from outside, in a louder, more intense tone than usual. The chickadee sang, crickets chirped. A cow mooed in the distance. Gently, Titus opened his eyes and saw Remus' concerned face.

"Nightmare?" asked Remus.

Titus nodded, looking at the sun rays streaming in through the window. He sat up, relieved to see his surroundings and took a deep breath as he wiped away tears from his face. For a moment, he glanced at the stone stool on the other side of the room, the table and chair, the cupboard, the window next to the front door. His fingers caressed the cool wall. He took Remus' hand.

"Are you alright?" asked Remus.

"I'm glad you're here," Titus replied.

Remus' surprised expression turned into a smile.

The following day, Titus walked to Nicopolis. Dark clouds adorned the sky, but it hadn't rained yet. The fields were muddy from the previous day, in contrast to the stone road, which remained passable thanks to Roman craftsmanship. At the gate, bored youths loitered, scanning their surroundings.

"There's Laelius, the one who turns stones into gold," one of them said. The youths burst into laughter. "Turn this into gold!" a burly youth with bushy eyebrows shouted, hurling a stone that whizzed past Titus' head. Images from his dream flashed before his eyes. Unconsciously, his legs began to move faster. Stones landed around him. A pebble struck his upper back. Titus' legs carried him into a covered gallery. His thoughts couldn't keep up with his body.

The gallery was bustling. Bakeries, shoemakers, jewelry shops, and clothing stores attracted a large crowd. Titus pulled his hood up and tried to move unnoticed through the crowd. The congestion, scents of perfume, freshly baked bread, melting iron, and the shouts of merchants reminded him of his former life in Rome.

Unrecognized, he hurried out of the gallery, through the streets, to his destination. Thunder rumbled in the distance. His hood shielded him from the first raindrops followed by a downpour. Before the rainfall intensified, Titus entered the residence of Caius Aelius Octavianus, who greeted the visitors with a haughty smile.

Titus waited under the porch by the patio until the lecture began. Zeus unleashed his fury from the heavens onto the earth, obscuring the view across the courtyard. Titus always found it a magnificent sight. The idea that such a downpour temporarily halted city life brought him peace.

The lecture hall was packed, forcing some guests to stand at the back and others to sit on the floor at the front. Today, a special guest from Rome was present, and thankfully, to everyone's relief, it wasn't Tiberius Sellus. Caius Aelius Octavianus joyfully announced the presence of Junius Rusticus[22], who sat at the front row, attracting the attention of Caius' teenage daughters with his dark brown locks.

The young Junius Rusticus turned out to be the grandson of Arulenus Rusticus[23], a prominent member of a group of Stoic philosophers who had opposed the rule of various emperors in the past. Caius explained with animated gestures that these philosophers of old refused to partake in the vulgar scenes of politics, thus opposing the tyranny of Nero and Domitian.

"It is an honor to welcome Junius Rusticus as our guest at today's lecture!" Caius said.

Epictetus had arrived in the lecture hall by then, and Caius Aelius Octavianus promptly handed over the floor to him. Arrian was ready with his pen and papyrus. Next to him, Titus sat slightly hunched over. He heard people

---

[22] Junius Rusticus (c. 100 – c. 170 AD) was a Roman Stoic philosopher and one of Marcus Aurelius' teachers. Some scholars believe that he might have attended Epictetus' lectures.
[23] Arulenus Rusticus (c. 35 – 93 AD) was a Roman senator and Stoic. He belonged to what is known today as the Stoic Opposition, a group that resisted what they deemed tyrannical and autocratic tendencies of certain emperors.

whispering behind him but tried to ignore it. Epictetus scanned the many visitors in the lecture hall. His gaze briefly settled on Junius Rusticus, then on the people at the back of the room. The Stoic sage spoke about the philosopher Helvidius Priscus, who was denied entry to the senate by Emperor Vespasian.[24]

"Helvidius firmly stated, 'You have the power to deny me a seat in the senate, but as long as I have one, I must enter.' The Emperor responded, 'Well, at least be silent when you're there.' Helvidius agreed on one condition: 'If you don't ask for my opinion, I will remain silent.' However, the Emperor insisted, saying, 'But I must ask for your opinion!' Helvidius replied, 'And I must say what I believe is right.' Then the Emperor threatened to kill him."

The room fell silent. Caius sat on the edge of his seat. Arrian diligently recorded Epictetus' words.

"But... Helvidius persisted in his virtue, saying, 'When did I ever tell you I was immortal? You will do your part by killing, and I will do mine by dying without fear. You can banish me, but I will leave without sorrow.'"

Cries of admiration echoed from the audience. Caius started clapping, and the rest of the hall joined in with applause and cheers. Titus clapped along, though his thoughts drifted to Alcander and Ariadne, and how they had denied him access to his children. He realized that in his life, Alcander was the Emperor. It was within his power to take his family away and ruin his reputation.

---

[24] Epictetus, *Discourses*, 1.2.19-21

But what is my part then?

Epictetus hobbled to the front row on his stool, toward the Roman who fiddled nervously with his toga.

"In such moments of challenge, we must distinguish between what is and isn't ours. What is your part? Your wife leaving you? Or enduring it without sorrow? Being treated unjustly? Or proving your innocence?"

"But what if no one believes me?" Titus asked. "What if all the lawyers are bribed and the advisors are too scared to stand by my side? I've done everything I could! Like Helvidius, I've resisted injustice. I've told the truth to anyone willing to listen, but it's gotten me nowhere."

"Examine the situation rationally and accurately, and you'll see it has yielded something for you, namely, that you've acted justly and with integrity, unlike those who lie and deceive, thereby harming themselves. You've done what you could, but the outcome is not yours. What is yours? To live well, in accordance with nature[25], to do what is right, using reason."

Titus sighed. His hand massaged his stomach. The unpleasant feeling was back. How could he live well under such injustice? What was there left to make of life? He might be just and integral, but what did that buy him?

---

[25] Stoics strive to live 'in accordance with nature.' This phrase can be interpreted in multiple ways. Often, 'in accordance with nature' is equated to 'virtue' or 'according to virtue.' Much has been written about what Stoics precisely mean by 'virtue,' but I will not go into detail here.

Helvidius could endure injustice without sorrow and find his happiness in virtue. But Titus was not Helvidius. The idea of letting this injustice go unpunished made him even angrier. The thought that those who had deceived him would get away with their actions only fueled his desire for revenge.

16. Party

In the fresh open air, significantly cooler than the previous evenings due to the summer rainstorms, Titus' belongings were still scattered around the outdoor kitchen. Remus had offered to clean up three times, but his master refused each time.

Despite Magnus' discouragement, Titus claimed he was more determined than ever to continue his experiments. Still, little evidence supported this. Usually quick to rebound from setbacks, this time seemed different. The regular spark was missing from his eyes as he observed his reflection in a bucket of water that morning.

Have I finally accepted it? Is it truly impossible to turn stone into gold?

Having cracked open his large wine stock of twelve jars, Titus spent the entire afternoon drinking. After sunset, Remus found him on the other side of the house, leaning against the wall beneath the window.

"Good evening, my loyal friend. What do you make of this? Epictetus says I should accept it all. I should 'live well,' he says. 'Live well.' Is this a good life? What do you think?"

Sitting down beside him on the ground, Remus pondered for a moment.

"You're healthy, have a roof over your head, and you

can still eat and drink. I'd say you're better off than many others."

Titus chuckled, taking a hefty swig from the jar.

"You must understand... they took everything from me. Everything was stolen. They deceived and betrayed me. Epictetus has it easy. He was enslaved like you. You're used to owning nothing. You are the owned. Slaves don't understand what it's like... what it feels like to have much and then lose it."

"You have a point. I indeed don't know what it's like to lose a fortune, wife, or children because I've never had them. But that's exactly why I think people can learn a lot from slaves."

"Oh? Like what?"

"Well, look. We live as others' property, unfree in a sense, subject to our owners' will. Every day, we see how other people live, freely, in luxury. But that's not meant for us. And yet, we make the most of it. I still see slave women laughing, servants joking with each other. If you, as a slave, can embrace your fate and even live contentedly, you've achieved a lot. A master may own your body but not your choice to be happy."

Titus stared ahead, momentarily contemplating happy slaves and trying to empathize with them. But a surge of emotion from seeing Ariadne on Alcander's villa terrace disrupted his reflections. A luxurious carriage discharged a party of four. Ariadne ushered the guests inside. Soon after, numerous carriages emerged from the darkness, each parking at the villa. Music echoed across the fields. Titus imagined the Nicopolitan elites and surrounding area's wealthy celebrating their fortunate lives, dancing, feasting, and, of course, drinking. Remus placed a hand on Titus' shoulder.

"Let's go inside."

From the shed, Titus peered through the window. Tree tops towering over the villa walls reflected the light from bonfires in the peristyle. *Are Ares and Faustinus part of the celebrations?* Perhaps Ares was paddling in Alcander's lavish pool, and Faustinus sat on Grandma Galyna's lap, nibbling on dried fruit. *They must be having such a great time,* he thought.

Remus lay on his side on the floor, eyes closed. Approaching him with a wine jar, Titus examined him closely. After hearing the first snore, Titus stepped back, tiptoed to the front door, and stepped outside. He navigated through newly planted olive trees and patches of dry grass where the soil remained moist from recent rains. Tripping over a stump, he fell, his toga smeared with mud. The jar lay on the ground, wine slowly seeping out. Cursing, he stood up, grabbed the remaining wine, and marched toward the villa.

On the veranda, by the front door, the drowsy doorman sat on a chair, eyes shut. The influx of guests had ceased; the party was in full swing. The many greetings had likely exhausted him. On his lap, the black cat slept. Two other guards patrolled the wall. Crouching in the bushes near the path, Titus waited until the two men turned the corner and crept onto the veranda toward the door.

The cat opened its eyes, meowed, and rubbed against the intruder's legs in confusion. Titus gestured for the animal to move, but it continued to weave between his legs. Stepping through the front door, Titus stumbled over the threshold but managed to save the wine jar from hitting the marble floor. He straightened up. The drowsy doorman remained motionless, like a hibernating marmot.

After a hearty swig from the wine jar, Titus meandered down a long corridor flanked by columns, marveling at the ceiling paintings he had overlooked during a previous visit. The paintings depicted the life story of Alexander the Great. His gaze shifted to a painting featuring two scorpions. A pang hit Titus' stomach. Music and murmurs grew louder. The doorway at the corridor's end resembled a moving painting. Through the frame, he saw an elegantly dressed woman dancing and laughing uproariously, surrounded by boisterous men in white togas raising their drinking cups.

Hesitating at the doorway, Titus watched the revelers. A group of actors and musicians squeezed through the entrance, entering the corridor. Titus turned his back to them, admiring the ceiling paintings until the group passed. On the floor lay a mask adorned with bronze ornaments and a sun god emblem above the eyes. One of the actors must have dropped it. Titus put it on and, sipping from the jar, entered through the doorway.

The grand hall housed a pool fed and drained by an aqueduct. The pool was crowded with bathers, both men and women. Numerous side tables bore wine jars and delicacies like olives, dates, ham, fresh bread, and cheese. Guests danced around the pool and lounged in the hall's corners or on benches and chairs. Some seemed engaged in heated discussions, while others played drinking games. The scents of freshly roasted meat and rose perfume intermingled.

Unnoticed, Titus navigated the crowd as inconspicuously as possible. Suddenly, a hand clasped his shoulder. Turning, Titus faced a man with a broad jaw holding wine jars in both hands, his bloodshot eyes looking at Titus excitedly.

"What a fantastic performance! Quite impressive!"

Titus remained silent.

"Don't be shy. If I say something, I mean it!"

Realization dawned on Titus as he touched his mask.

"Thank you. It was an honor to perform here."

The man hugged Titus tightly, kissed his cheek, and vanished into the noise of the party.

At the back of the hall, in the center, Alcander Cassius sat on a chair on a raised platform in his finest toga, surrounded by a few slaves, advisors, politicians including Praetor Gaius Lucullus Flavus, as well as his two constant bodyguards. Ariadne, in a beautiful dress and with her hair up, sat next to Alcander. A sharp, burning sensation returned to Titus' stomach, dulled somewhat by the wine. There was no sign of Ares and Faustinus. A wave of unrest surged through his limbs as if in flames.

Boldly, Titus approached the platform at the back of the hall. He ascended the stairs, grabbed Alcander by the throat, and repeatedly struck his eye. Some women in the hall screamed. The musicians ceased playing. All eyes turned to the intruder. Ariadne ran hysterically toward Titus, tripping and falling to the ground. Praetor Gaius Lucullus Flavus shrieked like a Vestal Virgin about to be flogged for being caught unchaste.

Four guards seized Titus by his arms and legs, struggling to restrain him.

"I want my children!" he screamed. "Give me my children!"

Tears streamed down his cheeks as the guards dragged him outside, like farmhands removing a cow from the barn for slaughter. The guards threw Titus onto the field. One kicked him in the stomach, another in his upper back.

"Wait!"

The guards turned. Behind them, Alcander's silhouette appeared.

"Pick him up."

Two guards firmly held Titus. Alcander punched him in the stomach and struck his face multiple times. Titus gasped for air. His nose bled. Alcander stepped back.

"Do what you will with him, but let him live. I don't want the murder of my wife's sons' father on my conscience." He turned to walk to the terrace. After two steps, he paused and glanced over his shoulder. "Oh, by the way, Titus, I would have liked to grant you some time with your children, but I'm afraid you've squandered your chances now."

Titus laughed, blood drowning his teeth.

"That... we'll see about that."

When exactly he lost consciousness was unclear. He remembered a wave of pain and violence transitioning into a lucid dream. His unconsciousness transported him back to his childhood in Rome, where he ran through his family's patio, around the pond, into his mother's arms for a tight embrace. On a summer day, he played in the park and walked with his parents along the Tiber.

However, he saw buildings across the river ablaze. Soon, buildings behind him ignited, even the river itself, as if it were oil. Screaming people ran through the streets, some spontaneously turning into black ash. Titus spotted a familiar figure moving from the burning Tiber to the shore. It was Magnus. His dark red toga was unscathed. The fire reflected in his gray irises. He laughed. Like a dry leaf catching fire, his body turned to ashes within seconds.

The sky turned red. The firestorm spreading from the Tiber inward engulfed his father. Titus clung to his mother's legs, which turned black, hard, and sinewy. His mother's face, now unrecognizable, lacked a nose and eyes. Sharp teeth protruded from her mouth, and her dark brown hair burned away. Titus released her legs and fled onto the road. Giant scorpions emerged from the firestorm.

Titus ran, surrounded by numerous giant scorpions. Realizing he was trapped, he curled up. The ground beneath him collapsed, swallowing the monsters. Rome shattered into thousands of pieces. Up became down, down became up. The endless darkness of the universe stretched around him, adorned with countless nebulae. Fragments of the Colosseum, Pantheon, and Circus Maximus drifted by.

Despite the distant sun, the emptiness felt cold. Titus' body shivered. Darkness cracked as if a knife sliced through black cotton fabric. Beyond the cracks, a rock ceiling illuminated by a dim lamp appeared. Waves of pain shot through his limbs. A warm woolen blanket covered his body. Slowly, he sat up, coughing. Rumbling from a corridor leading to the room grew louder. A shadow cast on the wall sharpened. Footsteps approached. A figure emerged from the corridor. Titus' breath caught. A surge of fear raced through him.

17. Cave

Drops echoed from the rock walls, accompanied by a serene hum, as if rivers flowed somewhere in the depths. Titus' throat felt parched, as if he hadn't drunk for weeks. His limbs were listless, like plants dying from drought. The walls reminded him of a vacation with his parents to the island of Capri years ago, where they visited the Blue Grotto by boat. Unlike the grotto on Capri's coast, there was no seawater in sight.

In the center of the room, Magnus refilled a burning lamp with oil. A wooden bench and two stools surrounded a table, resembling a crate typically used for transporting bread or fruit. Next to the rock wall lay a sleeping mat made of reed and straw, likely similar to the one Titus had awakened on. There was even a small cabinet containing several papyrus scrolls and a locked chest with unlit candles on top. From a large jug, Magnus poured a mug of spring water and handed it to Titus, who gulped it down.

"Where am I?"

"Exactly where you want to be."

Magnus placed a plate with sliced bread, goat cheese, and a bowl of olives in front of him. He examined Titus' face closely. Titus felt a painful swelling around his eye and touched the scratches and bruises on his arms and legs.

"They beat you up pretty badly."

Titus sighed, chewing a piece of bread, as brief flashes

of the beating flickered through his mind.

"What happened? How did I end up here?"

Magnus gazed into the distance before explaining that he had visited a tavern in Nicopolis that evening, engaging in a philosophical discussion with various travelers and locals. On his nocturnal return to the cave on horseback, he found Titus lying by the road and carried him to his dwelling, where, according to Magnus, he had slept uninterrupted for two days.

"Why did you even go there? You could have stayed home, avoiding a lot of pain and misery."

"They can't take my children away from me."

"Is that so?" Magnus stood and paced the room. "Isn't it up to the gods what happens to your children? According to Epictetus, children, like spouses and other family members or friends, are beyond our control. The gods take them back whenever they wish, and if they still live, they might assign them to someone else. Isn't that what the Stoics say?"

Titus recalled Epictetus' lectures, Arrian's notes, and the discussions echoing through the hall after class. He imagined Zeus taking his children from him and assigning them to Alcander, all part of a divine plan, ensuring they grow up happily under his guardianship. A burning sensation in his stomach now accompanied the aching pain of scratches and bruises.

"Yes, they do say that."

"So, the notion that they can't take your children from you is unreasonable. They certainly can, and they have indeed taken your children and assigned them to Alcander Cassius. A reasonable thought would be that it's a part of life for loved ones, including your children, to be taken from you, right?"

The Roman nodded, trying to find peace in the thought that losing his children was a common event, realizing that some die at birth, many don't survive infancy, and others perish from diseases before reaching adulthood. All this is the will of the gods, Zeus' plan, to which mortals must conform.

Do you resist? Then you'll experience great turmoil, as you're opposing matters beyond your control. Better to desire not what you wish for but what actually happens, for then you'll be at peace with any situation.

The burning sensation in his stomach intensified.

Magnus sat on one of the stools, his piercing eyes radiating a certain sadness, yet also anger. It was a quiet anger, as cold as the Alpine mountaintops, which could unleash a true avalanche with the slightest dislodged rock.

"But why didn't you consider this before deciding to invade Alcander's villa and punch the host? Had you lost your mind? How could you do the exact opposite of what Epictetus taught you?"

Titus' trembling hands clutched his abdomen. Tears welled up in his eyes as if the aqueduct's floodgates to his deepest pain had flung wide open.

"Because I *hate* him, alright? I hate him! And I hate her too! And no Stoic can change that!"

Magnus took a deep breath, watching Titus cry on the sleeping mat. The sadness in his eyes turned to compassion.

"I think we have an answer to my questions."

"What... what do you mean?"

"It's time you see the world in a different light. You possess a power far stronger than reason; a force beyond rationality that drove Alexander the Great to conquer India and the Spartans to stand against the Persians. It helps you attain what you deeply desire in your heart, things you believe are out of reach. Some believe, it can even change the course the gods set out for you."

Titus looked at Magnus curiously, memories of his early years with Ariadne, their marriage, and the birth of his sons flashing by.

"You know what I'm talking about," Magnus continued. "It's the pain that surfaces when you think of your children, that nagging feeling in your stomach when you act against yourself, but also the joy when you get what you long for. Ignore it, and you'll be lost. Listen to it, and you'll follow the right path."

The burning sensation in his stomach intensified even more. For a moment he saw Alcander Cassius and Ariadne crucified side by side.

"What power is this exactly?"

"Do you want to learn about it?"

He imagined himself strolling through the forum, receiving warm greetings, with some people even approaching him to apologize and admit their mistakes. *Wouldn't that be something?* The chances of it happening he considered slim. *But what was left to lose?* He was out of options. And since the night at Alcander's villa he lost all hope as well.

"Yes, why not."

Magnus stood, stretching like a Roman emperor after an afternoon nap, a satisfied smile on his face.

"I could try to capture her in words, but better I show her to you. Rest now. Tomorrow morning at sunrise, I'll be waiting at the abandoned shrine of Dionysus. Meet me there, and I'll teach you about this power. If I don't see you, I'll assume you're no longer interested. I'll disappear from your life and won't bother you anymore."

After leaving a mug of wine for Titus, Magnus vanished into the corridor leading to the room. Titus followed his fading shadow for a while, its outline growing dimmer with each distant footstep. With a lingering ache in the background, he pondered the mysterious power Magnus spoke of. *What force is stronger than reason? And could it possibly help me regain my children and achieve justice?*

18. Dionysus

Despite the nagging pain radiating from the bruises and scratches, Titus decided to explore his surroundings. After all, he had no idea where he was. The cave entrance hid behind a wall of vegetation consisting of trees, shrubs, and weeds, making the olive grove beyond inaccessible. Next to the entrance hung a rope ladder leading to the top of a large rock formation. From the top, he could see Nicopolis in the distance, which relieved him since he could have ended up on a deserted island for all he knew. On the other side of the rock formation, a sandy path with vegetation on both sides led to the lagoon.

Not far from the cave lay an abandoned shrine of Dionysus. From there, one could see the lagoon and the Gulf of Actium, with the temple of Apollo not far-off. The shrine was a ruin on a hill accessible by stairs. A battle from the distant past had razed what was once a temple to the ground, leaving only a few broken columns standing and remains of the foundation protruding from the ground.

On the narrow gravel path toward the shrine, Titus encountered a group of young women. Dressed in long animal skins and robes, they walked singing and dancing along the path, playing tambourines and sipping from drinking jugs. He walked past them with a polite greeting, ignoring their cries of seduction. Climbing the stairs, he found himself amidst the ruin, surrounded by chunks of meat and carcasses of various animals likely left by the women.

Candles warmed his skin in the cool morning. Watching the night fishermen guide their boats from the Gulf of Arta into the lagoon, he waited for Magnus. Soon after, as the sun's rays made the sea shimmer, he heard a voice greeting him from behind. Turning around, there stood Magnus, still in his dark red toga but this time also wearing a wolf skin.

"Dionysus loves dead animals, did you know?"

"I didn't realize you were a follower of Bacchus[26]."

"A follower? I wouldn't call myself that. But I do enjoy his company, just like the ladies who just crossed our path. You should spend some time with them instead of those dull, dusty Stoics, then you'd have some excitement and fun in your life."

"I think I've had enough excitement lately."

Magnus chuckled, shaking his head at the sight of meat chunks and carcasses lying next to wine and red petals. He then climbed onto one of the broken columns about a meter high. Like a teacher about to share his expertise, he looked down authoritatively at his one-man audience.

"Dionysus," he began, "represents everything the Stoics, the meek lambs of Apollo, abhor. Dionysus doesn't limit himself to reason and seeks neither peace nor virtue.

---

[26] Bacchus is the Roman name for Dionysus, the god of wine, fertility, insanity, ritual madness and religious ecstasy. The fact that Titus calls him Bacchus highlights his Roman origin.

Forget inner peace! Forget virtue! Vice? That's Dionysus!"

"What does Bacchus—or Dionysus, for all I care—have to do with the power you spoke of yesterday?"

"Impatient, I get it. The power I spoke of can be named but cannot be captured in language. As soon as you name her, she's gone; as soon as you try to explain her, words fall short."

Titus squinted at his enigmatic companion from head to toe while rubbing his stubbly chin. "You're talking nonsense."

"That's exactly it! The philosophy of the Stoics is reasonable, logical, understandable by the mind. But what I have in store for you is anything but! You must feel it, then you'll know, experience it, then you'll understand."

"So, how can I experience this power?"

"Do you want to?"

"Yes."

"Good." Magnus jumped off the column, walked up to Titus, and stood in front of him. "You can experience the power... by making a sacrifice."

Magnus grabbed Titus by the wrist, drew a knife out of nowhere, and cut his palm. Titus screamed like a pig being slaughtered. Blood flowed as if from a breached aqueduct. Magnus collected the blood in a wine cup, which he placed in the center of the ruin among the chunks of meat. As

Titus tried to stop the bleeding with the sleeve of his toga, he was astonished to see two scorpions crawl into the wine cup.

The soft hum of the cave calmed Titus, though he clenched his jaw and his eyes darted restlessly. Magnus had bandaged the wound with a cotton cloth. To ease the pain a bit, he poured a cup of undiluted wine.

"You've just mutilated me! This better be worth it!"

The wound stung as if he had plunged his hand into a nest of red forest ants. Sweat dripped down from his forehead. Blinking brought visions of the plains from his dreams into his eyelids. He smelled the sulfur rain in the distance and heard the clatter of scorpion pincers from the depths.

"Exaggeration is also a profession, huh? There's only one thing Dionysus loves more than dead animals, and that is human blood. You wanted to experience the power? Well, nothing in life is free."

"I don't feel… anything at all… except this pain you caused me. I think you're just a swindler! A sophist… with pretty words. You were supposed to teach me about this power you spoke of, but so far, I've learned nothing."

Magnus laughed, shook his head, donned his hood, and headed toward the passage leading outside.

"Rest well. We will see each other soon. May Dionysus grant you strength."

"Where… are you going?"

The words "I have some matters to attend to in Nicopolis," echoed through the corridor.

The pain in Titus' hand was throbbing, sharp with every movement, but generally dull. The exceptionally strong wine burned his throat but served as a better painkiller than expected. The alcohol made him drowsy, so he closed his eyes for a moment. When he opened them and the rock ceiling spun like a grain mill powered by horses, he quickly shut them again. It wasn't long before his attention drifted to the irrational; the dark, illogical realm beyond the reach of reason, where deeper forces reign supreme.

Cracks in the ground emitted darker, thicker smoke plumes than before, and volcanoes in the distance spewed lava. A scorpion's pincer grabbed Titus' ankle from the edge of a chasm. Soon, jet-black, segmented creatures climbed up from the darkness. With his other foot, Titus kicked the pincer off his ankle, sending the creature back into the abyss. However, he saw many more scorpions approaching and started to run. The harder he ran, the louder he screamed, the more numerous the scorpions became. His palm burned. The pain curled his fingers into a fist. A strange urge seemed to take over. His legs slowed, his shoulders retracted, his chest pushed forward. The red sky closed in with dark clouds, and it rained wine.

Surrounded by scorpions, Titus began to scream. The beasts charged at him, and as their pincers clamped onto him, they fused with him, causing Titus to grow and grow. His muscles lengthened and defined, his scream grew louder and deeper, his skin tore and fell from his body. A gigantic black abdomen with a sharp sting grew from his tailbone. His voice turned into a crow's caw but louder, higher, as if several crows made the sound together. His body tensed all its muscles, his abdomen went rigid, the tiny legs extended, and he screamed and screamed and screamed.

Echoing through the rocky corridors, Titus' voice found its way outside. Likely, no one heard him, except maybe the morning birds feasting on berries and brambles near the exit. Tense as the strings of a lyre, Titus sat upright on his sleeping mat when he opened his eyes. He was back in a world full of water, nature, fresh air, and a blue sky. He looked around. The rock wall seemed to close in on him. The background noise irritated him. He felt a strong urge to get up and leave the cave.

By the exit, Magnus had left a pair of trousers and a dark brown tunic. Titus dressed, leaving behind the blood-stained clothes, and hurried up the rope ladder. The bright sun burned his skin. After leaving the northern hills behind, walking past the vast olive grove, his shed came into view. His skin itched as if hundreds of grass blades brushed against it. He had a lump in his throat, sweat on his forehead, a knot in his stomach, trembling hands, shaky knees, a rock in his stomach, and butterflies in his belly.

In the front yard, Titus found a sea of shards. Various substances colored the glass like an exploded rainbow. The large pan that had been on the stove of the outdoor kitchen lay meters away on its side. His instruments and tools were scattered across the yard, some bent, others broken. The stone mold lay in two pieces under the window next to the front door.

Before his hand reached the latch, the door opened. Serious eyes looked at him.

"Where have you been? I was worried." Remus looked at the cotton cloth wrapped around Titus' hand. "What happened to your hand?"

"What happened here?" Titus tried to enter the shed, but Remus blocked the doorway. "Move aside."

"Wait... before you go in. We have visitors. Don't be shocked... please, don't be shocked."

"What? Who?" Titus felt his fingers curl, pushed Remus aside with force, and saw a presence in the corner at the back of the room, sitting on the stone stool. A familiar but distorted voice full of pain whispered his name.

"Flavia?"

Titus' fingers clenched into fists, his tense muscles nearly tore. Flavia's head had become unrecognizable due to the swellings. Blood ran from her nose down her chin. Like a miserable lump of human, she sat hunched over in the chair. Next to her sat Arrian, holding her hand. With a wet cloth, he dabbed the blood from her face.

"Who did this?"

"... Alcander and his men," said Flavia.

"Alcander and his bodyguards have paid some visits," said Arrian.

Flavia leaned forward. The swellings mostly hid her eyes, but it seemed she hadn't lost her sight when she addressed her younger brother with a stern gaze.

"… I stood my ground… they want us gone… but we're not going anywhere…"

Arrian stood up, took a deep breath, and walked to Titus.

"Alcander tried to persuade the magistrates and the senate to banish you and your sister from Nicopolis. He wants to confiscate the two villas and the piece of land based on criminal offenses. Breaking in and trespassing, violence, pimping. And whispers say he convinced Praetor Gaius Lucullus Flavus that you're Christians guilty of blasphemy. I did my utmost to convince the magistrates and the senate that you, despite some minor incidents, pose no threat… successfully. The magistrates have rejected Alcander's demand."

Titus' hand wound burned as if submerged in a bucket of vinegar, and if his leg muscles were strings, they surely would have snapped. He tried to speak but couldn't get a word out, as if his throat was being squeezed, leaving him breathless. Arrian's eyes moistened.

"I believe my actions have incurred Alcander's wrath."

Titus looked around. Not much remained of the cabinet but a collection of broken boards, and the contents were scattered across the floor. The old ugly chair and the wooden table had clearly been smashed with brute force. Only the stone stool Flavia sat on had survived. The wooden hatch to the crawl space stood wide open.

"They took them," said Remus. "The silphium too."

Arrian placed his hand on Titus' shoulder.

"The will of the gods is not always as we wish life to be. But they have given us the strength to endure."

Titus' stomach burned as if he had drunk a bucket of lemon juice. He imagined Lady Fortuna concocting such a tragic fate high in the clouds and mercilessly executing it; how his sister's pain apparently intertwined with Zeus' divine plan.

What kind of gods are these? Are beings that rain down such pain upon the world even worthy of worship?

"I spoke with Epictetus. He says—"

"I don't care what Epictetus says!"

Titus knocked Arrian's hand off his shoulder. He grabbed the wooden tabletop from the ground and threw it against the wall. Flavia, with some effort, stood up.

"Take it easy… take it easy…"

"Easy? They'll see what's coming to them!"

Arrian and Remus firmly grasped Titus' arms. He tried to break free, kicking wildly.

"Titus! This is pointless! You can't do anything to him! It's unfair, but that's how it's been decided! Accept it. Calm down, and then we'll see what we can do together," said Arrian.

His words brought Titus back to the lecture hall, facing the paternal gaze of Epictetus, the calmness, the reasonableness. His muscles relaxed. When Remus and Arrian let go, he fell to his knees and wept.

19. Woman

A diverse crowd filled the lecture hall. Titus' old neighbors, Plautia and Sejanus, had also come to take a look. *Surprising,* Titus thought, *as they didn't seem like the most philosophical types to me. Are they there for Epictetus' wisdom or just to be seen in the lecture benches?* After all, saying you were learning from Epictetus made an impression. If you wanted to impress even more, you'd throw some profound-sounding aphorisms on the table, such as: "Do not wish for things to happen as you wish, but wish for them to happen as they do happen," or "Do not say how one should eat but eat as one should," or perhaps even the best: "People are not disturbed by things, but by the view they have of them."

Caius Aelius Octavianus, for instance, had become known as the "real estate philosopher"—a slumlord and major landowner who also provided unsolicited life wisdom. In some of his properties, he even had Stoic aphorisms engraved about embracing fate and letting go of things beyond one's control.

But you'd better not dare to pay the rent late, or there would be trouble.

Fidgeting with his legs, Titus tried to focus on the lecture. The words of Epictetus sounded like an off-key orchestra with broken string instruments. Though the cut on his hand was still healing under the cotton, the pain had subsided after a few days.

Arrian, with wide eyes, wrote on the papyrus, eager for every syllable from the lame Stoic's mouth. Titus looked at Arrian and sighed.

"Tell me, why exactly are you doing this?"

"Is that a serious question?"

"Yes."

"Because Epictetus' wisdom must be preserved at all costs."

"But why?"

Arrian stopped writing. Frowning, he looked Titus in the eyes.

"Isn't that obvious? Epictetus is the greatest Stoic philosopher of our time. His lectures must be passed on to future generations. Who knows how many lives will benefit! Hundreds, maybe even thousands of years from now, people could still profit from his insights."

Titus imagined people in a distant future sharing the words of Epictetus, in enormous lecture halls equipped with advanced water systems in buildings reaching the clouds. Imagine: people in the distant future, living by the ideas of some Greeks, with Arrian's handbook as a guide.

A fascinating idea, but also highly unlikely.

After the lecture, another debate erupted in the hall, where Caius Aelius Octavianus and Arrian clashed like gladiators of reason. The overlapping voices, the cheers, and applause sounded like screeching birds fighting over a piece of bread on the forum. Without saying goodbye, Titus left the building, overwhelmed.

The street tiles gleamed from the morning drizzle that had given way to a dull sun. The morning in Nicopolis was in full swing. Beggars, sellers, local politicians, and temple priests moved through the streets. Horses pulled carts full of merchandise, and teachers guided groups of students. With his hood up, Titus tried to move inconspicuously through the crowd. Once past the busy streets, he slipped into an alley.

The alley was narrow with buildings on both sides. Rats ran along the side walls from crack to crack. It smelled of urine with a hint of burning wood, probably from one of the surrounding houses. Titus heard voices behind him getting closer. The talk stopped for a moment, followed by a whistle. Titus turned around. It was the same young men who had robbed him earlier.

As the two men chuckled and approached Titus, he quickened his pace to the exit of the alley. When he came out of the alley, he saw in the corner of his eye that their tall, skinny friend was just a few steps from the exit. Startled by the two city guards parading through the busy street, the bandit darted into the alley. Titus hurried to the two authoritative-looking figures, armed with short wooden clubs.

"Hey! Hey! Three bandits tried to rob me! They're in that alley there!"

The city guards stopped. One of them had a notably large nose. His muscular body towered over Titus. The other was a head shorter. His long, broad neck with a compact head atop reminded Titus of a hyena. The large-nosed guard examined the Roman from feet to crown.

"Aren't you Laelius?"

"Yes, I'm Laelius."

The guard with the hyena head looked at him with wide eyes. "The Laelius who turns stone into cat dung?"

"Yes, yes, that's me. Are you going to catch those bandits or not?"

The city guards looked at each other. The large-nosed guard shook his head. "No, sorry, but we're in a hurry. We have an important assignment."

"From the Praetor."

"Yes, from the Praetor."

Fidgeting from one foot to the other as if he urgently needed to use the latrine[27], Titus glanced at the alley and then at the city guards. His eyes dropped to the club in the hand of the one with the hyena-like head. As quick as a skilled pickpocket, he snatched the club and dashed into the alley.

Rats darted into holes and cracks, and a cat scrambled

---

[27] A latrine was a private toilet in the homes of ancient Greeks and Romans, usually constructed over a cesspit.

up the wall hissing and disappeared through a window. At the other end of the alley, he saw the bandits ducking into a bakery. He charged across the street, stormed into the bakery, wove through the customers, out the back, over a fence, through an old couple's backyard, another fence, down an alley, and back onto the street.

The skinny, tall bandit tripped over a protruding stone. He came to a rolling stop. Titus ran up to him, kicked him in the stomach, and struck him multiple times with the club. The other two ceased their pursuit. From a distance, they yelled incomprehensible shouts. From a side street, the two city guards, Hyena-head and Big-nose, rushed into the scene.

"There he is!" Hyena-head said.

"Laelius! You are guilty of theft and damage to government property!" Big-nose said.

Titus took a few steps back, ran back down the alley, jumped the fence into an old couple's house, out the front door, down an alley, in and out of gardens. Once at the western gate, it seemed he had lost the city guards. He slipped outside, along the wall out of the guards' view, through the cypress plantation into the coastal forests where he hid for the rest of the morning. Early in the afternoon, he walked northwards through the woods. By the Apollo temple, he fled through the hills to the east.

Titus burst into the cave. Magnus was slouched against the rock wall, intently reading a text on a small papyrus scroll as if Titus' entrance went unnoticed.

"You won't believe what just happened. They tried to rob me. I gave them a beating. And then I was chased by the city guards. Unbelievable…"

Other than a confirming grunt, Magnus did not respond. Exhausted, the Roman dropped onto one of the stools.

"What are you reading?"

"Nothing special, really. Just something I found in that chest this morning, hidden under a pile of old blankets."

At the top of the papyrus roll was the title: *That Women Too Should Study Philosophy*. Magnus chuckled and shook his head.

"I find it amusing how these Stoics always think they know how we should live. They have discovered what 'virtue' is, supposedly unique in all of human history. Then they come up with all sorts of ideas and rules we must follow to lead a virtuous life. This manuscript is a prime example of that."

"What does it say?"

"It's a lecture by Musonius Rufus, a grand Stoic, not long dead, once banished from Rome… just like you. He even taught Epictetus; imagine that. Not very surprising, reading all this."

Magnus' finger roamed the text, searching. "Ah, here it is: *'Above all, a woman must be chaste and self-controlled; she must be pure regarding unlawful love, exercise moderation in other pleasures, not be a slave to desire, not be quarrelsome, not be lavish in spending, and not be extravagant in clothing. These are the actions of a virtuous woman, and to these, I would add: controlling her temper, not being overwhelmed by grief, and being superior to uncontrolled emotions of any kind.*[28] "

"If you ask me, this Musonius Rufus describes the ideal woman," Titus said.

"Really?" Magnus said, throwing the manuscript across the cave. "What makes the ideal woman according to you?"

"The ideal woman is caring, obedient, faithful, kind…"

"Funny, the woman you describe doesn't quite resemble your former wife, does it?"

Titus chuckled.

"Yeah, now that you mention it," Titus said. "She possesses none of those qualities."

"Yet it's interesting that you married her."

"If I could turn back time, I'd choose a good woman: one who is faithful, can control herself, and doesn't do crazy things. One who supports me in my work, is caring and does what I ask of her."

Magnus burst out laughing.

---

[28] Musonius Rufus, *Lectures and Fragments*, Lecture III, That women too should study philosophy. I have used Cora E. Lutz'

"Oh yes, that sounds like a perfect woman. Submissive, useful, predictable. Breakfast ready every morning. She washes your clothes, cleans the house every day, takes care of the children, and massages your feet in the evening. And, not to forget: you just snap your fingers, and she neatly lies on her back with legs spread. What a wonderful woman that would be. Who wouldn't want that?"

The idea described by Magnus didn't sound wrong to Titus at all. Such a woman would be very valuable; an ideal partner for a man, supporting him in all facets of life, and always making herself available to him. Such a wife would never become hysterical, cheat, or waste money on unnecessary luxury items. With such a spouse, one would be free from the aura of drama and misery that surrounded Ariadne. No flying pots through the living room, no drunken spectacles, no unpredictable emotional outbursts, but loyalty, virtue, helpfulness, obedience, and moderation.

"What's your ideal woman then?" Titus asked.

"I don't have an ideal woman. I go with the flow, see what comes my way and how it goes. I especially don't let myself be guided by ideals and certainly not by Stoic ideas about virtue and vice. Those ideas are worthless. Every person is unique. And when two people merge, something unique again is created—that's something you should understand as a metallurgist. Why would you destroy that

---

translation of *Lectures and Fragments* as a source.

uniqueness by letting yourself be guided by all sorts of frameworks and rules? That would be a disservice to a special gift from nature."

"If not guided by ideals, by what then?"

"By the power you can't name! The power that brings you where you need to be, good, bad, pleasant, or... painful."

"Painful? Well, I could have done without the pain of my marriage."

"Not at all! Because that pain brought you here. It has made you what you are now, led to what you now feel. That too is the power, the indefinable, the all-encompassing. Her plans for you will soon become clear."

20. Urge

A gentle breeze cooled the landscape just before dusk. From the sanctuary of Dionysus, Titus watched the sun sink behind the hills. On a large stone, once the foundation of the temple, stood a wine chalice from which he and Magnus took turns drinking.

Music and loud cheering disturbed the dusk chirping of blackbirds and the chorus of crickets. Titus stood up and looked toward the gravel path. Dozens of men and women dressed in animal skins and masks, equipped with musical instruments and wine jugs, walked singing to the shrine.

Three men and three women carried the carcass of a wolf on a wooden stretcher. They placed the dead beast on a wide, broken pillar. As if madness had struck them, the three men and women danced around the carcass and doused it with wine. From a distance, Titus observed the scene. Magnus, on the other hand, joined the ritual dance, sipping from a wine jug. A man dressed in a wolf skin lit torches. The crowd feasted and sang, and the wine cups remained filled. Magnus danced with every woman.

Amid the festive noise, three stunningly beautiful women dressed in long but revealing gowns appeared. They danced gracefully, swinging their arms. The ladies reminded him of the descriptions his mother gave of forest nymphs. They possessed such indescribable beauty that his breath momentarily halted.

Magnus tapped Titus on his shoulder.

"They're pretty, aren't they?"

"Are they…"

"Yes, they're nymphs. Real ones. They're loads of fun. But never get attached, or they'll devour you. Otherwise, they're the best company a man could wish for."

Titus' gaze met with one of three nymphs. She had golden locks down to her buttocks and was dressed in blue. Along with the other two ladies, dressed in light red and green, she moved to the music around the carcass. She smiled at Titus. He smiled back. She emptied a wine cup in one gulp and danced gracefully toward him. The scent of wine grapes and rose petals surrounded her.

"What brings you here, new-face?" the nymph asked.

"Magnus invited me," Titus replied as his heart raced, the wine only dulling the sensation slightly.

"Ah, I heard about you. You must be his new pupil!" the nymph said, her eyes scanning him curiously.

Titus kept silent, his gaze drifting out over the crowd.

"I didn't expect you to be so handsome, though," the nymph continued, her tone teasing.

Titus, at a loss for words, moved uncomfortably, his gaze drifting out over the dancing crowd.

"You're not much of a talker, are you? I'm sure you know what I mean. The women in the city must be drooling over you. And men, too, probably," the nymph added.

"Not really…" Titus replied.

"I find that hard to believe," she chuckled.

"Maybe I'm just not paying attention."

"That must be it! So, why aren't you? You might miss out on your true love…"

"What's that supposed to mean?"

The nymph laughed, her eyes twinkling as she reached for his hand, dragging him into the festive noise. She embraced Titus tightly, pressing him against her chest.

"Do you believe love is predestined?" she asked, her breath warm against his ear. Titus' body tensed at her sudden closeness.

"I mean, have you ever met someone, and the moment you see this person, you just know you've found the one?" she continued.

Memories of the Odeon flashed by, images of Ariadne sitting among the audience, feelings of passion for a mysterious woman, longing without truly understanding why.

"I think so."

"Oh, yes?" The nymph surrendered in her embrace to him, as if trusting him like a child trusts its mother. "Who is it? Man or woman? Tell me."

Her intrusiveness caught Titus off guard, though he didn't mind. Hesitantly, he wrapped his arms around her and tried to relax his muscles.

"We've just divorced."

"Just divorced?" She rested her head on his shoulder, like a newborn puppy in its mother's lap. "Then she was not your true one."

"I don't think so."

She looked at him, her pupils seeming almost to encompass the whole world, nearly as large as her irises, as if they wanted to capture every detail of his face. Titus felt his heartbeat quicken. He hastily took a sip from the wine jug.

"You know it when it happens. Not because you have ever experienced it before, nor because someone has ever explained to you how it feels. You know it, like you know the seas are full of fish, even though you can't rationalize it."

"Have you ever experienced it?"

"I believe so."

"Do you believe the seas are full of fish? Or do you know it?"

"Sharp." Her hand covered her laugh, and her gaze dropped to his chest. "Sometimes doubts hide what you know for sure, like a cloud cover between Earth and the sun. Then you just have to wait for it to clear."

The nymph leaned forward, her eyes closed, and gently pressed her lips against Titus'. The torches became dim lights in the distance, people lost their faces, music its sound. Thoughts drowned in desire. Titus saw only her, the nameless creature with long, golden locks, until she too vanished into a vast, dark haze.

Titus woke up startled. The sound of the tambourine echoed in his head. The rock ceiling spun. His head felt as if it had been trampled by a herd of galloping horses. The girl with golden hair lay in his arms. She opened her eyes. Her fingers caressed Titus' face. A shout came from an adjacent corridor.

"You scoundrel! Arrogant jerk!" said a shrill woman's voice.

"What did I do wrong now?" said Magnus. "You came along with me, didn't you?"

"I can't believe I let myself be charmed again."

From the corridor, a young, dark-skinned woman dressed in green, with the look of a quarreling cat, hurried in. Titus recognized her. She was one of the nymphs who had suddenly appeared in the festive noise, just like the nameless woman in his arms.

"Play the victim again. That's what you ladies are so good at, right? You just don't want to admit how much you adore me."

"Adore you? I find you utterly despicable!"

"Utterly despicable, indeed. You thought differently

last night. You squealed like a piglet during slaughter. Out of pleasure, mind you."

"You have a vivid imagination."

The woman marched toward the exit with determined steps. Magnus followed her like a hungry goat.

"Stay a while longer, Nysa. I have guests. Let's have a cozy breakfast together."

"Are you crazy? I want to get out of this stinking cave as soon as possible!"

The woman with golden locks, still in Titus' arms, looked disapprovingly at the scene, as if she knew more about the relationship between the two. Her eyes followed the woman in green, apparently named Nysa, on her way out, then looked at Titus laughing.

The Roman felt his heart race. He ran his fingers through her golden locks. It felt like his fingers glided through the soft water of a hot spring. She jumped up and dressed. Her slender legs moved as smoothly as the sea.

"Where are you going?" asked Titus.

Without answering, she kissed him on the mouth and walked to the cave's exit. Titus pulled himself into his tunic and followed her. Before he reached the exit, he lost sight of her. He ran outside, climbed the rope ladder. From the rock, he looked around. There was no sign of her. Magnus and the woman in green had also disappeared. The orchestras of morning birds sounded muffled as if his ears were covered.

From behind, Magnus' voice sounded.

"Why bother with those creatures… so fickle."

Titus stared at the sea in the distance.

"She's the most beautiful thing I've seen since Ariadne."

Magnus burst out laughing.

"What's so funny?"

"You should have heard yourself yesterday. Caring, obedient, faithful… Your girl is a nymph! That goes for the hysterical lady in green, too. And I'll tell you: the nymphs of Dionysus are not exactly known for those virtues of yours. They are wild and unpredictable as the Aegean sea, seductive as the sirens that once enchanted Odysseus. Even married men fantasize about them while their obedient wives sleep. Even gods have a weakness for them!"

The dancing nymphs of Dionysus flooded Titus' imagination. Their graceful movements by the torchlight, fleeting as fireflies, ungraspable as the ripples of the sea, challenging as sirens, irresistible as Aphrodite herself.

"Why are you convinced you want one thing but fall for another?" asked Magnus.

"I don't know," said Titus.

Magnus laughed, then fell silent, as if taking the time to soak in the views from the rocky outcrop. The Ionian

Sea sparkled in his gray eyes that drifted to the stadium at the foot of the hill, the forest edge along the coast, and then to Apollo's temple, its columns shining as if they emitted light in the morning sun.

"It's because of that power that cannot be described in words, although some call it the *'Urge.'* But the Urge that can be named is not the true Urge, for the true Urge names, but has no name, describes, but cannot be described."

"The Urge…"

"It makes trees grow to great heights, fills oceans with fish, brothels with customers, and moves brave men beyond the known world's boundaries. The Urge does not heed reason. She desires what She desires, regardless of good or evil."

"So, the Urge is both good and evil?"

"What do the Stoics consider good or evil? Virtue is good, vice is evil. Virtue leads to inner peace and happiness, vice to misery. But the Urge operates differently. She speaks the language of our deepest self. The Stoics push you to make choices that go against the Urge. Think about it! Look at what happened to you! Good or evil, virtue or vice… these matters don't concern me. What matters to me is how your wife's betrayal, or any harm or alleged 'injustice' inflicted on you by others, affects you."

"It makes me angry. Angry and sad."

"Exactly. And the Stoics say that anger or sadness

comes from your attitude toward these things, or rather, the thoughts you form about them, right?"

"Yes, that's correct."

"If it's that simple, then they need to explain why animals show anger when something hurts or threatens them. Or why a dog is so happy to see its owner when he comes home. Is it because of their thoughts? Because of the stories they tell about these situations? Because of an attitude they consciously adopt? Or is it due to innate impulses that protect and make them survive?"

Titus thought of the neighborhood cat that fiercely chased away other cats entering its territory, the quarreling ducks, the howling of Mr. Evagrius' dog. The emotions of these animals were clearly natural phenomena. A cat doesn't seem to think about its anger, or to be persuaded by other cats to cool down. Ducks also don't seem to ponder the nature of what they're mad about. These animals just react.

"Animals act in harmony with the Urge," said Magnus. "They don't react because they find something 'bad' or 'good.' They're not concerned with ethics or morality. They do what they do because of the force that drives them."

"But aren't we humans different from animals? Didn't the gods give us the power of reason for nothing?"

"Reason is both a blessing and a curse. On one hand, it allows us self-reflection and the ability to grow and learn from our experiences and consider the future. On the other hand, reason can also lock us in a cage of ideas, categories, and rules, making us blind to the core of our being. And the more time we spend in this cage, the further we become removed from our true nature."

"But isn't it exactly that true nature that gets us into trouble? Our impulses, our desires... can't they be just as destructive as they are liberating?"

Magnus smiled. "They can indeed. And that's the beauty of it. The Urge is detached from good and evil, moral and immoral. The only thing that matters to Her is who you truly are."

Titus sighed, struggling with the concept. "So you're saying I should give in to every impulse?"

"Not blindly, no, that would turn out poorly. Reason is a tool. We don't have to throw it away to follow the Urge. We shouldn't allow reason to govern us; instead, we should be the ones governing reason.

"But how do we follow the Urge?"

"Forget virtue, let go of your morals, abandon your life rules. Look beyond reason, see ideas for what they are, namely, creations of our limited intelligence. Forget, and you shall know. Let go, and you shall find."

"But how—"

"Start by not asking questions all the time."

"But—"

"Stop asking questions! It's always the same with people who can't stop thinking. Philosophers, scientists, mathematicians... from Plato to Pythagoras to that lame loudmouth from Hierapolis. They question everything. And when all their questions are answered, they come up with new questions. And when those are answered, what do they think of? Right. Even more questions. Animals don't ask questions. Why would they? Their innate nature is more than enough to lead their lives. Mathematical problems, political issues, philosophical dilemmas, research questions... what use are these things, except to keep a bunch of half-baked, graying men in togas busy? Oh, dear, now I catch myself asking a pointless question."

"But aren't questions useful? How can we truly understand the world without asking questions?"

"Of course, there are also useful questions. But most questions are irrelevant. They only lead to confusion. The more we want to understand, the less we grasp. The more knowledge we gather, the less we actually know. 'Why are we here?' one asks. It doesn't matter. 'Is there life after death?' another asks. What do you care! You don't even know what life is!"

Silently, the Roman stared at a fishing boat sailing along the lagoon's spit.

What is life? Sailing the Gulf every night like a night fisherman? Pursuing a political career like a Roman senator with his carved-out smile? Living according to Zeus' will like a Stoic?

"What is life?"

"Don't overthink it. Don't doubt so much. There's only *one* important philosophical question, and that is: 'What do I want?' This question seems simple, but few can answer it. Most have forgotten what they want. For them, the answer is far-off. Some drift aimlessly, others cling to a belief. The latter group is the worst. They think they know exactly how everything works, why they are on Earth, how they should live, what they should and shouldn't want, but are secretly terrified of themselves. Because if they looked beneath the surface of their beliefs, they would discover what they truly desire. And what they truly desire, the Stoics, the temple priests, and other types who like to dictate how to live are not so fond of. They fear the Urge, dismiss Her as irrational, animal impulses. But that makes them afraid of life itself."

Titus, no longer daring to ask the enigmatic philosopher further questions, gazed at the fishing boats in the distance.

What do I want? Is it justice? Revenge? Wealth and power? Love? Acceptance, perhaps?

The more he thought about the question, the more the answer eluded him.

21. Chaos

Atop the rocky outcrop, Titus gazed beyond the lagoon, cautiously touching the cotton bandage over his slightly throbbing cut. The mountains that usually rose behind the Gulf of Actium were obscured by the hazy weather.

The surrounding vegetation seemed different to him than before. What once appeared as nature's peaceful green protrusions now spoke to him as a violent, silent force, struggling into life yet destroying everything alive. Even bird songs sounded less friendly. In a nearby cuckoo's call, he thought he heard a craving for living worms. He realized that cuckoos lay their eggs in the nests of other birds and, upon hatching, their young push other eggs or chicks out of the nest.

Where is virtue in nature? And often, one might wonder: where is virtue in humanity?

"Virtue is a mask we wear to show each other how good we are. Why does anyone want to be 'good'? Is it for the sake of goodness itself, or for what this goodness brings?"

Magnus had just climbed up the ladder and, like Titus, gazed at the misty sky where the mountain peaks in the east hid. He picked up a stone from the ground and threw it into the distance.

"We study philosophers' works, discern between right

and wrong, adhere to rules of conduct, and construct a massive tangle we then call 'society.' And as members of society, by contributing our goodness, we secretly hope the gods and our fellow men grant us a slice of good fortune." Magnus chuckled and threw another stone. "What a roundabout way to get what we want, isn't it?"

"But what do we want?"

Magnus laughed and pointed toward the lagoon. Fishing boats disappeared into the mist, seagulls circled above the water, and a flock of sheep grazed along the shoreline.

"Wherever She leads us."

"The Urge?"

Magnus nodded, his penetrating gaze locking with Titus' eyes. The afternoon breeze fluttered his long, straight black hair across his face.

"She speaks strongly within you. But you've forgotten to listen to Her. Most people, especially folks like the Stoics, deny Her presence because of the system humanity has created for itself. We've hidden Her behind a wall of thought constructs, ideas, perceptions, reason, you name it. She's like a mother, longing for Her child who doesn't want Her, even denies Her existence. It's sad, I know."

The burning sensation in his stomach overshadowed the pain from the cut.

"How can I hear Her?"

Magnus' lips curved upwards, laugh lines appearing around his gray eyes reflecting the cloud cover.

The starry sky was obscured by dense clouds that evening. Magnus placed a cup of wine on the remains of the foundation and lit the area with an oil lamp. Soon, the sound of musical instruments, singing, and cheering blended with the symphonies of crickets and night birds.

A group of about twenty men and women, led by three stunning nymphs illuminated by oil lamps, proceeded along the gravel path toward the shrine. Titus' heart raced at the sight of the nameless woman in blue, whose golden locks shone in the lamp light. He took a large gulp from the wine jug he had brought from the cave.

The procession halted at the broken pillar. A young woman with hair as wavy as the Ionian Sea stepped forward, cradling a dead animal in her arms. Titus felt a jolt in his stomach as the animal looked eerily familiar. The sturdy legs, the black-and-white fur… could it really be? Titus' face turned pale as he looked at Magnus.

"What's happening here?"

"An initiation ritual. An offering to Dionysus. After this, she will be a full-fledged follower."

The musicians played ominous melodies, percussionists ecstatically beat their hand drums and tambourines.

"But I know this animal," Titus said. "It's our neighborhood cat! What happened to it?"

Magnus laughed, dancing to the rhythm of the music.

"What a coincidence! The neighborhood cat! She killed the neighborhood cat in honor of Dionysus! The creature couldn't have met a better fate!"

Titus squinted at the animal laid out by the woman on the broken pillar, amidst wine cups and maggot-infested pieces of meat. The followers formed a circle around the neighborhood cat, their songs in an unknown language echoing over the hills surrounding the sanctuary.

At the ruins stood a human-height column dressed by some followers in a white toga and a mask with a laughing face, adorned with curly hair, grape leaves, and grapes. They placed a large earthen pot filled with wine by the dressed column.

Several followers in animal skins lit a bonfire. The three nymphs poured wine from jugs depicting Dionysus; a young, chubby man in a white toga exposing part of his upper body, sitting on a cheetah. In one hand, he held a wine cup, and in the other, a grapevine. Grapes and vine leaves grew from his hair. The nymphs distributed the full wine cups to the followers, who danced and sang ecstatically around the bonfire:

Struck by wine, a lightning strike so bright,
sorrow fades, easing the pain that grips me tight.
Forget what we know, let everything slide,
so we may rise again, with each pour, more refined.

Titus stared at the dead neighborhood cat, its fur gleaming in the bonfire light. He felt a hand slide over his back, turned around, and found himself face-to-face with the nymph in blue. He took a big gulp of wine and focused again on the dead animal. The nameless nymph caressed the back of Titus' head.

"Don't mourn. Let it go."

"Why did he have to die?"

"Nature and death are inextricably linked. Everything alive will eventually die. Yet, in death, there's also the promise of new life."

Titus remained silent.

"Did you know Dionysus' mother, Semele, died before he was born? Zeus saved him, and later, Dionysus rescued her from the Underworld. He possesses the power to make vines flourish, but also to wither them, to grant life and take it away. Our sacrifices are a way of thanking him for his role in the cycle of life and death."

Titus tried to understand the logic behind the ritual. He sought to decipher how consuming wine, dancing, singing, and offering sacrifices specifically benefited the followers.

What was the purpose? How did it work exactly?

Everyone he asked provided evasive, vague answers. No one could explain it. You had to experience it, and then it offered liberation. Wine was the first, essential step toward that liberation. And from that place, the blessing of fermented grape juice, you discovered who you truly were. The path of the Stoics was one of logic and reason; the path of Dionysus, one of madness and ecstasy.

"You won't find any answers, until you stop looking for them," the nymph in blue said. "The more you seek to understand, the more confused you'll get."

"What do you mean?" Titus asked.

"You think too much! I've known so many people like you. Theorists, analyzers, speculators. But you can only grasp Dionysus' rituals if you stop trying to understand them. You must surrender yourself completely."

The Roman kept silent, gazing how the bonfire reflected in the nymph's dilated pupils. She laughed and shook her head.

"It's like falling in love. Could you ever really explain why it happens? I don't think you can. Yet, we surrender to it, because we understand its essence beyond words."

"Well," Titus said. "I think it's quite simple. It's nature's way of letting us reproduce. You see, if we didn't fall in love, far fewer children would be born, and our species would risk extinction."

"So, you don't believe there's a deeper meaning to love, aside from reproduction?"

Titus briefly stared at the dancing crowd.

"No," he answered.

The nymph playfully slapped him on this arm.

"How disenchanting! I know you're lying. If you've experienced it—and I know you have—you know it goes way deeper than what you describe."

"Ah, is that so? Maybe I'm just more pragmatic about these heart matters."

"Are you? I think you're just being a tough guy afraid to admit that you, too, have fallen under love' spell... and have had your heart broken."

"Wait... what did Magnus tell you about me?"

"Nothing!"

"Really?"

"Really! It's just... You're divorced. You told me, remember? So, I thought..."

"I don't want to talk about it."

"Fine. But you know I'm right. You know that the passionate love for another is one of the most beautiful experiences. It's profound. It's divine."

"It's also dangerous."

"And well worth the risk. I couldn't imagine life without it."

The bonfire flames grew, soaring as if to touch the clouds. Magnus drank with two nymphs by his side; one had olive-colored skin and wore a brown dress with yellow cords and a floral wreath. The other was Nysa, still in green, adorned with a leaf wreath and braided hair. She watched the bonfire as if preoccupied with a thought that constricted her joy.

Magnus stood up. He walked to the ruin's center and leaped onto the broken column. With hand gestures, he commanded the musicians to halt. He cupped his hands around his mouth and howled like a wolf. All eyes turned to him.

"The flames reach the atmosphere! This is the sign! The world is off balance, Apollo's influence[29] has grown excessive! Dionysus calls us to restore the balance!"

The followers cheered. Titus looked skeptically at the tipsy attendees and then at Magnus, curious about his next words.

"We are the answer to excessive order! We fight against the tyranny of reason that oppresses many! Down with the life-deniers, down with the stifling morals! Away with order! Followers of Dionysus, what is your response?"

"Chaos! Chaos! Chaos!"

"Tonight, we enter the city!"

Wine cups clashed together. Followers extinguished the bonfire with sand. They donned inconspicuous, dark tunics. Titus caught himself with a subtle smile at the thought of delving into the night's depths. "Chaos" was, of

---

[29] Magnus refers to the philosophical concepts of the 'Apollonian' and 'Dionysian,' which represent a duality between the mythological figures Apollo and Dionysus, notably discussed by Friedrich Nietzsche. Apollo symbolizes the rational, order, logic, and art, while Dionysus embodies the irrational, chaos, passion, emotions, and instinct.

course, a broad term; it could mean anything. And that's what made it so exciting. It reminded him of his experiments, where he mixed and heated various elements, never knowing the outcome. Perhaps the most beautiful part of life was the unknown, the most memorable moments being those spontaneous ones that fell outside the norm.

The stadium and the adjacent theater and gymnasium were deserted. From there, it was a short walk past the baths and the cemetery to reach Nicopolis' northern gate. The gate was well guarded. In groups of three, the followers spread through the cemetery, moving cautiously toward the city wall, sneaking from tomb to tomb. Magnus carried a fabric bag. Titus could only guess its contents.

The followers reached the walls. The three nymphs hurried to the gate. Titus watched in amazement as they later led a line of night watchmen through the cemetery into the olive groves. The coast was clear. Titus and Magnus sneaked along the walls, through the gate, and saw the followers who had gone ahead darting into various alleys.

Magnus looked over his shoulder at Titus. He gestured for him to come closer.

"Follow me."

"Where are we going?"

"Don't ask questions. Just follow me."

Magnus turned into a narrow alley with residential

buildings and backyards on both sides. Shouts echoed in the distance, sounding like the city watch. Magnus climbed over a fence. Titus followed. They ran from backyard to backyard, scaling fence after fence, moving from alley to alley. In a side street off the forum, Magnus halted. From the fabric bag, he retrieved two masks resembling the Dionysus mask with which the followers had adorned the column at the ruins.

With masks on their heads, Titus and Magnus darted out of the side street onto the forum, where the other followers had already gathered. Wine jugs, drums, tambourines, string, and wind instruments emerged. A bonfire was lit. Singing and dancing, the crowd moved across the forum. From adjoining streets, the three nymphs appeared, also wearing masks, playing flutes. Behind them followed strings of people, men and women, seemingly enchanted by the music, joining the festive uproar.

More and more people appeared on the forum, curious about the festive crowd. Guests from nearby pubs, most of whom had long forgotten the wine god, joined the dancing throng. The wine, again distributed by the nymphs, was ever stronger and more flavorful than anything available in the pubs. Titus stood in awe, seeing the magic the Dionysian revelers cast over the surrounding people, as if their dance moves and songs took over the depths of their souls, liberating them from their inhibitions. Of course, the free wine could have played a role in this, too.

From a distance, city watchmen observed the scene. In the eyes of some, sparks of desire to join the festive uproar sprouted. Titus nudged Magnus and subtly pointed to the city watchmen.

"Do you think they'll intervene?"

"It's already too late. We are like the Trojan horse. The spirit of Dionysus already roams the city streets. His power has ignited the hearts of the people. They are afraid."

Familiar faces appeared on the forum. Titus' former neighbors Plautia and Sejanus watched the spectacle from a distance. Caius Aelius Octavianus walked disapprovingly past the crowd. When Quaestor Tiberius Sellus joined the revelers, even the many spectators, including Ptolemaios and his wife, dared to take the plunge. Luckily, Titus wore a mask, otherwise they would have surely recognized him.

Titus drank gulp after gulp. He felt his troubles slide off his shoulders. Thoughts sank to the bottom like sand in still water, thoughts melted like ice in a bread oven, categories lost their demarcations and boxes. The flames of the bonfire mingled with the buildings around the forum, the crowd was like a warm mash, stirring itself in a large stone pot. He danced with the nymphs, offbeat yet in rhythm, and flawlessly sang along to songs whose lyrics he did not know. He no longer knew, he had forgotten his name, he existed without existing.

22. Thalassa

High grass spread out beneath him like a soft natural mattress. A holm oak provided shelter from the blazing sun. Awakened by the sound of seagulls against a backdrop of gently rippling water, Titus sat up. His heart thudded in his head as if a surge of blood pumped upwards might explode his skull. The impulse to vomit was mild, though he suspected that standing and walking would upset his stomach.

Dragging himself through the grass like a dog with a broken paw, he made his way to the holm oak and slumped down there. His back rested against the trunk. Closing his eyes, he saw the flames of the bonfire, the dancing crowd, the city guards parading along the forum's periphery. The songs, the jingling tambourines, and the thumping percussion echoed in his ears.

"You must be thirsty for a sip of water."

The milky white legs carried grace; an impressive creation of mother nature after millions of years of practice. In her delicate fingers, she held a clay drinking cup.

"What happened? How did I end up here?" Titus asked.

The nymph laughed. Titus took a sip from the cup but felt his stomach rebel. The tears and mud stains on his tunic contrasted sharply with the nymph's spotless blue dress that looked brand new.

"Do you really not remember?"

Titus shook his head. Looking out over the lagoon, he tried to string together fragments of memories.

"I completely lost myself last night."

The nymph laughed.

"We discover who we are by losing ourselves."

Water lilies adorned her golden locks. It was then that Titus noticed small reddish fins protruding from the sides of her head, just above her pointy ears. She sat next to him and rested her head on his shoulder.

"Are you really a nymph?"

"Yes… is that so hard to believe?"

"I've never seen one before I met you. Do you have a name?"

"Thalassa. I am a nymph of the sea, rivers, and lakes. The lagoon is my home."

Thalassa stood up and took a few steps through the high grass. To Titus' amazement, seagulls landed on her shoulders. She opened her hand, and a sparrow from the holm oak landed on her palm. The water level of the lagoon rose. The high grass overflowed, reaching Titus' bare feet. Thalassa stood ankle-deep in the water, greeted by jumping fish and turtles and crabs attempting to climb up her legs.

"Do you believe me now?"

Titus watched the scene with his mouth open. Thalassa whistled with her fingers. The seagulls took off, the sparrow flew back to the tree, the fish swam to deeper waters, and the turtles and crabs dropped into the water as the lagoon's edge receded. As if floating through the grass, she moved back to Titus and sat down next to him again.

"What's a nymph like you doing in such company? I mean... the followers of Dionysus... I don't understand."

Thalassa looked at Titus with a lightly amused expression, as if flattered.

"Dionysus celebrates the passions of life. Like my waters, they are volatile and unpredictable. Lakes know the depths of emotion. Sea waves can be calm one day and wild the next. Rivers bring the landscape to life and thrive on their banks, just as wine immerses our souls in joy. Dionysus is life, but also death, exuberance but also destruction. An endless cycle of change and renewal."

Titus gazed at the swaying grass beyond which the lagoon sparkled in the afternoon sun. Thalassa kissed Titus on his cheek and nestled her head into his chest, her fingers playing with his tunic. As he stared ahead, he tried to understand her affection. For a moment, the nausea stopped, as did the thumping pressure in his skull. A feeling of weightlessness overcame his body, as if floating on the grass like on the sea, but without the waves and accompanied by the floral scent from Thalassa's hair.

The Roman thought of Ariadne, how they lay together

under the large olive tree at the stadium, or roamed the city inseparably for entire afternoons. It didn't matter where they ended up, as long as they were together.

"What are you thinking about?"

"Nothing."

"Liar."

The nymph stood up, ran through the high grass to the shore, and dived into the lagoon. Titus jumped up and walked to the water's edge, intrigued. A flock of ducks passed by, a fish briefly showed itself on the surface, a seagull skimmed its feet over the water's surface, but Thalassa was nowhere to be seen.

"You can't fool a nymph."

Startled, Titus turned around. Piercing eyes stared at him. Despite the events of the previous night, there was no trace of fatigue on his face. His dark red toga looked as if it had just come from the tailor; there wasn't a wrinkle or other imperfection to be seen.

"Have you been standing here long?"

"For a while."

Titus sighed. With his hands, he straightened his clothes, while his eyes looked around restlessly.

"Don't worry so much. I'm happy for you. Enjoy it while it lasts."

"It's not what you think. There's nothing between us. I

woke up here, we talked a bit, and that was it. I don't want anything more from her."

"Your eyes say something else."

"What are you talking about?"

A wide grin appeared on Magnus' face.

"Nothing… probably I'm mistaken. Thalassa is pleasant company. She's fun, adventurous, and incredibly intelligent. It's just…"

"Just what?"

"She remains a nymph," Magnus said. "She breaks hearts as quickly as she conquers them. I understand you. You're not the first to fall for her beauty and charm. But she doesn't have a loyal bone in her body, she's as changeable as the water in this lagoon."

The water level rose. A storm sounded in the distance. Seagulls circled over the raging waves threatening to splash over the water's edge. Thalassa's voice sounded from the sky.

"What did you say, Magnus?"

From the lagoon, a large wave crashed over Titus and Magnus, barely allowing them to remain standing. Strands of seaweed clung to Titus' body. Magnus jumped up and down like a playful deer.

"Ouch! Ouch! Ouch!"

Laughter echoed from the sky. Magnus tried with both

hands to rid himself of the crab clinging to his nose, but the crustacean only seemed to pinch harder.

"Let go, Aphrodite!" Thalassa said.

The crab dropped itself into the water. Magnus' hands went to his nose.

"Aphrodite? You name these pesky creatures after gods, do you?" he asked.

"All the animals in my lagoon have names. We have Athena the sea snail, Hera the seahorse, Apollo the turtle, and, not to forget, Hermes the parrotfish. Do you have a problem with that, Mr. Magnus? It wouldn't be the first time you get worked up over things that don't concern you."

Magnus laughed and shook his head, rubbing his red nose.

"You're like a child, giving names to a bunch of dumb animals. Don't you have anything better to do? Better to kill them and offer their bodies to Dionysus; that would be something useful. The Urge has clearly gone astray in you, crazy, crazy nymph."

"Crazy, crazy nymph? Look who's talking! What do you do all day in that cave? Mess around with sloppy city girls and married women?"

"Why? Are you jealous?"

"Give me one reason why I would be jealous of your victims."

"I can think of a hundred."

"Well, I'm listening!"

"Why do you even care about what I do in my cave?"

"I don't care what you do in your cave! I absolutely don't want to know!"

"Why ask then, crazy nymph?"

"That was a rhetorical question, you piece of shoe sole!"

"You two are like an old married couple," Titus said. "If you don't mind, I'll be heading home soon."

"No!" both Magnus and Thalassa said in unison.

Titus looked at his companions in surprise and laughed.

"Titus, Dionysus expects you at the ruins tonight for an important ritual," Magnus said.

"A ritual?"

"I assume you still want to learn about the Urge?"

"Yes," Titus hesitated.

"Tonight is your most important lesson. Come after dusk."

Magnus turned and vanished behind the trees and bushes that naturally bordered the lagoon's shore.

The sun reached its peak, though the cloud cover

softened its light. Thalassa and Titus walked eastward along the lagoon's shore, with the stadium behind them. Aside from a few farmers, there were no people around. Thalassa skipped stones, frolicked ahead of Titus, and then turned around.

"I heard you've been studying with the Stoics," she said.

"Not too zealously. I attended a few lectures by Epictetus."

"Epictetus, the herald of reason."

"So they say."

"Oh, those Stoics… They talk endlessly about virtue and freedom from passions. Do this, do that, don't get burned by things beyond your control. That's what they say, right? No, not quite my thing."

"Yet many benefit from it. My friend Arrian from Nicomedia swears by it. The Emperor also seems very interested in Stoic teachings. So Epictetus' lectures must not be that bad."

"Oh no, I don't deny that! Don't get me wrong, I'm not a Stoic-hater like my good friend Mr. Magnus. The path of reason can be very useful for those who aspire to it. But… it's not for me."

"Why not?"

"What would a lagoon be without the passions of life? My waters are chaotic. Fish eat each other. New creatures are born every day. My lagoon is a harmony of joy but also pain, of life but also death, of connection but also loss. Without one, the other does not exist. That's how I see life too. Imagine my waters without this harmony. It would be quiet and still, but also lifeless and cold."

"I see where you're going. The Stoics might avoid passions like anger and pleasure, but they are not entirely without emotions. Joy is allowed. Even desires, but in moderation and without craving."

"Oh, that would be a gentle breeze over the water. Or the rays of a dull morning sun that slowly fade into dark, lifeless depths. What is that compared to the spectacle you see here? The raw, untamed uproar of existence? Life in full glory?"

Titus observed the countless insects in the reeds, the birds along the water. He absorbed the sounds of crickets and croaking frogs. Thalassa crouched by the water's edge. Her hand floated in the clear water. Tiny fish the size of thumbnails circled her fingers.

"Oh yes, I understand why Epictetus is so popular," she continued. "Life is full of adversity. Imagine being unmoved in the face of tragedy? A lot of suffering is spared, oh yes indeed! But... that detachment also occurs with things that normally provide us with pleasure, joy, and even ecstasy."

"Things like what?" Thalassa kissed Titus passionately on the lips and then looked into his eyes. "I get what you mean," Titus said.

"What's life worth if you can't fully immerse yourself in it? Isn't it worth suffering if you get so much in return? Oh, many people want absolute solutions to their problems. They throw away the beautiful along with the ugly. Say what you will about Magnus; he doesn't shy away from the dark sides of life. In his own way."

"Magnus... How long have you known each other?"

"Years. He comes and goes. He belongs to the family of Dionysus, although he has his own ideas. Oh, poor Magnus. His hatred for the Stoics has grown over the years. Especially now that Epictetus' lectures are full but no one listens to what he has to say. People want logic, reason, one plus one equals two, if, then, therefore. They crave a system. That's what the Stoics offer. Because yes, who's waiting for vague descriptions of unfathomable forces that you can neither understand nor express in words?"

"The Urge..."

Thalassa laughed.

"Yes, the Urge, as Magnus calls it. As a true sophist, he parades Her around like he's the one who discovered Her. As if She's a product he's trying to sell. Hilarious! Too bad his marketing approach has yielded little fruit so far."

"Do you believe the Urge exists?"

"The concept of the Urge is not the Urge itself. As soon as you name Her, you lose Her. But of course, The

True Urge, Who cannot be named, no, I don't doubt She exists!"

"What is the Urge?" Titus asked.

"That's the big question. What do I win if I answer it correctly?"

"A kiss?"

"Come on, I've already had that. Think of something else!"

"I don't know."

"Interesting answer."

"Why?"

"You don't know. The unknown. How intriguing. This leads us to a crucial question. Do you know that feeling, that deep longing for something without knowing why? That no logic or reasoning can explain why you want what you want?"

Titus gazed into Thalassa's eyes. Just like Ariadne, she embodied everything Titus wasn't looking for in a woman. As a true Laelii, he was taught from an early age what to look for in a marriage partner. Faithful, loyal, obedient, modest. That kind of thing. The nymph didn't exactly fit the picture. She was unpredictable, strong-willed, confident, independent, seductive. She did exactly as she pleased, whenever it pleased her. And if he believed the stories about nymphs, she was far from reliable—a terrible homemaker.

No, this nymph was probably the last person with whom he would ever marry or entrust his life to. Yet, he felt a strong attraction to her, just like with Ariadne. What he intellectually wanted differed from what he deeply desired. The latter, he couldn't explain rationally. Titus nodded.

"Ah! See, that's because of the Urge!" Thalassa said. "It makes you long without telling you why. Many people don't want to acknowledge that power. They don't like the idea that something outside themselves determines their desires and influences their choices. Especially when those desires arise out of nowhere, without reason! They come up with rational explanations. It gives them a false sense of control. They tell elaborate stories about why they chose their partners or why they suddenly want to travel. But these stories never really cover it. Really, hilarious! Others fight against the Urge, but that leads to conflicts."

"What kind of conflicts?"

"The true desires always surface. If you deny them, they'll surprise you. They'll appear in ways you don't expect. Some people bury them so deep they're unaware of what they truly desire. At the same time, they condemn these desires in others but can't explain why, while the reason is hilarious: they see in others what they hate in themselves but deny in every way that the irritation at a neighbor visiting prostitutes actually stems from their own suppressed lusts, or the hatred toward rulers comes from their own suppressed desire for power.

These repressed desires can eventually lead to an

eruption, like a volcano that suddenly awakens after a long period of silence! People then make sudden decisions, overturn their entire lives, or act against their principles. Why? They don't know either! That's the funny part! But if they were aware of the force driving them, they could have chosen a path more aligned with their deepest desires, without it having to come to such an explosive, unexpected release."

"So we should follow the Urge?"

"Yes. But that's precisely the tricky part. The Urge has many different voices. And sometimes those voices are barely distinguishable from your own reasoning. And as if that wasn't difficult enough, these voices can also change and say something different! So how do you know which voice to follow?"

"Well? How do you know?"

"You find out by listening. Very carefully. If you listen close enough, you'll know which voice to follow. That's the true path; the rest are inferior—some irrelevant, others mere echoes, and a few even dangerous."

Titus closed his eyes. He tried to make sense of the images that passed by in the darkness of his eyelids, the sounds in his body, the voices in his thoughts.

"What are you doing?" Thalassa said.

"Listening."

Thalassa laughed, paced back and forth like a nervous, wagging dog, looked at Titus, and fell to the ground laughing. Titus, now with his eyes open, looked at the nymph disapprovingly.

"Am I doing something funny?"

"No, not at all! I just found it… cute."

Thalassa wriggled with laughter, arms and legs flailing.

"Glad you find it amusing."

"Oh, don't be so grumpy," Thalassa said. She kissed Titus on the lips.

23. Ritual

At the shrine, a few followers of Dionysus had gathered. The group, consisting of Magnus, Thalassa, Titus, two men, and five women all clad in animal skins, also included Nysa, whose dark eyes pierced Titus with their gaze.

"I don't think I've introduced you to Titus yet," Magnus said. He laughed, grabbed Nysa by her side, and pulled her toward him.

Nysa pulled Magnus' hand off her side and pushed him away.

"Don't do that. You know I hate it."

"Oh, come on, relax, girl! Tonight is a special night! A festive moment! We're opening all the sewers! Bringing everything out! It's time for truth with Dionysus himself as the ultimate witness!"

The group cheered, taking turns to gulp down from a passed-around wine jug. Thalassa clapped enthusiastically. Nysa's eyes scanned the attendees one by one, lingering particularly on Titus. Titus observed a dark concoction bubbling in a cauldron over a fire. Due to the lack of light, he couldn't discern its contents. It smelled of rotting leaves. Nysa ladled the brew into seven small bowls. Magnus jumped onto a broken column.

"Welcome, chosen ones! Dionysus has selected you to undergo a special ritual under my guidance. Tonight, you'll face your true desires. The many voices of the Urge will loudly make themselves known to you! But only *one* of these voices is strongest; it's the voice that all Her other expressions submit to: it's the Zeus among gods, the river from which smaller streams spring, the star that shines brightest among all others. Tonight, it will become clear what you desire most deeply. *That* is the Urge in its highest form. *That* is the path—the true path."

Nysa and Thalassa distributed bowls to the chosen ones.

"Drink," Nysa instructed. Titus took a sip of the brew. It tasted even worse than it smelled. As his body resisted, he downed the bowl in one gulp. The two men in the group, both fairly young, displayed looks of horror. One of the women had to gag.

"In a few moments, Dionysus will reveal the Urge to you," Magnus announced. "What you do with these revelations is up to you. Want to share them? You can. Prefer to keep them to yourselves? That's fine too. Ultimately, this is between you and Dionysus. But remember, the path of the Urge is there to be walked. This is the most important and final step in the process. Follow the Urge, and you'll end up where you need to be. And once you're there, my task is done."

Titus felt his legs weaken. He became aware of his breathing. The air moving in and out of his lungs felt like a cool spring breeze tickling his insides. The previously sharp outlines of the group began to blur, as if merging into one another. The sounds of crickets grew louder. He seemed to understand them, though he couldn't put it into words. The more he tried to control all sensations, the more he lost grip. He decided to let go. His body wanted nothing more than to lie down. It wasn't long before Titus could no longer differentiate between his inner world and the world around him.

He found himself in his old workshop in Nicopolis, stirring a large cauldron. Various ingredients lay scattered on tables around him. He scooped some of the golden concoction into a mold. Suddenly, he was kneeling before Emperor Hadrian in a crowded marketplace, presenting him with the most beautiful, brightly shining gold bar the world had ever seen. The crowd cheered. Those who once laughed at and ridiculed him blushed with shame.

Ariadne ran through the crowd and fell into his arms, followed by Ares and Faustinus. Ariadne kissed him passionately. They lay under the great oak tree just outside the city. "I've never felt this way about anyone before," Ariadne said. Titus burst into tears as a long-awaited summer rain showered down. It rained and rained until a giant flood wave swallowed the great oak.

Surrounded by water, Titus sought his way to the surface. Gasping for air, he swam through the darkness when a luminous being came to his aid. It was Thalassa. She pressed her lips to his and breathed oxygen into his windpipe. While her lungs kept him alive, she guided him to the water's surface. Once above, he coughed the water out of his airways. He looked around. He wasn't at Thalassa's lagoon and the nymph was nowhere to be found.

Surrounded by columns, doors, and withered plants, he realized where he was: on the patio of Caius Aelius Octavianus' building. He climbed out of the bath and walked through the hallway. A familiar voice echoed from a lecture hall. Titus entered. Epictetus was speaking to a large audience. His voice grew louder, but Titus couldn't understand him, as if he was speaking in another language. Incomprehensible words relaxed his muscles. He collapsed into one of the lecture benches. The hall's walls cracked. Flames leaped wildly from the floor.

Titus ran through the hallway and ended up in Alcander Cassius' bedroom. In the dimly lit room, illuminated by a single candle, he stood face to face with his rival. In his hand, he held a gladius. Alcander was defenseless, begging on his knees. From the shadows, Magnus appeared.

"Isn't this what you want?" he asked.

Behind him, Thalassa's voice echoed.

"Spare him, Titus. Don't do it!"

"Get lost, you crazy nymph!"

"Don't listen to him!"

Titus glared at his rival, tightening his grip on the sword as his legs trembled and his heart raced, pumping blood at a furious pace. The walls around him turned into hedges of flames. Thalassa screamed as the fire consumed her body.

"Isn't this what you want?" Magnus said. "Follow the true path."

With both hands, Titus raised the sword above his shoulders and, with a wide swing, hurled it forward. Alcander's head rolled across the endless plains, surrounded by storms and the smell of sulfur. Magnus had vanished.

Dropping the sword, Titus wandered the plains alone. Slowly but surely, his limbs became hard and sharp. Walking turned into crawling, with a swishing tail. He crawled through crevices and along rivers of lava, encountering no soul. Alone with his rage, he lost all sense of time. Years, perhaps centuries seemed to have passed, yet the past remained close; it weighed on him like a stone he couldn't shake off his back. Often, he saw Thalassa in the distance. He ran toward her at full speed, only to find she was a figment of his imagination.

Am I trapped in this nightmare forever?

His body jolted awake on the hard surface, as if struck by a torturer's whip. His throat was dry. His belly roiled. There was a strong need to throw up. Though he made an effort to resist, his body took over. He lurched to his feet and vomited. Drenched in sweat, he looked around. The rocky walls, sandy floor, and a cabinet full of papyrus scrolls revealed his location. Tears of relief streamed down his cheeks as he embraced reality once again. For moments, he wept, washing away the horror that seemed to last for eternity.

Titus allowed his senses to adjust: the feel of sand grains under his palms, the smell of vomit, the dim light of the oil lamp on the table. He struggled to his feet. His limbs felt heavy, like lead. He dragged himself to a bucket of water and splashed some on his face, which helped him wake up. He stared at his hands, surprised by the cold water slipping through his fingers, and realized he was truly back.

"Hello? Magnus? Hello?" he called in a hoarse voice. No response. His mind wanted to stand, but his body wanted to lie down. After a deep sigh, he surrendered to his churning stomach and weak limbs. He closed his eyes.

When he woke up after a dreamless sleep, his stomach seemed to have settled, and his muscles were willing to move again. He had lost all sense of time. The oil lamp had gone out by then.

Once outside, Titus found a cool afternoon accompanied by a gentle breeze. His stomach growled. He walked down the hill along the sand paths, passing the Temple of Apollo, to his shed.

Remus was brushing a roof tile. From a distance, it was clear where he had cleaned and where he hadn't. He threw pieces of moss down, forming a decent pile. As Titus entered the front yard, Remus jumped off the roof.

"Where have you been? I was worried!" Remus exclaimed.

"Worried? Why?"

"You're never gone this long! You're a homebody."

"I wasn't gone that long, was I?"

"It's been almost a week!"

Titus laughed. As he lost track of time, he found Remus' update quite handy.

"Did I miss anything here?"

"They've been looking for you. The city guards came by. I barely convinced them I had no idea where you were."

"They didn't harm you, did they?"

Remus shook his head no.

"Are the rumors true?"

"What rumors?"

"Everyone's talking about it. That you broke into Alcander's villa and got beaten up. And then you disappeared without a trace. Can't you see why I was worried?"

"Don't sweat it, Remus. I just took some time off. Needed to clear my mind."

"So it's true? You broke into Alcander's house?"

"Ah, it was nothing."

Remus shook his head, laughing.

"I'm glad they left you in one piece. Alcander's men

are notorious. They've beaten some so badly they couldn't tell the tale."

"Then I was lucky."

Remus came closer, his eyes scanning Titus from head to toe.

"Where have you been all these days?"

Titus averted his gaze.

"Here and there. Around the city."

"Here and there, huh? With that old friend?"

Titus nodded. Remus' eyes narrowed.

"By the way," Remus said, "Arrian stopped by. Because of the rumors, he came to check on you. He asked me to let him know when you're back. If you had stayed away any longer, he might have organized a search party. And your sister is doing well. Her wounds are healing, and she's speaking like usual."

"That's good to hear. I'll visit Arrian tomorrow."

Titus took a big gulp from the wine jug, sitting under the back window against the wall with his legs stretched out in the grass. Alcander's villa was suspiciously quiet. A dim oil lamp lit the veranda. As usual, the drowsy doorman dozed off in his chair. Through the cricket sounds, Titus tried to catch a scream or shout from his children, but in vain. He imagined them filling their bellies with delicacies from Alcander's kitchen, playing in his huge inner garden, and wading in the pool heated by the hypocaust system.

Titus turned his gaze to the lagoon. Thalassa's home was hidden somewhere in the distance, behind the trees and plantations. He wanted to be with her yet tried to understand why. She opposed everything he sought in a woman so it couldn't be her character.

Is it just lust after all, then?

No, his affection went beyond the physical. He found her the most beautiful creature he had ever seen, and that was no lie. But it wasn't just because of her hair, skin, eyes, nails, or other features of her outer beauty, nor even her wit or sense of humor. He couldn't find a rational explanation for his attraction; it seemed there was none. There was something profound about the nymph that he couldn't intellectually grasp or explain, but it was undeniably there, and it crushed all his previous concepts of what he looked for in a woman. It felt as if he was meant to merge with her, for no other reason than the merging itself, making it a masterpiece of his existence as a metallurgist, with himself as one of the main ingredients. The more he tried to resist his desires for her, the stronger they grew. He took another sip.

24. Brundisium

Remus was still asleep when Titus snuck out of the shed. He walked eastward through the olive grove toward the lagoon on a surprisingly warm late summer day. The sky was a clear blue, and the sun scorched his scalp, making his tunic cling to his body.

The lagoon's shoreline buzzed with life as usual. Insects busied themselves along the water's edge, and birds darted back and forth, signaling the start of mating season. Fish bubbles appeared on the water surface, not yet fallen prey to anglers quietly navigating the barricades in the distance. Suddenly, he felt a hand glide over his back and turned around in shock.

"Do you miss me?" Thalassa asked with an engaging smile, as if she saw the most beautiful thing ever in him.

"Yes," Titus replied.

Thalassa kissed him. "Have you recovered a bit?"

"I woke up in Magnus' hideout, clueless about how I got there."

"Magnus and I carried you to the cave afterward," Thalassa said, bursting into laughter, floundering on the ground. "Oh, you were so out of it! You should have seen yourself!"

She looked at Titus, and laughed some more.

"I'm glad you find it amusing."

"Oh, grumpy man, don't take it so hard."

"It was intense. I don't know what to make of those visions. Dionysus was supposed to show me my path, but the whole experience left me even more confused."

"You know, the Urge works differently for everyone. For some, the path is clear. For others, like you, it seems more complex. Dionysus sometimes shows multiple paths without indicating the right one."

"But how do I know which one to follow?"

"That's the thing! Some aspects of the Urge, like anger or hatred, can be overwhelming. They often overshadow quieter parts, like love or security. It's easy to think those loud emotions are what you truly want, but that's not always the case."

Titus nodded, lost in thought.

"It's a matter of introspection," Thalassa continued. "You need to look beyond superficial emotions and understand what your heart truly desires. Not everything loud is necessarily true."

Titus offered a faint smile and looked into Thalassa's eyes. Their lips met. He kissed her neck. Her hand caressed his thighs. Titus glanced around quickly. No one was in sight.

A soft wind caressed the lagoon. Titus' tunic and Thalassa's blue dress lay by the water's edge. As the two rested in the grass holding each other's bodies, Thalassa said, "Dearest... during the ritual... did I appear in your visions?"

"Why do you ask?"

"Just curious. And you don't have to tell me exactly! I just want to know if I was there."

"Yes, you were there."

"Oh, really!? And in what way?"

Titus laughed, coughing a bit. "But you just said…"

"Come on! Tell me! What was I doing in your vision? How did I look? What was I wearing? And how were my nails?"

"I'm not telling!"

Thalassa playfully hit his leg and pressed her forehead against his. "I want to know. Tell me. Tell me! Tell! Me!"

Titus playfully pushed her away. "Alright, stop! Magnus was right, after all."

"About what?"

"You really are a crazy, crazy nymph."

"Says the crazy Laelius!"

Thalassa stood up, slipped into her dress, and dove into the lagoon. Titus put on his tunic and ran to the water's edge. She was gone. He waited by the water for a while, calling out her name a few times, but the nymph was nowhere to be found. After waiting and walking back and forth along the water's edge, he headed home.

Titus trudged into the front yard. The outdoor kitchen looked tidy. Since his last futile experiment to turn stone into gold, his tools, bottles, and jars had remained untouched. He had finally allowed Remus to clean up the previous night, so he must have started that morning.

"You were up early, weren't you?" Remus said.

"I went to see Arrian. Then I took a walk by the lagoon."

Remus nodded, wiping a large glass bottle with a thin neck with a cleaning cloth.

"Aren't you going to the lectures anymore?"

"Maybe soon. I'm not really in the right mood."

Titus entered the shed. He felt exhausted and lay down on the bed. As he closed his eyes, he saw the lagoon, the many insects, birds, and frogs, the fish surfacing, Thalassa in her blue dress, dancing by the water's edge.

Just before lunch, Titus was awakened by the front door swinging open. The smell of freshly baked bread wafted in. He rubbed his eyes.

"Were you taking a nap?"

Titus sat up. It was Flavia, pulling out three pieces of bread from a cotton bag. Remus entered the shed with a bowl of olives and a pot of young cheese.

"I was exhausted. I went out early this morning."

Titus' eyes examined his sister's face.

"You look like your old self again."

"Thank you," said Flavia. "Are you okay? I never see you anymore. And what in the world happened at Alcander's villa? People won't shut up about it! Oh, and I ran into Caius Aelius at the market. He was asking about you. Aren't you going to the lectures anymore?"

Titus sighed and shook his head.

Why are people so fascinated by my life, which had been the case since I set foot in Nicopolis but had now reached a new peak?

"I'll drop by soon."

"You should. People are asking about you."

"Yes," Titus said, chewing on the bread. "So, how is that my problem?"

"They're just concerned."

"Oh sure, they're concerned. They're worried they'll have nothing to gossip about regarding crazy Laelius. I have no business with those people. If they all disappeared, I wouldn't shed a tear."

"It can't be that bad…"

"No, it is that bad." Titus pointed toward Nicopolis. "As long as I don't have to, I'm not setting foot in that city. I don't need to see anyone from that stupid folk."

"What do you want then? To live like a hermit forever?"

Titus shrugged and spit out an olive pit.

"I don't know. Maybe I just want to leave this place. Head to Brundisium."

"Brundisium?" Flavia said. "What on Earth would you do there?"

"Brundisium just came to mind first. What's wrong with that place? It's just another city like Nicopolis, with temples, a theater, houses, parks. The only essential difference is that I don't know anyone there. That's exactly what I'm after. And if Brundisium doesn't suit me, I'll just move somewhere else. It doesn't matter where, as long as I can start with a clean slate. I've got nothing left to look for here."

"What about your children? And me?"

"Remus can take care of you. I'll leave everything I have left to you two. And my children? As if I'll ever get them back in my life. I can hardly call myself their father anymore. They have a new father now. It's only a matter of time before they forget about me."

"You shouldn't think like that. You'll always be their father. Times change. Maybe Alcander will come around and—"

"After what happened? I doubt it. And the idea that it all depends on how that scoundrel feels... no, I can't live with that. Arrian was right. I can't do anything against that guy. So I see no other option than to pack my stuff and leave."

"That's exactly what they want. Then you'd be admitting defeat."

"I don't care." Titus spat out another olive pit with some force and pointed to the window. "Look at what I'm faced with every day when I look outside. You know what I see? Loneliness, loss, powerlessness, injustice. *That's* what I see. I'm sick of it. Either that scoundrel goes, or I go!"

Flavia placed her hand on Titus' leg and sighed.

"Why don't you visit Epictetus? He must have some advice. Arrian even asked—"

"Get lost with Epictetus, sis! How has his rambling helped me so far? Let me tell you. Not at all! Those lectures are just gatherings of self-absorbed individuals who love to call themselves 'philosophers.' They listen a few times to that drivel and then walk around as if they hold all the wisdom. As far as I'm concerned, they can burn down Caius Aelius Octavianus' place. Burn it to the ground! With everyone inside!"

Remus slowly chewed while staring at the ground. Flavia started sobbing.

"I'm just afraid you'll do something rash. Yes, you've lost your family. Yes, our family is out of money. I lost my husband to that strange disease. Our fate is unfortunate. But at least make sure you don't also lose your sanity."

"I've long lost that, sis." Titus stood up. "I'm going for a walk. I don't know when I'll be back." He walked out and slammed the door behind him.

25. Neptune

After crossing the olive grove, Titus arrived at the lagoon, where he encountered restless water. He paused until two hands covered his face.

"Do you miss me?"

Titus removed the hands and turned around.

"Sneaking up on me again? You scare the life out of me."

Thalassa laughed, dancing around like a dog who had just met a new playmate.

"I enjoy it. Seeing how you react."

"Well, this is how."

Titus grabbed the nymph and kissed her.

"Why do you just disappear suddenly? I waited for you, but you didn't return. I just went home."

"I'm sorry. I'm a nymph. This is what we do."

"Well, then I guess Magnus' prejudices about nymphs must apply to you, too."

"No!" said Thalassa. "That's not true. We're not all the same! It's just... it's something most of us do. And we always come back, you know!"

"Please don't do it again. I hate it when you do."

"I'm so sorry. I will do my best to change. I promise!"

The lagoon started to wave, with thunder rumbling in the distance. A deep, resonant voice echoed over the water, though the words were unclear. Thalassa froze like a startled squirrel.

"What's wrong?" Titus asked.

"Hide. Behind the hedge. He's coming."

"Who?"

"Just hide. Quick."

The voice grew louder, the water more turbulent. Crouching, Titus peered through a gap in the hedge to see what was happening. With splashing waves and gusts of wind, a bearded figure appeared, floating above the water surface, with a body that would make Alcander Cassius jealous. Thalassa looked up, her face a mix of irritation and displeasure.

"Why must you always disrupt the harmony in my lagoon with such fanfare?"

Holding his trident firmly, the figure replied with slight irritation in his voice.

"What do you expect? I'm the God of the Sea! Thunder and lightning are my aliases. Do you want me to make my entrance like a tame earthworm? That would be unworthy of a god!"

"Oh, don't make me laugh. No one here enjoys your

godly display. The fish are terrified of you."

"Fear? That's not fear. That's respect! They need to know who's in charge here!"

"Are you a god or a tyrant? You don't earn respect from sea dwellers by scaring them. They'll fear and hate you. That's not respect. But tell me, why are you here? Do you need something from me again?"

"Come with me to Delphi."

"Delphi? What for?"

"Apollo is hosting a big gathering. I'm going there. I want you by my side."

"Those gatherings of Apollo are boring! Why don't you go alone? Ah, I see. You probably want to show me off again, to affirm your prestige among the other gods. You want to parade me around like a trophy so everyone can see how great and attractive you are. Because, after all, you've courted a nymph."

"That's not true at all."

"Then why?"

"Because… because I'd feel incomplete without you."

"Incomplete? If you feel so incomplete without me, why haven't you showed yourself for three months?"

"Ah, woman. Three months… what are three months in three thousand years?"

"What is one of Apollo's gatherings in the ten thousand that bore already hosted, all with the same, dull prattle about ethics and order. It's maddening! Why not ask one of your concubines? They'd probably love to make an appearance with Poseidon! Oh, Poseidon, the God of the Sea. Yes, they'd surely feel very special! The lucky one gets to dine with the gods, drink the finest wine in the highest company. Sounds like a perfect transaction to me, where both parties come out satisfied."

The god hung his head and sighed.

"I'd be very disappointed if you don't come."

"Been there, done that. Too many times, if you ask me."

Poseidon waved his trident. Dark clouds gathered. Lightning struck a tree by the lagoon in half. Titus recoiled in shock and fell into a mud puddle.

"I've heard enough," said the god. Floating above the lagoon, he rose, cast a final glance at the nymph, turned, and shot into the sea as fast as lightning. After a deafening thunderclap, the weather cleared. Titus crawled from the bushes and walked to the water's edge, wondering if he was hallucinating or dreaming.

"Was that really…?"

"Yes, that was him. The one and only. Are you surprised?"

"Yes, well… I've seen more unusual things in the past few weeks than in the rest of my life."

Thalassa kept silent. Titus stared at the water recovering from the disturbance.

"So… you two are a couple?"

"Poseidon, whom you Romans call Neptune, is my husband."

The Roman felt a pang in his stomach.

"I'm sorry," the nymph said. "I wanted to tell you, but…"

Titus paced along the water's edge, wondering what he gotten himself into now. He couldn't decide which was worse: finding out the woman he liked was married, or that she was a god's wife.

Imagine if Neptune[30] found out! He'd skewer me on his trident and feed me to the sharks. Or tie me to a sea rock where vultures would pick out my intestines.

Titus shuddered at the thought. His legs moved as if he was about to run away.

"Why are you doing this?"

"Please stay. I'll tell you everything."

An open space in the woods at the lagoon's edge offered a view through the trees to the water, while the surrounding nature provided shelter. Titus watched as Thalassa greeted the frogs in a ditch that flowed from the

---

[30] Titus stubbornly continues to call Poseidon 'Neptune,' which emphasizes his Roman heritage.

olive groves to the lagoon. Her slender, white legs made a graceful jump to the other bank, and she sat down. She gestured for Titus to sit next to her and started telling him their story.

"But why did you marry him then?"

"I was naïve, young. Who wouldn't want to marry a god? It was something I dreamed of. Little did I know he would treat me like this. That he wouldn't give up his concubines. That he would be away for months, sometimes years. That I would merely serve as a trophy and he would have absolutely no regard for me, let alone my lagoon. And then he complains that he feels incomplete! What a joke. Truly hilarious."

"Even though he's a god, why wouldn't he appreciate you more?"

"A man is as faithful as his options."

"That applies to women too, you know! Believe me, I know. By the way, you're not faithful either. Regardless of what your husband does, you're making the same mistake. You're just as wrong by hanging out with me."

"I know, I know." Thalassa picked up a small frog, letting it rest on the palm of her hand, inspecting it closely. "Well, what does 'wrong' mean anyway," the nymph said. "Is he wrong for doing what he does? Am I wrong for doing what I do? Maybe, according to some ethics and ideas about morality. Yes, probably most people will say what I'm doing is wrong. But it certainly doesn't *feel* wrong being with you. That's why keep doing it."

"What do you mean?"

"If what I do is wrong, why does She tell me otherwise?"

"The Urge, you mean?"

Thalassa nodded, putting the frog back in the ditch.

"What does She say then?"

Thalassa took Titus' hand and kissed him. She rested her head on his shoulder and looked at him in a way that would melt even a god.

"She is clear about my path."

Titus stared at an oversized toad that jumped from the bank into the ditch. The cries of seagulls echoed from the lagoon. That a nymph so beautiful she could leave gods speechless would fall for a mere mortal like Titus remained a mystery to him.

"The Urge within you… can you hear what she says about me?" the nymph asked.

"You keep trying, don't you?"

"Not true!" Thalassa stood up and jumped over the ditch. "Why don't you just tell me? I want to know!"

"Well, I can't explain it. The Urge cannot be expressed in words. It goes beyond our understanding," Titus said with a grin on his face.

"You!" Thalassa said. She grabbed Titus by his tunic

and kissed him. He caressed her slender legs. The sky darkened. Thunder rumbled in the distance. Titus stopped kissing and looked toward the lagoon. For a moment, Titus thought he heard the almighty God of the Sea. Fortunately, he was nowhere to be seen. Of course. He was in Delphi. Probably with one of his concubines.

"Don't worry," Thalassa said. Her blue irises undulated like the Mediterranean Sea on the wild coast of Iberia. The longer Titus looked into her eyes, the greater his disbelief that she had chosen him.

This can't be real. Am I still under the influence of the foul-smelling ritual brew? Am I lying unconscious by the ruins, completely unaware of reality, only to awaken from this dream?

He hoped not. If it was a dream, he definitely didn't want to wake up.

26. Elysium

Clouds gathered over Epirus. From afar, Titus saw rain pouring down from a thick, gray mass. A group of five seagulls skimmed along the coastline as if fleeing from something. To his right, Titus saw the spit of land separating the lagoon from the Gulf of Arta. To the left, the coastline extended northward but soon turned eastward. Following it would lead around the entire Gulf and, after a short crossing, back to the lagoon.

Near the spit, Thalassa stopped walking and whistled with her fingers. The five seagulls turned around, flew toward Thalassa and Titus, and circled around them.

"Kallias, Daphne, Zephyros, Helios, Iris! Where are you hurrying to?"

The seagulls screeched, still circling around Thalassa and Titus.

"Seeking shelter from the storm? Where? In the caves on the hills? Oh yes, that's a good spot! Oh yes, yes, I'll be careful! Who this is? This is a good friend of mine! No, we're just friends, nothing more, nothing less! Why do you think I'm lying? Oh, please, just fly on. Take care!"

"Can you understand those creatures?"

"Of course! I can understand all animals, at least those in and around my lagoon. They often bring very useful information."

"Like what?"

"Well, whether a storm is coming, for example. Or what people in the city are up to. Or who enters my lagoon…"

"That explains why you always manage to sneak up on me."

Thalassa laughed and extended her arm. One of the seagulls circled down and approached her hand. Titus remembered his visit to the seer. Images of the Persian carpet flashed before his eyes, the seagulls circling like a dark cloud above the apple tree. Startled, Titus took a step back.

"Don't be afraid, it won't harm you," said Thalassa. The seagull perched on her hand and allowed her to stroke it.

"I'm not afraid. It's just…" Images of his nightmares flashed before his eyes. The vast plains, volcanoes in the distance, scorpions climbing out of the crevices.

Helios screeched and flew to his group. The five seagulls made a few more circles and continued on their way.

The cloud cover had thickened, and the wind had picked up. Thunder rumbled in the distance. A few drops heralded a downpour. Thalassa grabbed Titus' hand and pulled him into the wooded strip along the coast. A narrow path led them to an abandoned stone building, resembling a small temple. Part of the roof had collapsed. Holes in the wall indicated the building had once been attacked by catapults.

"We can take shelter here," said Thalassa.

The afternoon was as dark as dusk. Titus had managed to find dry pieces of wood.

"Now I'll do something I'm good at."

He arranged a number of stones in a circle and placed the wood in the middle in a pyramid shape. Titus took flint and a piece of metal from the pouch under his tunic. He pressed the metal piece against the flint.

"Do you always carry that with you?"

"Yes, you never know when you'll need to make fire."

With a skilled motion, he struck the metal against the flint, producing sparks.

"You remain an odd duck."

"Me an odd duck? You're the one who talks to animals."

"Hey!" Laughing, Thalassa gave him a gentle push. "Speaking of which… Helios saw something in you."

"Helios? The seagull?"

"Seagulls are very intuitive. He sensed a conflict in you. Something you're holding back. Is there something you want to share?"

Titus shook his head. A few sticks caught fire.

"There's nothing."

Titus gently blew on the small flames, his face illuminated by the growing fire. The larger pieces of wood started to burn as well.

"It's about your children, isn't it? You miss them. You're angry, but you also want to move on with your life. A fresh start. Is that it? Tell me if I'm right!"

"Nothing gets past you, I see."

"So, am I right? Just tell me."

The fire now crackled lively, its flames dancing and lighting up the surroundings.

"I'm considering leaving. My children, my wife... I've lost them and can't get them back. Every day I look out the window and am reminded of it. I can't change this situation. I'm broke. Half the city laughs at me. The other half hates me because of the lies they've spread. What am I doing here still? I want to leave everything behind and start anew. Just fly away like your seagull friends."

"But where do you want to go?"

"To Brundisium. Or maybe even further away. Remus can take care of my sister. They'll manage. I'll leave my last piece of land and the two villas in Nicopolis to them."

Thalassa stood up and paced around the fire. She seemed to be conversing with herself, whispering, sighing. Like a tidal wave, she threw herself at Titus. Her large pupils pulled him in.

"Take me with you."

"You? With me?"

"Yes!"

Titus sensed an unexpected joy within himself, which also immediately frustrated him. In his mind, he would set out alone, and in deliberate, chosen solitude, spend the rest of his life. Having Thalassa by his side would likely bring him a lot of turmoil. Such an unpredictable, whimsical presence didn't fit at all into the hermit life he had set his sights on.

"What about your lagoon?" asked Titus.

"It can take care of itself by now. We'll go together and make the best of it! Together we are stronger! We'll join forces! Maybe we'll become very rich and successful! We'll found our own little village, somewhere far away, high in the mountains. And when the time is right, we'll return to Nicopolis, and you'll reunite with your children and tell them the truth."

"I don't know, Thalassa. You're a nymph. Human communities aren't suitable for you."

"Oh, don't worry about that. Wherever we go, they'll surely have a lagoon, or a river, or these beautiful mountain lakes."

"But, suppose we do it. You know it will end. You are immortal, I am not. You'll have to continue without me afterward."

Thalassa sat up straight.

"I can give up my immortality!"

"But how?"

"I know some people. Underworld people. I'm sure they can help me."

"And then? You're ending something that could have lasted for thousands of years just for me? Who knows what you're missing out on. It's quite a big decision. I'd think it over carefully."

Thalassa sighed. She fidgeted with her dress. Titus took her hand.

"I've been here for ages. Surrounded by life, yet so alone. Yes, I've loved, but I always felt something was missing. Even my marriage didn't help. In fact, it deepened my loneliness. For centuries, I swam in the lagoon, cared for the animals, and sought distraction with Dionysus, drinking wine to forget my sorrow. I was like an empty shell. Until I met you. I would rather die with you than facing that emptiness again."

"Why me?"

"You're fun, handsome, interesting. I feel good around you... But it's mainly because I believe we didn't meet by chance. She brought us together."

"I don't know about that..."

"Imagine how vast the universe is, our planet alone.

Huge! What are the odds that two beings meet, one desires the other, their paths lead to each other. It must be Her will for us to be together. I know you are the one for me, I just know. At least now, today. Why, you ask? What does it matter! It's not about that. I want what I want. That's enough."

Titus tried to understand Thalassa but found the more he tried, the less he understood. His lack of understanding didn't keep him from seeing her, and the more he did, and with each encounter his affection for the being behind the pretty face became stronger and the more he wanted to merge with her. At the same time, he dreaded being drawn to her and kept fighting it to no avail.

Marrying Ariadne was a big mistake he made before. He surely wouldn't stumble over the same stone a second time, would he? No, definitely not. If he ever remarried, it would be to a woman who fully met his strict criteria. No compromises, no exceptions. But this nymph threw all this out the window. She wanted Titus, and that was that. The fact that she was married—to a god, no less—seemed to be just a minor detail to her.

"But how about…"

"Yes, yes…" Thalassa hit her forehead. "I'll find a solution for that. It will probably take a while before he realizes I'm gone."

"Can't you divorce him?"

"Divorce a god? That's something. Divorcing the God of the Sea is not that simple, you know."

"What if he seeks revenge? We're powerless against him. I don't even dare imagining his wrath. He'll probably turn all the seas and oceans inside out. Even in the mountains, he would find us."

"Yes, you have a point. That guy can really lose his temper, I admit. But I'll think of something."

The nymph's devotion to their relationship kept surprising him. At the same time, Magnus' warnings echoed continuously in his mind as she stroked his hair. He could feel her affection, and it was mutual, but he dared not surrender to it.

Thalassa jumped up.

"I've got it! We'll go to Elysium!" she said.

"Elysium?"

"Yes, Elysium! The land of the blessed. It's a paradise even more beautiful than the Alps, full of nice people, animals, expansive fields, countless lagoons. One valley is more beautiful than the next, one waterfall higher than the other. Paths everywhere, and I've heard your legs never get tired when you walk on them. It's huge! Endless!"

The rain pelted the roof, streaming down the walls. The fire attracted mosquitoes.

"It sounds like a beautiful place. But… why go there?"

"Elysium is a secluded place, ruled by a separate authority. They're very selective about who they let in. And, the great thing about it is that Poseidon has no power there."

"I see. But if they're so selective, why would they let us two in?"

"That's a good question. I can put in a good word for us with Kronos! He will help us. I've got connections, you know. Gods and Titans. I know them all. I'm sure I can arrange something."

Titus shook his head silently, his eyebrows furrowed upon hearing Thalassa's claims, which sounded so wrong and implausible in many ways.

"How do we even get there?"

"You know, the story goes that there once lived an ocean nymph named Halimede who gave up her mortality and married the fisherman Nikandros. Their marriage was so harmonious that even the gods were jealous. Out of respect, Hades granted them access to Elysium so their bond could live on eternally, provided their ashes were scattered in the same place. Nikandros had his ashes scattered at the bay, waiting for Halimede, so they could depart for Elysium together."

"And, did it work?"

"No, sadly. The jealous god Phthonus intervened. After Halimede's death, he stole her ashes and threw them into the volcano Nisyros, which erupted shortly after and spewed lava for weeks! No one knows what happened to Nikandros and Halimede. Some say their shadows went to the realm of the dead, others believe they did indeed go to

Elysium, separately, and have been searching for each other to this day."

"Sounds like a tragic fate," said Titus.

"I say, the lagoon!"

"What do you mean?"

"If we die, we'll have our ashes scattered at the lagoon! Then what happened to Nikandros and Halimede won't happen to us. Who knows, we might actually go to Elysium. And then we can be together forever! Imagine. All those beautiful walks we can take, all the places we can visit, getting lost in the endless landscapes that keep surprising. In Elysium, everyone is happy. Everything is in harmony."

Titus stared ahead. *Could such a place really exist?* It would surely be much nicer than the harsh, cold world where people made each other's lives miserable, where you could lose your loved ones right before your eyes, where justice was hard to find. Lady Fortuna would have everyone's best interest at heart. In such a world, he could trust both gods and people.

"Maybe it's a bit far-fetched," Thalassa continued. "What are the chances they'll let us in? Ah, we can at least try, right? Who knows, it might work! Wouldn't that be wonderful?"

Titus nodded. Maybe Elysium really existed, and he might even see it with his own eyes someday. Maybe not. What was certain was that his faith in Thalassa's suggestions was wafer-thin.

27. Nysa

The first sun rays pierced through the openings of the abandoned building. *How long had I been asleep?* He couldn't recall actually drifting off. A small pile of ash lay among the stones where the fire had been. A few raindrops trickled down from the roof. Titus stood up, walked around the building, and returned inside. Thalassa was nowhere to be found. "You left again without saying a word," he muttered.

A scorpion scuttled near Titus' feet. Startled, he stepped back. Two scorpions fell from the roof's edge. More crept in through the wall gaps. Titus danced in panic, jumping over the scorpions converging on him from all directions. He maneuvered his way out unharmed and ran through the forest strip toward the coast.

The sun hung low over the Gulf of Arta. He saw a familiar figure standing in the water, back facing him, his dark red toga fluttering in the morning breeze. "Magnus?"

The figure walked toward the sun until his head submerged under the water. Out of the corner of his eye, Titus noticed movement. He turned his head to the left. Countless scorpions crawled toward him. Screaming, he ran along the coast toward the lagoon. In the distance, at the start of the spit of land, he saw the philosopher in the red toga again.

"Magnus! Help!"

From the spit of land, a dark swarm flowed toward Titus. Black scorpions charged at him from two directions. Titus had no choice but to head inland, up the hillside path. He sprinted uphill. Some scorpions gave up, but many still followed. The higher he climbed, the fewer scorpions pursued, until he seemed to have shaken them all off.

Titus stood before the cave entrance, his wide eyes carefully scanning the ground and walls. It seemed safe. He entered. "Magnus? Magnus?" he said, his voice echoing off the rock walls.

Light shone in the cave. "Magnus, are you there?" He moved toward the light emanating from the philosopher's living space. "Magnus?"

A lamp burned on the table. Two chairs lay on their sides. The scrolls in the cabinet were scattered. The chest was open and empty. Footsteps sounded. A figure appeared from one of the tunnels. It was Nysa, adorned with a crown of branches and leaves, embellished with golden threads and emeralds.

"Magnus isn't here. He won't be back for a while."

"I just saw him by the coast."

"Is that so? He's not here."

Nysa approached. A sweet floral scent surrounded her. She put her arms around his neck.

"I must go."

"Why the hurry? Stay a bit longer. Talk to me. I want

to get to know you better. I don't bite, though I might seem like it."

Titus escaped her grasp and charged back.

"I can't…"

"She really has a hold on you, doesn't she?"

"Who? What do you mean?"

"You know who. Let me guess. You're the best thing that ever happened to her. You're meant to be together! And she can't get enough of you, right?"

Titus remained silent.

"Tragic, isn't it, how men keep getting seduced by her, time and time again, in exactly the same way. She makes you feel like you're her entire world, but sooner or later, she's had enough of you. Then she drops you, just like that, moving on to her next prey."

"What are you talking about? Thalassa and I…"

"The truth isn't pleasant, I get it. I feel your pain. Haven't you noticed how she sometimes just disappears and then suddenly reappears? Have you ever wondered why she does that?"

"Isn't that what nymphs do?"

Nysa laughed.

"Not every nymph is the same. Magnus and I have known her longer."

"What do you mean?"

"Let's just say you're not the only one."

The Roman shook his head. He felt a sudden burning sensation in his stomach. The times she had disappeared and then reappeared like a runaway cat that strolls back in through the front door after days of absence, acting as if nothing happened, raced through his mind.

Could it really be? And how many others might there be? Three, five, ten?

"But... everything she said. Escaping together, toward a new beginning. To be together forever."

"Together forever! In Elysium, right? That's a classic. An elusive, unpredictable creature—I know because I am one!—who even gods find appealing would suddenly commit to you, a mere mortal. She's married! To Poseidon, God of the Sea! Don't you smell something fishy? You're just a nice bit of fun for her, just like the rest."

Titus felt a surge of anger and sadness wash over him. Shaking his head, he paced through the cave. He collapsed onto the reed mat.

"Don't blame yourself. Thalassa is good at what she does. She carefully chooses her victims, usually men like you. Men with big hearts. Magnus and I just want to protect you from her."

"What's her endgame?"

"She wants attention. That's all. Her husband doesn't give it to her, so she seeks it somewhere else. It must feel great to save a damsel in distress, victimized by her unavailable, cheating husband. It must make men like you feel very special."

Nysa poured two cups of wine. She sat down next to him.

"I should have known," Titus said, taking a big gulp.

"We all make mistakes."

Nysa stroked his back and kissed his cheek.

"You deserve better, Titus. You're a good person."

Her dark eyes were mesmerizing. Her lips shone in the lamp's light.

"Don't mourn. Everything comes and goes. The universe is subject to constant change," the nymph said. She kissed his neck, held his hands, and looked into his eyes. "Surrender to that change. Allow yourself."

Titus couldn't completely shake off the echo of Thalassa's presence. Her image flashed through his mind.

"I… this isn't right."

"What's right? What's wrong? They're just ideas. Let go…"

"I can't do this."

"I understand. Don't worry. I only meant to offer some

comfort."

"I'm sorry."

As Titus stood up to leave, he felt a pull to turn back. In a spontaneous act, he grabbed her and kissed her. She ripped his tunic off his body. As if completely overtaken by his animalistic instincts, he eagerly kissed and caressed the nymph's sweaty, dark skin, losing all sense of self in a fleeting moment.

As he pushed Nysa's clammy body away, Magnus' laughter seemed to echo from the corridors. The nymph stood up, put on her chiton, and cast a glance over her shoulder with a laugh. Without exchanging another word, she left the cave.

Titus sat on the reed mat. Each time he closed his eyes, he saw Thalassa's captivating smile, her eyes and the little fins protruding from her neck, felt her passionate kisses and hugs, her fingers running through his hair, her snuggling up to him. That sparkling look in her eyes when she gazed at him, that hopeful smile. The more Titus pondered, the more astonished he became that the nymph shared the intense affection she showed him with others.

Was it all fake? Or was her love so vast that there was enough for many? Well, perhaps nymphs could do just that. After all, they were divine beings capable of superhuman feats.

While he tangled himself in thoughts of all the ways Thalassa might have deceived him, the notion that Nysa's entire story could be fabricated crossed his mind. With a lump in his throat, he wrapped his torn tunic around his body. His limbs felt hollow, as if an evil spirit had drained all vitality from them.

The fire from the oil lamp had become colorless, as cold as a winter night in the far north. He wanted to cry, but an icy emptiness held back his tears. Again, he heard Magnus laughing. Titus stood up. He surveyed the room and peered into the deep darkness of the adjoining corridors.

"Magnus?" He took a few steps into the dark corridor. "I know you're there. I can hear you."

A sound approached from the darkness, indiscernible at first. Thousands of tiny footsteps grew louder. He stepped back. From the shadows, a writhing, black mass appeared, covering the floor, the walls, the ceiling. Screaming, Titus ran out of the cave.

Through the drizzle, Titus hurried home. Remus sat under the porch awning, studying lantrunculi pieces arranged on the board.

"What happened to you?" asked Remus.

"Torn by a thorn bush."

Remus narrowed his eyes.

"A thorn bush, huh?"

Titus sighed and entered the shed. Everything was meticulously cared for. The modest, old furniture shone as if new. The floor was so clean one could eat off it. Titus' scrolls were neatly arranged in the cabinet. He nodded as he looked around.

"Arrian stopped by yesterday afternoon. He helped me cleaning things. Putting your stuff in order. Flavia helped too, actually. They waited for you until dusk and then went back to Nicopolis together."

"Oh? Is that so? If I had known…"

"Arrian said you never visited him. He's still terribly worried."

"Oh, yes! That's right. I forgot to mention, but—"

"You don't have to justify yourself. I'm just wondering what's going on with you. No, Lady Fortuna hasn't been kind lately. But your sister is right. After all you've lost, don't lose your sanity too. You still have a whole life ahead of you."

"Remus, that's enough! You're not in a position to lecture me! Know your place!"

Remus looked at Titus for a while and then turned his gaze back to the lantrunculi pieces.

"Understood."

Though he could have had his torn tunic repaired, Titus chose to discard it. In his eyes, the piece of cloth had been tainted and he wanted to rid himself of it. Lost in thought, Titus was barely aware of the cold water enveloping his body as he washed thoroughly. He dressed in his chiton and sat briefly beside Remus at the front door.

Without exchanging a word with the servant, he stood up and walked eastward.

A gray cloud cover hovered above the lagoon. Crickets dominated the soundscape. With small steps, Titus walked to the water's edge. His shoulders slumped forward. He stared at the bubbles on the water. Two hands squeezed his waist.

"Missing me?"

Titus exhaled deeply, still staring at the bubbles. Thalassa wrapped her arms around his waist and rested her head on his shoulder, kissing his cheek.

"Where were you this morning?"

"I'm sorry. I had to rush here."

"You promised me."

"I'm so sorry. Truly. I didn't want to wake you. You looked so peaceful. I had promised to try to change. But this was an emergency. Come, I'll show you!"

Thalassa took his hand and hurried to a nest by the water's edge, made of twigs, seaweed, and other materials, where four chirping chicks were nestled. From the lagoon, a seagull hurried to the nest.

"It's alright, it's alright," Thalassa said. "Your children are safe." She petted the small seagulls' heads. "A gang of foxes had their eyes on the nest. Four seagulls were facing them, clearly outnumbered and powerless against those vile creatures. That's why I rushed here and chased them away."

Titus stared blankly ahead. He felt his face grow pale. Thalassa grabbed his shoulder.

"What is it?"

"There's nothing."

"Yes, there is. Tell me."

"So… you have no one else?"

"What are you talking about? You thought I… Of course not! I have you! Finally! After thousands of years! When will you realize how important you are to me?"

Titus' eyes moistened. It didn't take long before his dam of sorrow burst open. He wrapped his arms around her, burying his face in her golden hair as he sobbed.

"What… what's wrong, dearest?"

Thalassa cried. Her hands rubbed his back.

"I did something stupid. I don't know what came over me."

Thalassa grasped Titus' shoulders.

"What happened?"

Titus recounted his flight and the events in Magnus' cave, and of course, what Nysa had told him about her. Thalassa took her hands off the Roman. She stepped back a few paces.

"Nysa. That filthy, lying hag." She seemed to struggle to contain her anger. "Where was Magnus? And what were you fleeing from?"

"I felt his presence, but perhaps I imagined it. And I had to flee because masses of scorpions were chasing me, in numbers I've never seen before. No idea where they came from. It was terrifying. Absolutely terrifying. Maybe I've gone mad, who knows."

"Scorpions, huh? That was Magnus. The scoundrel. It's all clear to me now. Don't you see? They lured you into a trap! What a dirty trick. I never want to see those two again! You won't find me at the shrine anymore, that's for sure!"

Titus remained silent. Thalassa hugged him tightly. She pressed her head against his.

"I forgive you, dearest. I forgive you. It wasn't your fault. They tricked you!"

Titus stepped back. He shook his head. For a moment, he forgot his surroundings. He wanted to believe her so badly. He wished that Nysa and Magnus had indeed twisted reality to manipulate him, and that Thalassa wasn't really as they had described her. But taking her words for truth was still groping in the dark. There was no proof. It was one word against another.

One thing Titus knew for sure was that he didn't want to risk being deceived again. Especially now, as he also had to digest the sorrow about his children and the betrayal of Ariadne that still haunted him daily. It would consume him. His grief would be endless.

He stared at Thalassa's face. She was still the most beautiful being he had ever seen in his life. If he said goodbye to her now, their shared dream would shatter, but at least he would be spared the potential pain of betrayal.

"I see no future for us," said Titus.

Thalassa ran to him. She grasped his hands.

"What do you mean? I don't understand! Don't worry! I forgive you, right? It's not your fault!"

"There's no Elysium, is there?"

"What are you talking about? Elysium exists!"

"How can you prove that?"

"I can't! You can only see it once you're there! Why don't you believe me? Why are you asking all this?"

"I don't trust you. I've tried, but I just can't."

"Nysa and Magnus are trying to drive us apart! Don't believe everything they say! What do they know? They want you to take a different path, but this is the right path. The path with me. I'm sure of it! Give me at least a fair chance!"

Titus pulled his hands away.

"I'm sorry," said Titus. He took a few steps back and turned his back on Thalassa. "I don't think we're meant to be."

"Listen to me! You're taking the easy way out! You're running away from what you truly desire because you're afraid of being hurt again. But by running away, you deny life, while you could embrace it, both good and bad, happiness and sorrow! True affirmation of life as Dionysus celebrates it means welcoming everything! Forgiving after anger, allowing joy after sadness, and choosing trust after betrayal. That's the hard path I want to walk with you! And I won't let you down, I promise you! After all you've been through, I could never bring myself to hurt you!"

Titus took a deep breath. For a moment, he thought of the eternal togetherness in Elysium.

"I can't do this," the Roman said. "I'll choose the easy way, then. So be it. I don't care what you call it. I'm leaving soon. I'm leaving all this behind. I'll spend the rest of my life alone, in peace, until I die. Maybe as a hermit, maybe as a traveler. I don't know yet. But I'm done with it. That's for sure. I've been through enough."

He walked to the hedge, stopped, looked over his shoulder, and saw her kneeling down. His limbs felt heavy, his stomach as if something was fermenting inside. But it was for the best.

28. Helios

A lightning bolt illuminated the northern hilltops. Carrying an oil lamp, Titus trudged through the olive grove toward his shack. He wrestled with a gnawing sense of discomfort. His conscience felt filthy, as if tainted with a disease that had caused irreparable damage. He heard Magnus' laughter again. At the end of the path lined with olive trees, Magnus stood like a scarecrow, laughing, his red toga fluttering in the stormy wind. Titus clenched his fist, feeling his pulse in his palm. He threw the oil lamp to the ground.

"So, this was your little plan, right? Well, you've succeeded!" Titus said.

"Oh, why the fuss? You kept heading down a false path. You were almost done for. Desperate times call for desperate measures. That nymph can't be trusted. Be glad you see this now."

"Who says you're not spouting nonsense? It's her word against yours!"

"Is that so? You're not the first one she's done this to, and you're certainly not the last. Oh well, you don't have to take my word for it. But believe what you will: she is married. Already has been for three thousand years. That says enough."

Titus fell silent.

"Deep down, you know what's going on. You feel it in

your gut, your bones, your muscles. Your body is always right. That nymph spells trouble. Don't let her distract you from your true path anymore. The Urge is clear. Follow Her, and you'll end up where you're supposed to be."

"The Urge can kick rocks. You can keep trying to convince and manipulate me, but I make my own choices. I know the path you want me to take. I've seen it. It's a direction I don't want to go. I don't care how loudly the Urge screams and yells; I refuse. I'm above this."

Magnus looked at Titus as if he had anticipated his reaction, with a smirk that seemed to derive pleasure from the accuracy of his prediction.

"Resist the Urge, and She becomes stronger. Suppress Her, and She will triumph. You might be done with the Urge, but the Urge isn't done with you. That's my final lesson."

"Good. I was done with your lessons anyway."

With a faint smirk, Magnus brushed past Titus, his shoulder grazing the Roman's. He inhaled deeply, like a dignitary before delivering an important speech to the people.

"I never told you, but I used to be a Stoic. I was fervent, always prioritizing virtue. Married a good, virtuous woman. At least, that's what I thought. I was a merchant. Often away from home, sometimes for weeks on end. I trusted her as I trust the sun to rise each morning. Later, it turned out she participated in orgies in my absence, with wealthy people at their luxurious parties. My world collapsed."

Magnus' confession struck a chord with Titus, reminding him of his own experiences and the agony that rushed back into his body as if it all just happened again.

"From my Stoic beliefs, I forgave her. I sought solace in Seneca's works. I even visited Musonius Rufus in Rome, after his return from exile, shortly before his death. I believed the Stoic path would help me process my grief, calm my anger. But in vain. The more I tried to let go and accept, the sadder and angrier I became."

Overwhelmed by Magnus' sudden confession, Titus turned to him curiously.

"After years of practice, I lost faith in the Stoa," Magnus continued. "And then She found me. The power I had long suppressed burst forth and engulfed reason, virtue, logic, ethics, morality; everything I had stood for so long. Although I feared Her, I decided to heed Her call. What did I have to lose? Through Her guidance, I overcame my grief, my remorse, my deep sense of humiliation."

"What happened?" Titus asked.

"All those years as a Stoic, I had hoped our marriage would flourish again, that I could inspire my wife to lead a virtuous life too. But no. Years later, she was still secretly participating in orgies. So, I followed her. And then I killed her—no, I slaughtered her. Not just her, but the other participants in that filthy debauchery as well."

Magnus chuckled. He stared ahead as if he could see his memories in front of him.

"I fled to a remote corner of the Empire where no one knew me. I feared a huge sense of guilt would overcome me. After all, I had 'harmed myself' by my deed. That's how Stoics reason, at least. But to my surprise, I felt relieved. I had settled the score with Fate. I felt better and stronger than ever before. What reason couldn't achieve, the Urge did. Surprising, isn't it?"

The philosopher glanced at his pupil one last time, then walked past the olive trees and disappeared into the darkness. Titus felt uneasy hearing Magnus' words. It was a reminder of his own desire for revenge and how he continually tried to bury it.

Titus flung open the door of his shack. He found Remus, sprawled asleep on the floor. Quietly, he stepped over the snoring servant's body toward the wine jars along the wall. With a full jar, he snuck outside. Sitting against the shack, he watched Alcander's villa, the drowsy doorman on his stool, the cats creeping along the outer wall. An unknown voice sounded from nowhere.

"Why are you still listening to that sophist? He doesn't know what he's talking about. He's overflowing with hate. He pretends to want to help, but he'd rather see the world burn, dragging everyone around him into misery."

Titus jumped to his feet.

"Who are you? Where are you? I can't see you."

"Above you."

Titus scanned the dark sky and then the shed. On the edge of the roof, just above the rear window, perched a seagull. The bird spread its wings, performed an elegant hop, and glided to the ground. As if witnessing olives sing, Titus watched in astonishment as the seagull addressed him.

"I apologize for dropping in unannounced, but it's urgent. At least, I believe it is. The truth is always urgent."

"But how… I don't understand… Helios?"

"Surprised? There are stranger things in the world than talking seagulls, I assure you, human."

"Like seas of scorpions attacking out of nowhere, or nymphs married to gods falling in love with mere mortals."

"Indeed, those aren't everyday occurrences. But their rarity doesn't make them any less real."

"What do you mean?"

"Do you doubt Thalassa's love for you is real?"

"I don't know."

"I've known her since I was a chick. She raised me as she raised my parents, and their parents before them, and so on. My family knows her history. My distant ancestors even witnessed her wedding to Poseidon, that arrogant pest of a god. Throughout the centuries, she remained closed off, like a flower waiting for the first rays of morning sunlight. But those rays never came, until you entered her life."

"I don't understand. She's married to a god. She's encountered countless souls over millennia. How can I, a mere mortal, fulfill her after all this time?"

"Yet you do, human. It may seem unlikely at first glance. But sometimes, even the most unlikely beings find a resonance, an unexplainable connection that goes beyond our understanding, beyond time and place. You see yourself as a mere mortal, but to her, you're as special as she is to you. Can I explain why? No. But does it matter?"

"I want to understand."

"Why? You're trying to comprehend something that goes beyond limited human comprehension. That's why you see it as illogical, irrational. Because it is, human! And so what? Sure, you could concoct all sorts of rational explanations for why things happen the way they do. Maybe she's just using you to satisfy an insatiable need for attention. Maybe she's using you as a tool to get a rise out of her husband. Maybe she sadistically enjoys toying with the hearts of helpless mortals. Maybe, maybe, maybe. Trying to rationalize irrational events is a dangerous game. The more you try to unravel, the more the truth eludes you. You end up making decisions based on assumptions about something fundamentally incomprehensible."

"It's for the best. She's a nymph."

"So, what? Nymphs can't be trusted? That's Magnus

talking. He blames the Stoics for being locked in a cage of ideas, categories and rules. He claims that every person is unique. Yet, he applies a broad-brush approach to the nymphs when it suits him. Don't you see how hypocritical that man is?"

For a moment, Titus stared in the distance. "She's married. I can't give myself to her. If you knew my history, you'd understand why. I just don't trust her."

"And she sees you as the best thing that ever happened to her in her life. She radiates joyfulness. Everyone in the lagoon is talking about it. Don't believe me, human? Ask the frogs, the bees, the crabs, the sparrows."

Titus glanced at the cat that had meanwhile settled on the drowsy doorman's lap, pushing its backside into his face with a meow. The seagull's revelation indeed shed new light on the matter, although it was naturally hard to verify since Titus couldn't communicate with those animals. At least, as far as he knew. And even if what Helios claimed was true, perhaps her affection—or whatever it should be called—might just be a temporary flood, soon to ebb away.

Why would I commit to such transience?

"All your life you've dreamed of turning stone into gold. Do you know why? I think it has nothing to do with wealth, recognition, or revenge. I believe you wanted to become so powerful because you thought it would bring certainty in an uncertain world, so no one could touch you, not even the gods. Your fear corrupted the Urge, blinding you to what you truly want. But no matter how powerful and wealthy you are, you can't escape the uncertainty of existence. Even mountains of gold as high as Olympus can't protect you from the whims of fate."

Titus, reluctant as he was, acknowledged a kernel of truth in Helios' words. The world was uncertain. This uncertainty bothered him, especially after he lost his wealth, faced his wife's betrayal, and suffered the loss of his children. These events fueled his obsession with producing gold. After enduring so much pain at the hands of Lady Fortuna, his wish to overcome uncertainty was stronger than ever, despite the fact that it was impossible.

A mortal cannot triumph over the will of the gods, as the Stoics justly observed. Life is uncertain.

But within this general uncertainty, there were degrees. Some things were more certain than others. It was more certain that the sun will rise in the morning than that a golden ring will still be on the street where it was left the night before.

The same went for people. Some were simply more reliable than others. A person couldn't have complete certainty, but a well-considered choice could significantly increase the degree of certainty. Hence, Attius Laelius had taught his son the characteristics of a good wife; a woman he could rely on, who was stable, obedient and predictable. She would make a man's life easier and more secure. "Such a woman is worth her weight in gold," he argued. In this regard, Thalassa appeared as an ill-suited partner for life, much like Ariadne.

Helios spread his wings and hopped toward Titus.

"Give her a chance. Of course, letting her go might spare you possible grief. But wouldn't you also lose what you long for?"

"What do I long for?"

"That's for you to figure out, human. Don't listen too much to Magnus and his ilk. Don't let their influence determine your direction. Their motives are self-interest. Remember that."

29. Gladius

Sleep eluded Titus that night, while Remus lay as if drifting into the arms of Morpheus himself. Lost in thought, Titus lit an oil lamp and descended into the cellar. The dim light cast long shadows on the dusty relics of his past. He noticed a long object wrapped in cloth, but he couldn't remember what it was. Carefully, he unrolled it to reveal a gladius, adorned with carvings, stirring memories of bygone days.

Titus' father had given him the gladius in his teenage years, undoubtedly hoping his son would follow in his footsteps as a skilled swordsman. To Attius' disappointment, that never came to pass, as young Titus showed little interest in the martial arts in any form.

Drifting into memories of his youth, some painful, as he recalled his father's ongoing discontent over his life choices and character, he placed the gladius near the cellar's hatch. Then, he lay down on the couch and finally fell asleep.

The next morning, Titus woke up with a headache. From outside, he heard the sound of metal and stone grinding against each other, feeling it deep in his bones. He jumped up and stormed outside, where he found Remus holding the gladius. He moved the sword along a sharpening stone with graceful movements as if he had done it many times before.

"Good morning, Titus, I hope I didn't wake you."

Like a cat, Titus' gaze followed Remus' movements. "I had to get up anyway," he replied.

Remus held the gladius in the air, the metal gleaming in the morning sun. "As sharp as the sword of Ares himself."

Titus stared at the sword. Images of Alcander on his knees flashed before his eyes: the sword swinging, Alcander's head rolling across the plains. Titus stepped back and clutched his forehead.

"Headache?"

"Yes."

"I fetched some water from the well this morning. It's by the door."

"Thank you, Remus."

Titus sipped water from a stone mug. He rummaged through the papyrus rolls in the cupboard. Hidden behind a large bundle were Arrian's notes. Titus took the notes outside. With a view of Alcander's villa, he sat against the wall by the window, holding the Stoic wisdoms in his hands.

"Never say of anything, 'I have lost it'; but, 'I have returned it.' Has your child died? It has been returned. Has your wife died? She has been returned. Has your property been taken away? And isn't that likewise returned? 'But the one who took it is a bad person.' What does it matter to you who the giver appoints to take it back? As long as he gives it to you to possess, take care of

it; but do not consider it your own possession, just as travelers consider a hotel."[31]

Were all those things I had lost never really mine? Were my properties, my lands, my family never really my possessions?

According to Stoic logic, all the things he valued so much, even his own children, even his body, were not within his power. Lady Fortuna could take them from him and allocate them to someone else, whenever she desired.

Staring at Alcander's villa, Titus took a sip of water. Maybe it was supposed to be this way; a comforting thought. All that fuss over something he couldn't change anyway. It had been nice, though he wished it had lasted longer. Instead of sorrow, perhaps gratitude would be more appropriate, Titus reasoned: gratitude to the gods for what they had given him on loan. Yet the words Magnus had told him the previous evening kept echoing in his head. Then he recalled Helios' visit, wondering whether it was a dream or if he was losing his mind.

On a homemade stand, Remus displayed the gladius by the door. The weapon sparkled in the lamplight.

"Attius would be proud. Such a fine sword shouldn't be left to gather dust in a cellar," Remus remarked.

With a modest chuckle, Titus took the gladius from the stand and wielded it like a Roman soldier.

---

[31] Epictetus, *Enchiridion*, 11

"My father once taught me some techniques," said Titus. He swung the sword around with both hands and made a stabbing motion as if piercing his opponent's torso.

"You can tell immediately. You could join the army," said Remus with a laugh.

"They probably wouldn't want me."

Someone knocked on the door.

"Are you expecting company tonight?" asked Remus.

Titus shook his head. Remus opened the door. Titus dropped the sword. Remus' mouth opened in shock. Titus searched for words. His limbs trembled. His stomach turned. The inside of the shed started spinning. Tears flowed through his nose.

"W… wh… who did this?"

In the doorway stood his oldest son with swellings around his eyes, scratches on his face, a bloody nose, and lips as swollen as freshly picked grapes. Tears ran from the swellings down his cheeks. Titus puffed out his chest and clenched his fists, as he didn't want his son to see him as the pile of misery he was collapsing into.

"Ares, son, tell Daddy who did this."

The boy was silent. He stared into his father's eyes.

"Who did this? Tell me, son. Was it Alcander? Yes, it was Alcander, wasn't it?"

Ares nodded. Remus took a deep sigh, shaking his

head, and glanced through the window at the villa. Like an angry bull, Titus stomped through the shed.

"That dirty, filthy bastard. That cowardly, filthy bastard. That filthy bastard!"

"Titus," said Remus. "I'll go to Arrian tomorrow morning. We need to resolve this through legal means."

"I'll flatten him to the ground!"

"Titus! I understand, believe me. I'd love to beat him black and blue too, but it's not the way. Your son needs you. He's seen enough violence, don't you think?"

Titus punched the wall, walked over to Ares, and embraced him. Ares cried.

"You're safe here, son. You're safe with Daddy."

Remus extinguished the oil lamp. He locked the door.

"I wouldn't be surprised if Alcander's men come snooping around here. We'll pretend we're not home," whispered Remus.

"Do you hear that, boy? We're playing hide and seek. So the three of us will be absolutely silent, so everyone thinks there's no one home. Agreed?"

Ares nodded. Remus peered through the window. It seemed quiet around Alcander's villa. A lamp burned on the veranda. The drowsy doorman slept in his chair. Remus stepped back.

"What is it?" asked Titus.

"Someone's coming. I couldn't see who it is."

There was a knock on the door. Remus grabbed the gladius from the stand, positioning himself to the left of the door. The knocking sounded again, this time more urgent, almost serious. Titus crept toward the window next to the door. Carefully, he looked outside and encountered a familiar figure. A surge of rage coursed through his body. He flung the door open, grabbed the visitor by the collar, and dragged her into the shed.

"What did you do to my son?" he roared.

Ariadne, sobbing, collapsed into Titus' arms.

"I… I'm at a loss. I tried to stop him. I don't know what to do anymore. Ares won't listen. He's becoming unruly. Alcander couldn't take it anymore. I'm caught in the middle!"

"Caught in the middle? He's your child! Exposing your children to such a monster… Of course, he's becoming unruly!"

"Yes, but—"

"You're simply a terrible mother! That's what you are!"

"I'm not a terrible mother," Ariadne sobbed. "I've done nothing wrong! I had no idea Ares would be so difficult and that Alcander would react like this! I'm at my wits' end. It all just happened to me and it's ruining my relationship. I'm the real victim here!"

"What a nasty, filthy, selfish, irresponsible wretch you are! You're not only a terrible mother; you're also a terrible person!"

"And I'm tired of your insults and scolding. Who do you think you are? He is coming with me. I'm taking him to my parents. That settles it!"

"Not a chance I'm letting you take him!"

"Oh, yes! I'm his mother!"

"Definitely not! Not as long as you're with that brute! My son won't step foot in that villa again. Even if I have to kidnap him!"

Ariadne's shoulders drooped in defeat. She collapsed onto the couch, tears streaming down her face endlessly.

"What am I supposed to do now? He's going to ask questions. What should I tell him? I'm out of ideas."

"Listen. Here's what will happen. You'll go back to that scoundrel and tell him nobody was home here. Tell him fishermen saw a boy at the lagoon. Alcander's men will search there. Tomorrow morning, I'll take him to my sister. Then we'll figure out what to do next, because his men will undoubtedly check Flavia's place too."

Ariadne nodded in agreement, dabbing her now bright red face with a handkerchief.

"I'll sue Alcander and take away his custody."

"You won't succeed. He's covered all his bases."

"We'll see about that."

Ariadne crouched in front of Ares.

"Mama's going home. You're staying with Daddy tonight."

Ares didn't respond. His eyes blankly looked past her.

"See? Look what you've accomplished," Titus said. "Well done."

Ariadne stood up, mumbled something inaudible, and slammed the front door shut.

Early in the morning, before sunrise, Titus and Ares left for Flavia's place. Remus had informed Arrian, who rushed to Flavia's, accompanied by two friends, namely Gnaius Cornelius Severus and Quintus Fabius Valens.

Gnaius Cornelius Severus was a stout Roman lawyer who had recently moved to Nicopolis and, according to Arrian, had not yet been bribed by Alcander. Quintus Fabius Valens was a young censor who, Arrian knew, detested the corrupt gang running Nicopolis.

"In a normal situation, you'd have a strong case. Child abuse is no minor offense," said Gnaius Cornelius Severus. "The problem is, this is not a normal situation. Remember Alcander's party recently? Since then, he's also bribed Tiberius Claudius Scipio, the legate from Rome. He's had the praetor and the duumviri in his pocket for a longer time. And, it seems, even the pontifex has taken bribes."

"We're playing a dangerous game here," said Quintus

Fabius Valens. "The risk of a lawsuit backfiring is high, especially considering your past."

"Alcander will twist the truth and lay the blame on you," said Arrian.

"So what options do I have?" asked Titus.

"My advice is this: flee," said Gnaius Cornelius Severus. "Take Ares and Flavia and flee. As far away from here as possible. Head to Hispania, Egypt, even to the Frisians if you must. I have friends in Córdoba. They can help you with housing and work."

"And Faustinus?" asked Flavia.

"Indeed," said Titus. "We can't leave Faustinus behind."

"You have to make sacrifices in this situation," said the stout Roman.

"Isn't there another way?" asked Arrian.

"Kill him," said Quintus Fabius Valens. "Someone has to kill Alcander Cassius."

"And then face the wrath of the Aelianii? That would be the end of you, for sure. No one dares. At least, no one with family or dear friends whose lives they care about."

"What about the slave? Can't he do it? He looks like he's up for the job."

Quintus Fabius Valens pointed at Remus, sitting in a corner, who looked around in surprise.

"No way!" said Titus. "I'm not sacrificing Remus."

"Why not? He's just a slave."

"And my most loyal friend. He's like a brother to me." Titus nodded at Remus, who gave a modest smile back. "Why don't you send your own slaves to their death?"

"Because I'm not going to harm myself! Alcander Cassius knows I'm not fond of him!"

"Do you think that doesn't apply to me? What kind of censor are you?"

"Hey, hold on! *You* are the one with the problem here! Not me! So it would make sense for *you* to make a sacrifice!"

"As if you're not benefiting from this! You're trying to use me for your own ends!"

"Gentlemen, this isn't helping," said Arrian. "I'll talk to the duumviri. Our families have good relations. You try convincing the legate and the praetor. Maybe they'll agree that it's time for Alcander's reign to end."

"Agreed," said Gnaius Cornelius Severus.

"And Ares?" asked Flavia. "It won't be long before they come looking here."

"I have an idea. Remus, get a horse, a cart, and some blankets," said Arrian. "I'll take the boy to my place. They're less likely to search there."

Arrian grabbed his notes from the table, walked over

to Titus, and pressed them against his chest. The Nicomedian looked at him intently.

"*Now* is the time to heed Epictetus' lessons. *Now* is the time to stay calm and rational."

Titus nodded. Quintus Fabius stood up, walked over to Ares, crouched down, and examined his face.

"He's a terrible man. Pure evil."

30. Scorpius

Titus had to go to the latrine for the second time that night, which was next to his shed. His stomach felt as if a school of pufferfish were swimming around, inflating themselves now and then. After throwing up once, his stomach seemed to calm down a bit.

He lay down on the bed. Remus' sawing snoring prevented Titus from relaxing. He tried to relax his muscles by breathing deeply through his nose, holding it for a few counts, and exhaling through his mouth. His breathing abruptly stopped when he saw something moving on the ceiling. Small, black shapes were crawling above his head. They were also walking on the walls, on the floor, and even on his bed. Frozen with fear, he started to scream.

"Remus! Remus! Help! Wake up, Remus!"

Remus didn't respond. The creatures crawled over Titus' arms, chest, back. He felt them crawling on his neck and head. He closed his eyes and screamed and screamed. Thunder sounded from the sky. Titus opened his eyes. Surrounded by plains, with spewing volcanoes in the distance, he was buried under scorpions. He stood up, started running, and managed to shake most of them off. A window appeared in front of him. He walked toward it. Through the window, he saw Alcander's villa. The villa got closer and closer until right up to the veranda. Scorpions were crawling over the floor and walls.

Titus woke up with a start and jumped out of bed. Remus was still snoring. He dressed in his tunic, put on his shoes, and grabbed the gladius from the stand. Like a gladiator facing his death, Titus marched past the shed, toward the tall grass. Large eyes appeared in a burning sky. The Apollo hill was spewing fire. The Gulf of Arta was a sea of lava.

"Titus!" a voice called from behind. "Titus, stop!" Without responding, Titus kept marching. "Don't do this! Don't risk your life!"

"He has taken everything from me!" Titus yelled. "My family, my life... He must pay for what he has done!"

Thalassa jumped on Titus' back. She wrapped her arms around his neck. She was light as a feather, but her grip was strong.

"Revenge is not the answer! Revenge only leads to destruction that will not spare you either. And then Magnus says the Stoics are life-deniers! What is a greater denial of life than destroying everything you dislike, paid for with your own existence?"

"Destruction is the womb of creation. That's the essence of Dionysus' teaching. I am that destruction! It's all clear to me now. This is my path. Magnus is right. This is what I want. I can no longer deny it."

"Magnus is wrong! You don't want this! I can see into your heart. Beneath all the anger lies a deep desire for love... love that I can give you!"

Titus tried to push Thalassa away, but her grip tightened.

"I beg you… don't let this be the end of your story, of our story. Think of what we can have, together! Elysium! Think of Elysium!"

"Let me go!" Titus pulled Thalassa's arms. "I care nothing for you! That's why I did it with Nysa! You mean nothing to me! And Elysium is a myth! Nonsense! And so is our love! Do you hear that? You're just a whore who betrays her own husband!"

Thalassa let go. She stood frozen, the pain of rejection clear on her face. Her red fins hung sadly by her head.

"Let me love you."

"I'm sorry."

Titus marched through the tall grass. Alcander's villa approached. The drowsy doorman was sitting in his chair, sleeping. A cat dashed away behind a wall. Lava shooting up in the distance. Scorpions were crawling out of the windows, over the veranda floor, along the long outer walls, over the drowsy doorman.

The front door swung open. Thousands of black arthropods poured out. Against the stream, Titus walked inside. The hallways had turned into a black sea of arachnids that were also crawling along the walls and ceilings. At the end of the hallway, he saw Magnus standing in his dark red toga with a hood over his head. His eyes were bloodshot. He pointed to a door and disappeared.

The scorpions were up to Titus' knees by then, as he shuffled toward the door. The door burst from its frame. A black tsunami poured over him. He struggled through the doorway. The arthropods scurried away behind him through the hallways, rushing outside as if fleeing from something. After the last scorpion left the room, Titus walked through the doorway.

Alcander was sleeping. An oil lamp burned on a small table. Titus saw his reflection in the large mirror where Alcander probably admired himself several times a day. He moved closer. Behind him, he heard a whisper.

"What do you want? Is this what you want?"

He raised the gladius with both hands above his head. Footsteps approached.

"Stop!"

Titus turned around. In the doorway stood Ariadne in a white, translucent nightgown. Alcander's eyes opened. He sat up abruptly, looking at the gladius Titus held above his head.

"Titus... dear Titus," Alcander said, his voice trembling.

"Get on the ground, on your knees."

Alcander carefully lifted his legs out of bed and knelt.

"I... I think I know why you're here. I'm sorry. I

might have been a bit too harsh on him. But… he needs discipline. That boy is uncontrollable. It was for his own good. It… it… was out of love, believe me, truly."

"You will not lay a finger on my son again," Titus said.

"I'm sorry, I'm sorry! Have mercy. I'll give you a few properties. And you can always visit to see your children, whenever you want, if you spare my life!"

Titus still held the gladius above his head. His arms were starting to feel heavy. He noticed Alcander's eyes drifting toward Ariadne, who stood behind him. Titus turned his head. Out of the corner of his eye, he saw Ariadne approaching. He spun around, dodging a dagger aimed at his upper back. With a feint, Titus thrust forward. Alcander screamed. Without fully grasping what had just happened, he pulled the blood-stained sword from Ariadne's body. She collapsed. Blood flowed from her mouth and nose.

"Ariadne… darling… Ariadne… What have you done?"

Titus turned around. A door slammed in the distance. Footsteps approached. With both hands, Titus lifted the gladius above his head. Voices grew louder.

"… we've searched almost the entire coast. No trace of the boy…"

"Help! Help!" Alcander cried.

Footsteps quickened. With all his strength, Titus

swung the sword in front of him. Alcander's head rolled across the floor, and his body fell sideways to the ground.

A wave of clarity overwhelmed Titus. He realized the gravity of his actions. He had committed murder—not one, but two. He stood up against injustice. An act driven by a deep desire for justice. Emotions overwhelmed him, anger but also sorrow. And so, it happened. The great conclusion had unfolded. The Urge had spoken, Her words realized.

Titus dropped the gladius, ran through the door, turned right into the corridor, heading toward the courtyard. Alcander's men chased after him. Titus dashed across the courtyard, climbed over the outer wall, crossed the path, ran through the tall grass. Like an Olympic sprinter, he sped past the shed, heading toward Nicopolis. Alcander's men were far behind.

Upon reaching the city gate, Titus stopped running. Out of breath, he walked to the night watchmen at the bottom of the watchtower. They were playing a Persian-looking board game. He met their shocked but slightly irritated glances. One of the watchmen slouched, sipping from a wine jug.

"What do you want?"

"I… I… have killed two people. I… want a fair trial… according to Roman law," Titus said.

The slouched watchman dropped his wine jug. One of the watchmen, a burly, balding Roman with a face that had seen many crimes, stood up.

"Son, tell me. What's going on?"

"I… have killed two people. These people were residents… of the territory of Nicopolis. Their names are… Ariadne… daughter of Echemus and Galyna… and Alcander Cassius Aelianus."

The irritated glances turned into looks of astonishment. Some even had a surprised smile on their face. From the window, the watchmen saw torches approaching.

"There are… Alcander's men," Titus said.

"The bloodhounds," the balding watchman muttered. "But without a leader." He gestured with his hand, and all the men in the room went outside and gathered in front of the gate.

"Sulla, give us Laelius," one of Alcander's men said.

"Why?" asked the burly watchman, apparently named Sulla.

"By order of Alcander Cassius Aelianus."

"Is that so? I've just learned that Alcander Cassius Aelianus was killed by Mr. Laelius."

Alcander's men looked at each other silently.

"Mr. Laelius has just confessed to his deed," the watchman continued. "He will be placed under house arrest by the city guard and tried according to Roman law."

"Give us Laelius! He must pay!"

"Oppose us, and you'll have a problem," Sulla said.

After dawn, a procession of seven city guards took Titus to the shed in the pouring rain. Staring at the ground, he walked along without any resistance. Dozens of citizens followed the procession. Rumors probably spread through the streets, alleys, and forums of Nicopolis. It was yet another piece of bad news about the Roman who had settled in the city of Augustus years before and undoubtedly the most dramatic.

With a defeated look, Remus stood by the shed as Titus and the procession approached. He watched the city guards escort Titus into the shed. Two of them went inside with him. Four stood guard outside. Sulla spoke to the crowd gathered at the shed.

"We're still investigating, ma'am. No, we can't confirm anything, sir," Titus heard him call out. The city guards were suspiciously tender. No pulling, pushing, or beating. One of them even poured some wine for him.

From the window, Titus saw city guards parading around Alcander's villa. Two carriages stopped in front of the veranda. From one carriage, Praetor Gaius Lucullus Flavus and the pontifex disembarked. From the other, Galyna and Ptolemaios stepped out, looking twenty years older.

The drowsy doorman on the veranda looked around confused, as if he had woken up from a years-long coma. In the following days, there was a constant stream of visitors. Ariadne's family was probably busy arranging the cremation. Alcander typically had no family in Nicopolis. The Aelianii were based in Athens, although their diaspora spread widely across the empire. Once the news reached them, they would travel to Nicopolis, although they would likely not arrive in time for the cremation.

Four nights after the murder, funeral attendants carried the two bodies out the front door on portable beds, followed by Galyna, Ptolemaios, family members, and intimate friends. It was crowded. Friends, acquaintances, and Alcander Cassius' many business relations waited in front of the villa and joined the procession. Musicians accompanied the procession, the pontifex and his helpers spread incense, women sprinkled perfume.

From the window, Titus saw the crowd glance his way. The distance was too great to see their facial expressions, but he expected no happy, friendly faces. He moved a few steps away from the window. The procession moved eastward, toward the stadium, and would end at the northern cemetery.

Titus' shed was still guarded by four city guards, who rotated twice a day. Remus was free to keep the household running as usual and do the shopping. In Nicopolis, he had heard the rumor that Alcander's men had skipped town before the cremation. Farmers had seen them on the road to Buthrotum. Apparently, and not surprisingly, many had a score to settle with Alcander's so-called "bloodhounds." Without Alcander Cassius' protection, these mere mercenaries—for whom virtue, ethics, and morality were foreign concepts—were vulnerable.

About a week after the cremation, the parents, two brothers, and sister of Alcander Cassius arrived, finding only the ashes of their loved ones in the mausoleum. Rumor had it that the Aelianii wanted to build a grand tomb at the cemetery, where Alcander Cassius' ashes could be stored upon completion, but they refused to include Ariadne's ashes. Why this was the case was unknown, although it was suspected that the Aelianii were unhappy with Alcander's choice of partner. To Titus' discomfort, Alcander's two brothers sat on the veranda every afternoon, staring incessantly at the shed until the family delegation left after a market week.

31. Noctua

Over the past few weeks, Titus had barely eaten anything. Sometimes, he went the entire day without eating. On the days he did eat, he usually consumed no more than a piece of bread and some water. His thoughts often drifted to Thalassa, the cabin in the Alps, her red fins. To what could have been, but what he had squandered.

If only I could lie in her arms by the waterfront, just to gaze at the fishing boats in silence.

The trial was lengthy, yet the outcome seemed almost certain to Arrian: a double murder would undoubtedly result in the death penalty. The city guard immediately rejected Titus' requests for fresh air, making him realize his only time outside would be on the day of his execution. Flavia escorted Ares and Faustinus to visit him three times a week; a lenient arrangement, pushed through by Arrian.

After much effort and discussions with the duumviri, Arrian managed to secure permission to visit Titus, even bringing an unforeseen guest, who arrived in a carriage on a sunny autumn morning. Titus never expected to be so pleased with the visit of the Stoic philosopher Epictetus, who, at Arrian's insistence, wanted to accompany him in his final days.

According to Epictetus, it was never too late to make progress; every step in the right direction counted. It would make dying easier; reduce the fear of death. The philosopher spoke about Seneca the Younger, who, like Socrates, faced his end with complete serenity. Like a child being read to by his mother, Arrian hung on every word from Epictetus' lips. Titus listened intently to the sage's discussions about the transience of life and the acceptance of death.

Epictetus made several visits, always accompanied by Arrian, who occasionally took notes. The Stoic views on life, death, and transience had been thoroughly discussed, always boiling down to the calm acceptance of the inevitable. The conversation was starting to repeat itself until Epictetus addressed the elephant in the room.

"Can you explain what exactly drove you to your actions?" he asked. Arrian sat up straight. Remus, who had almost dozed off in a corner, seemed fully engaged again.

The burning sensation in Titus' stomach returned, albeit mildly and bearably. He had to share his story, or they would never understand his actions. He detailed his first encounter with Magnus in the courtyard after class, Magnus' visit to his home, his awakening in the cave, the sanctuary of Dionysus and his followers, his relationship with Thalassa, seeing Neptune in the flesh, the ritual, and the eventual murder of Alcander Cassius and Ariadne. He talked about the mysterious force called "The Urge" and Her role in human desires.

"The Urge, you say?" said Epictetus. Using his staff, the philosopher lifted himself from his stool and shuffled around the room. "When I lived in Rome, a gladiator named Horatius regularly attended my lectures. He was a brave man, fought lions, wild boars, bulls, and, of course, human opponents. But other gladiators mocked Horatius for studying philosophy. One day, he stood in the Colosseum, face to face with a bear. The bear was large, fast, and extremely aggressive. Though not normally afraid, Horatius turned pale. His limbs trembled, his sword and shield quivered. Despite this, he defeated the bear. Afterwards, they ridiculed him. 'Wasn't he a Stoic? Why did his body suddenly experience a wave of fear?'"

Arrian leaned forward in anticipation.

"Our initial emotional reactions are beyond our control. They emerge before reason even notices them.[32] When he noticed his fear, Horatius used reason to regain his inner calm. He realized he had nothing to fear, that everything happened according to Zeus' will. The only thing that mattered was how he faced his fate: his actions. After his realization, his fear subsided, and he defeated the bear with skill and clarity of mind."

Titus looked down at the floor. *What was Epictetus trying to say? Could reason tame the Urge? Was the Urge subordinate to reason, contrary to Magnus' claims?* Remus appeared lost in thought. Arrian stood up.

"So, if I understand correctly, the Urge is just a physical impulse that can be overcome by reason, right?"

"The ideas of this sophist Magnus are misleading,"

---

[32] The Stoics accepted so-called 'proto-emotions' or 'pre-emotions' as involuntary, inevitable precursors to full-blown passions.

said Epictetus. "They deceive us into thinking our urges determine our choices. They tell us to follow not our reason but our emotions. But if Horatius had followed his emotions, fear would have dictated his actions. What would have become of him then? Or what do you think would happen if a man followed his lusts at the sight of every attractive woman? His marriage would be ruined, his children would hate him, and he'd soon be ostracized because no one could trust him anymore. But why? He's just following his desires, isn't he?"

Titus nodded. "So, I followed my anger. I let my passions guide me. And it cost lives and now also my own life."

"You mistook your anger for guidance. The question 'what do I want?' is not a bad question, but it is when passions overpower you. As Seneca once observed, soldiers consumed by rage make poor decisions. Initial anger in response to betrayal is human. The art is in what you do with it. So, what do you want? Do you want to give your passions free rein and let them grow until they completely possess you? Or do you want to use reason to maintain control over your choices and lead a virtuous life?" asked Epictetus.

Titus sighed and shook his head.

"A virtuous life guided by reason. I get it. Serving the greater good, moderation over excess, wisdom over impulse. It sounds like a life devoid of flavor or scent. Can't we just follow our desires as long as we don't harm others? No, it's not always right to follow your emotions.

My actions prove this. But aren't our passions there for a reason? This is what Thalassa was trying to convey, and she's right. Our strong emotions, the yearning for something, falling deeply in love, the intense joy of your children's first steps, your favorite chariot racing team winning, aren't these also what make life beautiful?" asked Titus.

An unexpected voice came from the corner of the room.

"If I may." Remus stood up. Epictetus answered Arrian's surprised look with an approving nod. "I was born a slave, just like you, Epictetus. Now, I've been blessed that the Laelii always treated me well. But I've also faced tough times. Not being free, not being allowed to speak up against my masters, always having to do what you're told. All this requires a thick skin. I've learned that desiring can be dangerous. Get what you want and the monster is quelled, but only temporarily. Don't get what you want and the suffering is endless. I may be a slave, but I'm also human. A human with desires. I've had to set aside many of these desires. Why? Otherwise, I would have gone mad. I might have wished life to be different, just like the beggar in the forum or the lively child who dies of malaria, but the gods have decided it so. Your desires, Titus, are what have destroyed you."

"You should free this slave," said Epictetus. "He could become a philosopher. Probably doesn't have much more to learn. It's exactly as he says. Your inability to accept the unfortunate events in your life has led you down a path of destruction. The Urge, which that sophist speaks of, is nothing more than a collection of unguided impulses and passions, unreasonable, irrational, and blind to virtue. It's the worst guide to a good life you could possibly imagine."

Dusk was falling. That evening, four city guards guarded his shed. Two stood watch. The other two played the Persian-looking board game at a table in the front yard and drank wine.

Titus peered through the back window. The crickets' chirping was drowned out by the hooting of an owl, growing louder. A city guard blocked his view of Alcander's villa. With a long stick, he poked something on the roof. The owl flew to the tree next to the shed, continuing its call.

Remus lay on the bench with Arrian's notes, which he had read several times since Epictetus' visit.

"Epictetus was impressed with you," said Titus. "You, a philosopher? I'd never seen you that way. But it would suit you well."

A faint smile appeared on Remus' face.

"I'd never seen it that way either."

Titus pointed to the notes.

"What do you think?"

"It's the first time I've delved into this material. It seems to describe how I've lived in recent years. Not everything, but much of it. I find it fascinating."

"Maybe you should pursue it. Apparently, you're already advanced on the Stoic path. Study with Epictetus. You two would get along well. Maybe you'll even teach others yourself someday. You might even become an advisor to the Emperor."

"Are you mocking me?"

"No, not at all. I'm dead serious. What do you say?"

"Say to what?"

"Dedicating your life to philosophy. In freedom."

"I don't quite understand what you mean."

"I'm setting you free. You are a free man from now on."

Remus stared ahead, as if his spirit had left his body. Titus looked around uncomfortably. He had considered freeing Remus since deciding to leave Nicopolis. Epictetus' remark was the final push. Yet, he had imagined Remus' reaction differently: perhaps more joyful.

As if drawing his spirit back into his body, Remus took a deep breath.

"But I was already free," he said.

"What do you mean?" asked Titus, puzzled.

"Forget what I just said. I appreciate it. But if I'm truly free to choose, I choose to spend the rest of my life caring for Flavia and the children. My loyalty lies with the Laelii. You've been good to me."

"Oh, stop it. Flavia will manage fine with the children. She's not wealthy, but she can afford a servant. Arrian will keep an eye on her and the children. You're healthy and hopefully have many years ahead of you. Seize that freedom. Do something with it. If you were still my property, I could command it!"

Remus laughed.

"I'll think about it."

"Can you promise me one thing, though? Consider it my last wish. I want you to scatter my ashes at the lagoon. Can you do that?"

Remus nodded.

32. Magnus

Through the window next to the front door, Titus saw Arrian approaching on horseback. As usual, he first greeted the city guards, cracked the typical joke about whatever, and if they were favorably inclined, he squeezed his way inside. Arrian was cut out for a brilliant political career in Rome. He possessed the dignity of a praetor, the charm of a senator, and the intelligence of an army strategist. He was driven and believed in serving the greater good.

In all these respects, he and Titus were opposites.

After closing the door behind him, Arrian's grin turned into a serious expression. He sat down. Remus offered him a cup of wine. Even though officially a free man, Remus continued his service as if he were still under his master's authority. Titus let him be, assuming he needed time to figure out how to use his newly acquired freedom.

Could freedom also be a burden? Perhaps because suddenly you have to think about all sorts of choices that captivity spared you?

Arrian gulped down a large swallow of wine.

"I've made some inquiries in Nicopolis about that Magnus. I visited every bar, every brothel. I went to all the temples, spoke with market traders, farmers, and city guards. I even asked beggars. No one, absolutely no one has ever heard of a philosopher named 'Magnus.' No one has ever seen a middle-aged man with graying long hair in a dark red toga in Nicopolis."

"That's odd," said Titus. "Magnus often said he had to deal with matters in Nicopolis. So, someone should have seen him."

"Yet, that's not the case. Well, sure, only Theophanes, that drunkard, claimed to have seen him, but that man is as blind as a mole. What's going on here? Are you pulling our leg?"

"Why would I do such a thing?"

"Remus," said Arrian. "Have you ever seen this Magnus?"

Remus shook his head.

"Titus, I understand the events have taken a heavy toll on you. It's quite a lot what you've had to endure. But… well, how should I put this…"

"Do you think I made up Magnus?"

"I'm not saying that."

"He really exists. I'd stake my life on it."

"It's not the only thing. What about Thalassa the nymph? I've never seen a nymph in my entire life. It's questionable if they even exist."

"Thalassa is real! She lives in the lagoon! Go see for yourself if you don't believe me!"

"And that story about Poseidon. I mean... the gods are real, but what are the odds..."

"But it's true! I saw him with my own eyes!"

Arrian stood up and paced back and forth like a confused old man who didn't know where he wanted to go. Remus stared at the floor. His glassy eyes told he didn't want to be there. He was now free to walk out the door, yet he stayed.

"Epictetus and I want to help you. I just don't know what to make of this."

"What does it matter? I'm dead anyway. So, do me a favor and leave me alone. I don't want to spend my last days with friends who doubt my reality, my truth."

"No, I won't leave you alone. I want the best for you. I want you to spend your last days in peace and quiet."

"You're doing a fine job disturbing my peace and quiet, so maybe it's better if you just..." Titus sighed. He looked at Arrian's concerned gaze. "I'm sorry. You've meant a lot to me. I appreciate everything you've done for me, my sister, and my children. But believe me. I'm not making this up. Everything I've experienced is real."

"Let's drop it," said Arrian. "Let's focus on philosophy; on things within our control."

Three city guards played their Persian-looking board game in the front yard, while the fourth guarded the back of the shed. Through the back window, Titus watched as an army of city guards with torches paraded past

Alcander's villa. No one knew exactly what would happen to the huge property. Some thought Alcander's family members would move in. Others claimed the Aelianii would soon put the villa up for sale. Rumor had it that some wealthy senator from Rome had already shown interest in the property. Ariadne's family also hoped to claim the villa, but the Aelianii had excluded them from any form of inheritance, which Titus secretly found amusing.

Remus was not home that evening. After many encouragements from Titus, he had gathered the courage to attend Epictetus' lectures. Epictetus and Arrian then invited him to discuss philosophy at the forum in the evening. Flavia and the children had still visited the shed that afternoon. Flavia mentioned that Ares was again suffering from nightmares. Still about scary men. Faustinus quietly played in a corner with the latrunculi pieces, without any knowledge of the game rules. As agreed, they left before dusk.

Titus leafed through Arrian's notes. The letters seemed to dance on the papyrus. Words came and went like fish at the water's surface. And the more he tried to catch them, the faster they escaped his gaze. He put the notes on the table, picked them up again, put them away again, picked them up again. The third time he tried to read them, the words turned into black spots, from which legs and large pointy tails grew. The black beasts multiplied like dandelions in the front yard and swarmed over the papyrus. Titus threw the sheets across the room.

"Good. Throw that nonsense away."

Magnus climbed through the back window.

"What are you doing here?"

"I'm just visiting. Those men are busy with their game. They probably don't mind."

"Any moment now, they will see you."

"The only thing they see are the bottoms of their mugs. Anyway, you've got yourself into quite a mess, I hear."

"You set me up. You convinced me to follow my anger. If I hadn't met you, none of this would have happened. I would have had a long life ahead of me."

"A life as a coward who didn't dare to follow his true desires."

"As a coward, I would have spared two lives. My children are about to become orphans."

"How quickly a hero falls from his pedestal. First, he deals with his greatest enemy, thereby freeing the city from the iron grip of the Aelianii. He followed the right, true path. But then? Yes, then, overwhelmed by a sudden sense of morality, he condemns his actions and seeks solace with the old cripple, cowardice personified, to bear his deeds and upcoming death. Tragic, cowardly, and weak. You were on the right track."

Titus shrugged.

"You're just angry because I turned my back on your

Urge. My reason has triumphed over her."

"Me, angry? Far from it. Rather amused. I find it amusing to see how the Stoics push reality aside by hiding behind reason. They think they are in control, but they are not. When they feel the beast stirring beneath the surface, they grasp fearfully at their empty rationalizations, their comforting logic, their distorted worldview. They celebrate their power to 'choose,' but time and again they choose against themselves."

"So I choose against myself by choosing inner peace?"

"Denying the Urge is choosing against yourself. You can't escape Her. She will always be there. Deny Her and She becomes stronger. Perhaps that's what She wants. Perhaps She wants you to hold Her back, like a dam holds back a river. When the water builds up, there comes a moment when it breaks free with devastating force, destroying everything in its path. Ironically, I realize now: your denial of the Urge has always been the Urge."

"Let your fantasies run wild. I'm locked up here. My execution is in a week. I'm ready to die. I won't harm a fly anymore."

"Ah. Then I wish you peaceful last days. If you need me, I'll be around."

Titus stood in front of Magnus and looked him up and down.

"Who are you?"

"What do you mean?"

"Arrian has made inquiries in Nicopolis. No one has ever heard of you. No one has ever seen you. Who are you?"

Magnus chuckled, took a few steps back, climbed through the window, and disappeared.

Titus picked up Arrian's notes. The letters no longer danced. Words formed powerful sentences. Sentences created clear messages.

Loud laughter came from outside. Titus looked through the window next to the front door. One of the night watchmen hurled the Persian board across the front yard, narrowly missing the second. The third sipped from a wine jug while urinating over the weeds. The fourth marched past the back window.

33. Aelianii

Empty wine jugs lay among the weeds in the front yard. Four city guards arrived to relieve the night watchmen and found two of them asleep in their own vomit. One of the men poked the bodies with his foot. No response. The men looked at each other in bewilderment and took up their posts.

Titus fiddled with bottles and jars in a corner of the shed. The rest of his belongings were in the crawl space, which he wasn't allowed to enter due to the risk of escape. The likelihood of Titus digging a tunnel to the outside in such a short time—he was expected to receive a verdict within a week, followed swiftly by his execution—was very slim. But the Aelianii wouldn't forgive the city guards if they let him escape in any way.

An angry voice sounded from the front yard. Titus looked through the window. Sulla, whose full name was Publius Tullius Sulla according to Arrian, stormed onto the property, red-hot with anger. Since Titus' house arrest, he checked the shed and its surroundings daily. A city guard rushed through the weeds with a bucket of water and doused the sleeping night watchmen. They crawled like shipwrecked sailors washed ashore, coughing. One of them vomited the last of his stomach contents over Sulla's shiny shoes, which the hefty night watchman answered with a flying lesson, straight through the garden gate.

"Anyone who drinks even a drop of wine today gets

expelled. This is an extremely serious matter. Mess this up, and we'll have a big problem," said Sulla.

The door swung open. Without greeting, Sulla inspected the shed like a farmer checking his cowshed for intruders.

"What are you up to?" Sulla asked, pointing to the bottles and jars spread out on the floor.

"Nothing, really. Just rummaging through my old stuff," Titus replied.

Sulla nodded, his eyes scanning the ceiling, walls, and window.

"I've spoken to the higher-ups. They'll probably make a decision before the end of the week," he said.

Titus stared at the long glass bottle with a slender neck.

"I once tried turning stones into gold. They laughed at me, called me crazy. Imagine if it had ever worked out. How would my life have turned out then?"

Sulla scowled like a dog hearing its owner sing for the first time. He grabbed the bottle and tapped it with his nail in a catchy rhythm.

"I once wanted to become a traveling musician. My parents wouldn't hear of it. Now I'm happily married, two children. Would my life have been different? For sure. But it goes as it goes. The gods must have wanted it this way."

Voices sounded from outside. A loud thumping. Sulla pulled the door open. Flavia was jumping up and down in the doorway.

"Ares!" she cried. "Ares is gone!"

Titus leaped to his feet.

"What do you mean? What do you mean 'Ares is gone'?"

Flavia tried to squeeze words from her throat. She paced in and out of the doorway. Her arms flailed along her body. "He's gone! He's gone!"

"Please sit down, Ms. Laelia," Sulla said. He offered her a chair. "Breathe calmly, in and out. In through the nose, out through the mouth. There, there."

Titus paced around the room. He looked through the window next to the front door.

"Tell me, sister, what happened to Ares? And where is Faustinus?"

Flavia took a deep breath through her nose and exhaled through her mouth, repeating this a few times.

"I woke up this morning… He was just in his bed last night… But when I entered his room… He was gone… Gone! I searched everywhere. Inside and around the house, at the neighbors'. No one has seen him!" She took another deep breath through her nose and exhaled through her mouth. "I went with Faustinus to Arrian's house. He immediately informed the city guards. His wife is looking after Faustinus until I return."

"Arrian, huh? Who did he talk to?" Sulla asked.

"I don't know. I really don't," Flavia said. She collapsed to her knees. "How could I let this happen? It's all my fault!"

"That's not true, sis. Maybe he just ran away. You know Ares. He does crazy things sometimes," Titus said.

Sulla paced back and forth through the shed. "I'm going to Nicopolis," he said. "I'm going to organize a search. I swear by Zeus that we'll find the boy."

The morning wasn't over yet, and groups of city guards walked past the shed. Arrian popped in briefly and mentioned that Leonidas was combing the forest with his hounds. Together with Remus, Arrian left to search the Apollo hill. Flavia returned to watch over Faustinus, promising to keep a close eye on the house.

The news of Ares' disappearance must have spread quickly, as even citizens were out searching for the boy. Titus watched groups trekking through the fields. Teenage boys dispersed through the olive groves. Seeing the searching crowd made Titus grow increasingly worried.

Feeling powerless, he gazed through the back window. Two seagulls skimmed past the shed and circled above the tall grass, interspersed with dives as if chasing prey. Three seagulls joined the group, then another two, then five, three, four, until Titus lost count. From all corners, a mass of circling seagulls gathered like a dark cloud over the shed. The four city guards ran to the back of the shed with looks of astonishment.

One seagull broke away from the mass and descended in circles toward the shed. The bird flew to the back window and perched on Titus' shoulder. It pressed its head against Titus' head. He heard a woman's voice, screaming, shrieking. Images of Thalassa flashed in his mind. She was lying by the lagoon, crying. The water turned red. Her arms were covered in blood. The seagull pulled its head back, screeched, and flew back into the mass.

"Get Sulla!" Titus shouted to the city guards. "Someone, get Sulla! I know where my son is!"

***

The intense chirping of the seagulls fell silent, as if nature itself held its breath. The oppressive silence that followed sang an ominous song of ignorance. The uncertainty about the future, always gnawing at his thoughts, now showed itself in all its power.

Every few seconds, Titus peered through the window next to the front door. Every sound from outside, no matter how soft, seemed a forewarning of impending doom.

Two city guards stood resolutely at attention at the corners of the front yard. People walked through the fields in the distance. He saw the city guards shift their stance. Their faces turned eastward. Titus stuck his head through the window.

"What's happening? What do you guys see?"

Without responding, the city guards paced restlessly through the front yard. Their faces were grave. Titus burst through the front door.

"What's going on?"

"Mr. Laelius!"

"You're not allowed to—"

"Where is my son?" Titus screamed. From the front yard, Titus saw a group of city guards approaching, led by Sulla. Two of them carried a stretcher with a body under a cloth. Titus screamed again. He tried to run toward the group, but the city guards grabbed him and dragged him back into the shed.

As Titus bombarded the city guards with questions, a suffocating silence fell. Time seemed to stretch, each moment becoming an eternity. And then, with the creaking of the door, the inevitable truth was ushered in, heavy and final. The Roman collapsed. He lay on the ground, squirming like a wounded gladiator facing death in the arena.

Ares' small body lay on a raised platform. Flavia had washed him, dressed him, and covered him up to his neck with a cloth. Silence filled the shed. Titus stared at Ares' face, which, despite his violent death, looked peaceful. Remus and two city guards sat silently. Arrian, usually so talkative, seemed to have no words for this event.

The door slowly opened. Sulla's large frame entered the shed and took a place next to Titus. The city guard glanced at the small body and whispered in Titus' ear.

"They're onto them. Farmers saw them. A bunch of bandits from the mountains."

Titus turned to Sulla.

"It doesn't matter who they are. The Aelianii are behind this. How many times do I have to say it?"

"Let's not jump to conclusions."

Titus stood up.

"Why would a group of bandits kidnap a boy, stab him to death, and leave him by the lagoon? Why? There was nothing valuable to gain. This act is completely senseless unless you're a total, deranged sadist or out for revenge. As for the latter, the Aelianii have a motive. I killed their son, so they killed mine. Now tell me, Sulla, as an experienced city guard, what seems most likely to you?"

"The Aelianii are known for their blood feuds," said Arrian. "Take a son of theirs, and they take a son of yours. It's very likely they're behind this."

"I understand," Sulla said, "but the problem is they probably left no traces. Without evidence, you're powerless against the Aelianii. And that's not even mentioning their influence here. Alcander Cassius was just one branch of the olive tree. His family's power is profound and widespread."

"So they just get away with it?" Titus asked.

"The murderers of your son will be caught. I have no doubt about that. But those who ordered it? I'd keep my expectations low if I were you."

Titus sat down again, disbelieving, as he looked at his deceased son. His attempt to enforce justice cost him a child. Such was his fragile hold on the world. He could take justice into his own hands, force his fate—at a high price—but before he could savor his victory, Zeus handed him a new tragedy. Misfortune is life's plague.

Try to eradicate it, and it pops up elsewhere. Thus, we lead lives constantly extinguishing fires while the eternal flame never goes out.

The procession to the cemetery was long, as if the entire city participated. Titus saw many unfamiliar faces drawn to the event. Apparently, Nicopolis did not take child murder lightly. Titus even recognized some drunkards who had abstained from wine that morning to pay their respects. Neighbors, Plautia and Sejanus, and the stone-deaf Mr. Evagrius also joined. Unlike Alcander's ceremony, the procession was silent. No musicians, no singing. Only sobbing and footsteps on the path could be heard.

A contingent of city guards—including Sulla—escorted Titus, Remus, Arrian, and Flavia to the cremation site in the necropolis. Titus' eyes briefly met those of Galyna and Ptolemaios. Their looks showed not anger but defeat. After all, they had lost a daughter first, then a grandchild.

Who was to blame here? Was it me, unable to control my anger? Or was it actually Ariadne's infidelity? And wasn't her betrayal due to her childhood trauma? And couldn't the fault for that be laid at her father's feet? But why had he never returned from Egypt? Whatever the cause, it seemed this was all the will of the gods. They have defeated us—as always—in the battle for external circumstances, reaffirming that their power over such matters cannot be surpassed by mortals. What response is left but defeat? What else can one do but submit to their decisions?

Through tears, Titus watched as funeral attendants laid Ares' shrouded body on the pyre. Flavia poured a cup of olive oil over the body to appease the gods. Galyna placed a basket of fruit, bread, and olives on the pyre, believing Ares' favorite foods would travel with him to the afterlife. The attendants lit the pyre. A temple priest offered a prayer, though he spoke no words.

Days passed like a dream in which Titus had no sense of time. Sometimes he rummaged through his bookcase or storage chest in the dead of night. During the day, he often slept. Sulla still dropped by every morning. Arrian brought him food in the afternoon. Flavia kept him company, along with Faustinus, though the visits were brief.

As Flavia's health deteriorated, she and Arrian discussed Faustinus' fate, as he was about to become an orphan. When Arrian proposed Epictetus as a well-suited adoptive father[33], Titus was skeptical. *Did that mouthy philosopher have any idea how to raise a child?* He'd rather have Arrian raise his son, but, due to his large ambitions he was afraid he'd fail that task.

Remus attended Epictetus' lectures every morning but then faithfully returned to stand by his former master; even if only by being present. In the late morning, about a market week after the cremation, Titus woke to the front door opening. Remus had brought his teacher along. Arrian was also there.

Titus got up and offered Epictetus a chair. Arrian and Remus sat on the floor. Epictetus talked about virtue and the gods but soon got to the heart of the matter, stating that losing loved ones is part of nature and therefore no reason to be upset. Titus understood the logic. Yet, he felt the burning sensation in his stomach flare up again.

"Have you ever lost a son?" Titus asked.

"No," replied Epictetus. "I have no children."

"Then you have no idea what you're talking about. Some thugs murdered my son. But since murder and death are natural phenomena, I shouldn't get too worked up, right? It's all the will of the gods, so we should just accept it with satisfaction, correct? It all sounds very logical and rational. But you conveniently forget how it feels to lose a

---

[33] Historical evidence suggests that Epictetus adopted a child in his later years, which was otherwise left to die. He raised the child with the help of a woman, although their relationship remains unclear.

child."

Epictetus nodded.

"Your pain is understandable. You remain human. But view the situation from that stance. A human is powerless against the gods. Do you really want to rebel against what you're powerless against? Do you want to fight a battle you've already lost? Look at where that has gotten you so far."

"Maybe the gods want us to rebel against them. Maybe this is a test of human will, and they want to see how hard we fight back, even though we're ultimately powerless. Why else would they give us strength and determination? Just to submit to their whims? Who knows, maybe they admire our fighting spirit, our refusal to accept the inevitable," said Titus.

"That's absurd," said Arrian. "To engage in a battle you can never win is absurd! It's illogical and irrational. Besides, it's a sure path to misery."

"Does everything in life have to be logical and rational?"

Titus noticed something black moving in the corner of his eye. He turned his head. A small scorpion scurried across the table. Remus jumped up, caught the creature with a cup and a piece of parchment, and threw the intruder outside.

34. Athens

Volcanoes in the distance erupted like never before. Titus marched across the plains, ready to confront any scorpion bold enough to emerge from the crevices. Yet, no scorpions appeared. Two large eyes in the red sky observed the seething magma flowing across the vast landscape, focusing on Titus. Red drops appeared on his skin, which, upon tasting, turned out to be wine, not blood.

The rain intensified, the water level rose, and a tsunami engulfed the distant volcanoes, rushing toward him. Running became challenging as the wine reached his knees. When the crest of the tsunami loomed over him, it rained tiny scorpions. Turning around, Titus saw the wave consisted not of water but of millions, perhaps billions of scorpions. Just before the tsunami crashed over him, he spotted a young man with a vine wreath on his head, laughing and drinking from a jug.

Titus woke up startled. It was dark outside, and he tasted wine in his mouth. He felt the scar on his palm, as if freshly cut, though it had long since healed. The interior of the shed seemed to spin around him. The flame of the oil lamp on the table appeared blurry, as if obscured by tears. He rubbed his eyes several times, but his surroundings still appeared blurred. He grabbed Arrian's notes from the cabinet, where the letters danced on the paper, sharpening and then blurring again as if his eyes struggled to focus. He felt pain in his stomach, opened the back window, and vomited.

"Are you okay?" a voice asked as one of the guards approached.

"I'm fine," Titus said.

"If you need anything, just let us know."

Titus coughed, cleared his throat, and spat out the last bitter fluid onto the ground. The taste of wine lingered in his mouth, and the shed continued to spin. Realizing that keeping his eyes open would only make him nauseous again, he decided to lie down and close his eyes.

The next morning, Sulla burst into the shed and ordered Titus to sit. Sulla's eyes conveyed the gravity of his forthcoming message, but Titus already anticipated the news. The events surrounding Ares' death had delayed the decision regarding Titus' execution. The time had finally come. Sulla informed him that his execution by beheading would occur in two days.

"Do you have any final wishes?" Sulla asked.

The taste of wine still hadn't left Titus' mouth, although his surroundings had stopped spinning, and his vision had cleared. He pondered for a moment and then sighed.

"I've told you that I dedicated my life to turning stones into gold. I'd like nothing more than to try it one more time. That's my final wish."

Sulla scanned the shed, his eyebrows betraying some doubt. He was well aware of the risks associated with Titus' endeavors. He could set the place ablaze just like he once did in Rome. But to be fair, since arriving in Nicopolis, there hadn't been any real dangerous incidents.

"Alright, but under strict supervision," Sulla said with a deep sigh.

Under Sulla's watch, two guards brought various items from the crawl space, including glass bottles, different types of stones, tools resembling torture devices, and jars and boxes with dubious contents. Titus sent Remus to the market with a shopping list he had compiled.

Moments later, a makeshift laboratory was set up around the outdoor kitchen. The guards watched curiously as Titus brought a large iron pot filled with a dark substance to a boil. Remus handed over the ingredients, which Titus stirred into the mixture one by one.

Sulla breathed down Titus' neck, and the other guards followed his movements like kittens trailing their mother. With trembling hands, the Roman opened a wooden box containing a colorful, sparkling powder. He glanced at Remus, who sighed and gave the most subtle nod he could muster.

"Pay attention to this dead man, folks, I'm adding the secret ingredient now," Titus said. He elegantly tossed the contents into the pot. Sulla and the guards watched the concoction like children at a magic show. The pot emitted a burst of bright green smoke that rapidly spread across the front yard.

Remus covered his eyes with a handkerchief. "My eyes! It stings!" the guards cried out. "Laelius, what are you pulling off now!" Sulla yelled. The green smoke gave way to a thick, purple fog that soon surrounded the shed like morning mist. And as if that wasn't enough, squealing, blue projectiles shot out from the pot, exploding upon contact with the ground.

Titus ran through the olive groves like a hare fleeing Arrian's greyhounds. He raced past the lagoon, sparing a glance for Thalassa, but quickly continued northward without looking back, fearing it would slow him down. As if chased by millions of scorpions, he hurried along the coastline. Mountains, trees, and fishing boats whizzed by. The sun scorched his neck. His legs could no longer carry him, but he kept placing one foot in front of the other until he heard a voice.

"There you finally are. I was wondering when you'd show up." A familiar figure appeared in the corner of his eye.

"Magnus?"

"You can stop running now. You've long lost those fools. Great stunt, by the way. Your skills came in handy after all."

Titus glanced over his shoulder. Beyond the landscape, the sea, and a few distant boats, he saw no one. Titus slowed to a brisk pace as Magnus matched his stride.

"Why are you following me?"

"You know why. To support you in making the right choice. You're on the correct path. You're following the

Urge. I'm proud of you."

"I have no idea what you're talking about."

"Oh, come on. You know exactly what I mean. I know where you're headed and what you're planning to do."

"This has nothing to do with your Urge," Titus said.

"You still deny what brought you here; the all-encompassing power, intertwined with every thought, every decision, every emotion. You're like a fish denying the water it swims in."

"Listen closely, Magnus. I don't have time for your theories. The Urge or not, I couldn't care less. I'm doing this in honor of my son and for my sister. The Aelianii cannot get away with this! Their time is up!"

"And I'm coming with you to help. You could use some assistance."

In the evening darkness, Titus and Magnus swiftly navigated the narrow streets of the Athenian residential area. Small houses and apartments gave way to luxury villas surrounded by high walls. The visitors had been busy since arriving in the Greek city, where Zeno once founded the Stoic school.

After a thorough search—taking them three days—Titus and Magnus had obtained two city guard uniforms from a corrupt official. They also inquired about the Aelianii and their residence, leading them to a vast complex; a collection of houses teeming with guards.

In their disguises, Titus and Magnus approached the complex's back entrance, encountering a group of guards who, judging by their loud and incoherent speech, were well on their way to drunkenness.

"Eutropios and Antigonos reporting for duty," Titus announced.

One of the guards stood up, his head as barren as a desert devoid of trees, proudly displaying his belly and scratching behind his ear.

"Eutropios…? Antigonos?"

"Correct, sir," Magnus replied. "My name is Eutropios, and my companion is Antigonos. We're at the service of the Aelianii, ready to report for duty."

"I must admit… those names don't ring a bell… I've never seen you here before."

"And where's that accent from?" another guard with notably deep crow's feet asked, taking a swig from a wine bottle. "Sounds Roman. But I could be mistaken."

"Nicomedia. I was born in Nicomedia," Titus said.

"Nicomedia, eh?" the bald guard said. "Have you been living in Athens long?"

"For years. Many, many years," Magnus said, sighing and shaking his head. "Things have really gone downhill since Domitian's time as emperor, and it hasn't improved under Trajan. They care nothing for us in Rome. All they do is take. But give? Not a chance."

"That's the absolute truth," said the guard with the crow's feet, now even more accentuated. "They say Hadrian will do better, but I don't believe a word of it! It's all nonsense!"

"Hadrian? Just another puppet of the Senate," Magnus said. "If he lifts a finger for Athens, I'll eat my uniform."

"Me too!" the bald guard said. "To pieces with those in Rome! They're nothing but a bunch of thieves! A corrupt mess! It's high time someone drained the swamp!"

"Absolutely!" Titus agreed. "Down with the Romans!"

The guard with the crow's feet signaled him to lower his voice.

"Don't let the Aelianii hear that. They're Greek on the outside, but on the inside they're Romans through and through," he whispered, glancing around nervously. "They live here like gods. They've got a big say in things here. The Quaestor is terrified of them."

"I heard they don't even pay taxes," the bald guard added. "They buy properties for a pittance. If you resist, you're done for. Then they rent those properties out for hefty prices. Yes, they're good at that."

"But are you Antigonos or Eutropios?" the bald guard asked.

"I'm Antigonos, and my companion is Eutropios," Titus said.

"Where's this companion you speak of?"

Titus looked around. Magnus was nowhere to be seen, as if he had vanished into thin air.

"I... I don't understand. He was just here!" Titus said.

"Oh, really? I didn't see him. Did you guys?"

"No, we didn't see him either!"

"Ah, must be the wine," the bald guard concluded, taking another hearty gulp. "You're a scrawny little fellow but I like you, Antigonos. Or was it Eutropios? Ah, what does it matter? Just be warned. As long as you remain loyal to the Aelianii and do your job well, all is good. But don't try to mess with them. Those who have tried are now scrubbing the floors of Hades' palace."

"Thank you... thank you for the warning, sir. I'd better go inside. Duty calls," Titus said.

A tall wall surrounded the Aelianii housing complex. Inner gardens with mostly exotic plants and trees distinguished the buildings housing various family members, including the family of Alcander Aelianus Cassius' brother, Claudius Aelianus, who lived in the largest villa in the complex. Magnus was still nowhere to be found.

From the inner garden, Titus looked up at a window on the villa's first floor. The ceiling reflected the yellow glow of flickering light. Behind him, a whispering voice sounded.

"There's where we need to go," said the voice.

"Where were you?"

"I slipped inside. Those men were stone drunk. They didn't even notice."

Titus silently met the philosopher's gaze. His gut feeling was telling him something was off, but the intensity of the moment left no room to dwell on it.

"Well, what are you waiting for?"

After hesitating, Titus approached the wall beneath the window, pulled himself up using protruding stones and holes, and climbed inside. Magnus followed. An oil lamp unveiled a glimpse of the detailed paintings on the ceiling and walls. In the center of the room, a bed held a sleeping boy, as deep in slumber as a hibernating squirrel. He must have been Ares' age, maybe slightly older. Titus' hands began to tremble. He drew the sword from its sheath at his waist. Magnus stood right behind him, his breath in Titus' ear.

"Son for son, remember? Son for son."

Titus watched the boy's breathing body, oblivious to the intruders.

"I can't do this," said Titus. He sheathed his sword, climbed out the window, and walked into the darkness of the inner garden. Magnus followed.

"What's wrong with you?"

"He's an innocent child."

"Yes, and...? Wasn't Ares an innocent child too? They took a son from you, now you take a son from them. They deserve it. It's as simple as that."

"Just because they kill children doesn't mean I have to do the same. It's wrong," said Titus.

"Whether it's wrong or not is irrelevant. You feel a deep need to avenge your son, out of love and a natural desire for justice. That's what counts. If you ignore the Urge, you'll always regret not being true to your deepest desires," Magnus said.

"This solves nothing. It's pointless."

"Then let it be pointless! It's about staying true to yourself! About listening to what the Urge tells you, whether you solve anything or not! That's your path! The true path! The only path!"

Memories of Ares flashed through his mind: holding him for the first time, his first steps, playing with his brother. Intense anger surged as images of his son, battered by Alcander, flashed through his mind. Magnus' voice seemed to nest deep in his thoughts now. "Son for son," the voice said. "They murdered your child. They brutally took his life. They deserve to be punished. Such is life, such is nature, such is your will and true path."

Scorpions swarmed through the inner garden, climbed up the wall, into the window. As if Titus stood with his back to the sea, black waves pushed him further and further toward the window. A giant wave lifted him and swirled him into the room. The walls turned black. The squirming mass on the floor moved Titus toward the bed. He drew his sword. A voice sounded in the distance, yet so close.

"Don't do it! They'll seek vengeance again! On Flavia! On Faustinus! There will be no end!"

"Thalassa," Titus said. "I must. This is my path. This is who I am."

"Not true! Don't listen to that harbinger of doom! Death is certain. Murder is permanent. Hatred is safer than love, destruction easier than creation. That's why Magnus' path is so tempting. But it's not your path! Yours is one of life, with all its risks and uncertainties included! I'm certain of it! She told me so! And She's trying to tell you too, but your anger refuses to listen! Let that dark cloud pass, and your path will become clear."

"There's no turning back now. Don't try to stop me."

"There is a way back. Flee. Come to me. I will help you break free from this. It's not too late."

"What does it matter? I'm marked for death, no matter what I do. If I flee, they will search everywhere for me. It's only a matter of time before I end up on the block."

"We'll flee together. To the Alps, remember? No one will find us there."

"Ignore her," Magnus said. "She is unreliable, unpredictable as the Ionian Sea. She lies and deceives. No, not all nymphs are the same, but she is as treacherous as they get. I know her well and let me tell you: She cares nothing for you. She promises you Elysium? What a joke. There is no Elysium! That's a lie designed to hold you, to drain you until you're completely empty, and then she'll move on to her next prey."

"Don't listen to him!" Thalassa said.

"But it's true! She's been doing nothing else for centuries. Which men have you devoured? Quintus, Leonidas, Theodoros, Scipio, Archimedes? How many of these fellows have you lied to? Who all have you deceived? Can you tell us that, Thalassa? And all the while being married. This remorseless nymph is deadly. She spares neither man nor god!" Magnus said. Silence fell, then Thalassa's sobbing filled the space.

"I've been lost, confused. I did many things I regret, desperate to fill the void. But meeting you changed everything—it's as if my entire life was a search that led to you. Please, give us a chance. Without it, you'll face your final moments haunted by what could have been, regretting that you chose death over life. And Elysium is real. Doubt me? Let me prove it to you."

With the sword in his hand, Titus gazed at the young Aelianus offshoot still sleeping undisturbed, oblivious to the intruder. Scorpions now crawled over his bed and body, tensely awaiting Titus' next move.

But what am I to do? Whom can I believe?

Ultimately, only one could decide, and that was himself. Deep in his soul, the voice spoke, the guide of his existence: the Urge. Titus closed his eyes for a moment.

"I know what I want," he said.

With a smooth motion, he turned the sword in his hands and plunged it into his chest. The scorpions burst apart like stars imploding under their own weight. Magnus, suddenly standing before him, grabbed his shoulders.

"What have you done?"

Light rays pierced out of Magnus' eyes. Smoke in every color of the rainbow rushed out of all his orifices. He screamed like the giant scorpions on the plains, but louder, hysterically like a tortured animal. Titus fell to the ground. At foot level, he saw the room's door open. People whose names he didn't know stormed in. A child's cry, a woman's scream, the roar of an outraged adult man. None of it mattered to him anymore. He had sealed his fate by his own hand, ending his life in this world.

Titus moved beyond all voices and thoughts, across the plains, past the volcanoes, through the red cloud layer while swarms of angry scorpions tried to pull him down. Slowly but surely, the sky cleared. Athens shone in the morning sun. He soared over the Agora, straight through the Stoa Poikile, where Zeno of Citium once began Stoic philosophy, and students tried to rid themselves of passions amid the hooting of owls.

Swiftly he rose above the cloud deck and shot westward with the speed of a thousand seagulls, toward Nicopolis. He flew through the streets, past the Odeon, through his sister Flavia's house where Faustinus lay in his crib. In an instant, years passed, his son growing strong and bright, his sister happy and tranquil in her later years. The cycle of violence was broken, and the Aelianii turned their anger on each other, feuding and bickering until in turn their family fortunes were ground to dust.

Wide-eyed, Faustinus sat beside Epictetus as he lectured the people of Nicopolis, absorbing the philosopher's words. Tears streamed as Titus saw his son grow into manhood in mere moments, wiser than his father could ever have hoped for.

Through the backyard, he blasted upwards again, as fast as Zeus' lightning bolts, skimming past the moon, racing by the stars, until a blinding mass of light surrounded him.

Snow-capped mountain peaks approached in the distance, with deep, green valleys at their feet with flowing water. The sky radiated a deeper blue than he had ever experienced, the sun shone brighter, while a gentle breeze caressed him. The surface approached. Like a bird that forgot how to land, he descended onto the green hills, faster and faster.

He closed his eyes.

A period of nothingness transitioned into the sound of a mountain stream, clear as the brightest diamond. The grass prickled his skin. As he rose, he saw grazing cows and goats and a waterfall in the distance, so high it vanished into the clouds. Along the stream stood a house, about the size of his shed. A door opened. Two slender, white legs stepped out. A laugh warmer than the summer sun welcomed him.

The myth was true. Elysium revealed itself in full glory. Mountain peaks scratched the clouds, streams twinkled, livestock grazed on grass shining in eternal dew. Thalassa ran into his arms. Titus held her and pressed her against his chest. He still found it hard to believe that the nymph, the most beautiful creature he had ever encountered, wanted to bind herself to him forever.

But what does it matter? The Urge led me to her.

This was his path. A new beginning with Thalassa in the land of the blessed, gifted with eternal life. After all he had been through, he felt hopeful.

He never wanted to let go of Thalassa. But when she freed herself from his embrace, he realized that even in Elysium, only his own choices were under his control. Everything else was beyond his reach.

Epictetus' logic still applied in paradise, which, just like the ordinary world, was subject to constant change; beautiful waterfalls and mountain tops could not make one defy transience. Titus' desire was eternal togetherness, but reality offered no guarantees. He could lose Thalassa, just as he once lost Ariadne. She could deceive him, leave him, and exploit him. The boundless eternity provided her ample time to confirm all prejudices about nymphs. She could hurt him on a scale that would make Ariadne's infidelity pale in comparison. Thalassa was as much out of his control as his children, his wealth, and his reputation. Eternal love meant eternal uncertainty. As long as he clung to her, the pain of loss, betrayal, or any feared outcome loomed.

The Urge leads you to what you desire most deeply in the world. But there's always a price to pay.

The Stoics warned that desiring things beyond our control would inevitably lead to pain, so we should not cling to them. "Be prepared to say that these things mean nothing to you," Epictetus once said.[34]

But isn't that much easier said than done? And is this the path we should be taking?

Titus certainly failed to do so. Among all the desires he cherished—justice, fame, and the peace of solitude—a fire burned within him that reason couldn't extinguish: the passionate love for another. By yielding to this desire, he became vulnerable, placing him at the mercy of Lady Fortuna, whose power reached even into Elysium.

Every commitment to something beyond our control is a leap of faith. It demands trust, a reach into the unknown. For some, this leap is an affirmation of life which, with some help of the gods, can yield a fulfillment that justifies the risk. Others see it as playing with fire, a fool's game that will inevitably get you burned. But maybe getting burned is exactly what the Urge seeks.

Who can say? Her motives remain a mystery.

---

[34] Epictetus, *Enchiridion*, 1

Printed in Great Britain
by Amazon